Dear Reader,

Every time I see a film ~~of the Indiana Jones or~~ ~~myself in the shoes of t~~ hero). How exciting! How romantic! Except...I'm not sure I'd have the guts, wits, strength and stamina to face and conquer all the physical and mental perils. Still, that doesn't keep me from imagining and pretending.

When I wrote *Out of Eden* and introduced the heroine's brother, a hunky celebrity treasure hunter, I knew my romantic-treasure-quest adventure was just a book away. *Into the Wild* afforded me the chance to live and love dangerously. I based Spenser and River's quest on an actual legend—the lost treasure of Llanganatis. Though I couldn't actually travel to Ecuador, I did research heavily and fell in love with the country. What started off as a jungle adventure in the Amazon stretched on into the Andes Mountains. Although I tried to stay true to the region and the legend, remember this is a work of fiction and I have quite the imagination.

As an aside, this past year I traveled to Wyoming with one of my sisters and had my own mini adventure in the wild. I drew from many of the challenges I experienced (altitude sickness, unpredictable weather, strenuous climbs into mountains) when I wrote this story. And most of all, the determination to push beyond your physical limitations as well as conquering (or at least taming) your fears.

As for the romantic aspect of this tale, all I can say is... *Be still, my heart.* Brace yourself, folks. You're in for a wild ride!

Cheers,

Beth

BETH CIOTTA
into the wild

HQN™

ISBN-13: 978-0-373-77467-8

INTO THE WILD

This book is dedicated to Barb Justen Hisle—a fellow adventurer, fantastic writer and awesome sister. Flat Creek Ranch, Yellowstone and the Grand Teton Mountains. We did it! Here's to our next Sister Adventure!

Acknowledgments

Special thanks to my critique partner (and sister), Barb, who read every chapter as I wrote it and bowled me over with her enthusiasm and insight. I am blessed.

To author-journalists Joe Albright and Marcia Kunstel—owners of Flat Creek Ranch, our fabulous guide Shelby Scharp and everyone at Flat Creek who contributed to my amazing adventure…thank you for your fantastic hospitality and for sharing your own awesome tales!

To my support system, my cheerleaders, my friends, Cynthia Valero and Mary Stella—you inspire me, personally and professionally. You're the best.

To my agent, Amy Moore-Benson—you are my rock!

To my editor, Keyren Gerlach, who inspired *Into the Wild* with her own jungle adventure—I'm in awe of your courage (as well as your editing skills and patience). Thank you for everything!

I'd also like to acknowledge every department and every single person at HQN Books. I so appreciate your dedication to my stories and all you do for *romance*.

Lastly, to all the readers, booksellers and librarians who share and support my love of romantic adventures—wishing you love and laughter, peace and joy, and a multitude of satisfying reads!

into the wild

CHAPTER ONE

Maple Grove, Indiana, USA
Altitude 810 feet

"AMAZING. ABSOLUTELY stunning!"

Melinda Clark, soon to be Mrs. Mark Donovan, pored over the sample wedding album with unabashed enthusiasm.

River Kane, owner and head photographer of Forever Photography, held silent as the woman gushed. Normally, she felt a surge of pride whenever someone complimented her work, but given the recent upheaval in her personal life, all she felt was numb.

Mark, in an attempt to curb his fiancée's blatantly expensive taste, looked at a photo and shrugged. "It's okay."

"Okay?" Melinda palmed her heart, her three-carat engagement ring glittering as brightly as her wide blue eyes. "Look at the expressions Miss Kane captured. So much love. You can just *feel* the joy."

"It's a wedding, honey. I'd be worried if the bride and groom weren't happy."

"Not just the bride and groom." She tapped a manicured nail to a five-by-seven of the Sweeny bridal party.

"There are…*twelve* people in this photo and every one looks fabulous, even the flower girl and ring bearer. How often does *that* happen? Usually at least one person blinks or sneezes, or scratches inappropriately. Remember your cousin's wedding album? Obviously that photographer didn't have the sharp eye and skill of Ms. Kane. Just look at these images of the ceremony!"

"They're kind of artsy."

"They're unique!"

Mark leaned in and muttered something to Melinda, who muttered something back.

Wishing she were anywhere but here, River gripped the padded arms of her floral upholstered chair. Drumming her fingers wouldn't do. Where was the tolerant patience that used to come naturally? It's not as if this moment, these prospective clients, were out of the realm of her normal world.

She was used to people admiring her work. She was used to those who criticized. Some splurged on her top package. Some budgeted for a lower tier, while others haggled over even her most basic package or, in some cases, walked away. After several years in the business, she'd pretty much seen it all. As a levelheaded professional, she was equipped to handle any situation.

She also had good instincts.

River was certain, by Melinda's enthusiasm, her extravagant ring and Mark's sagging shoulders, that they would commit to her premium package. That meant major dollars for Forever Photography. Yet River couldn't dredge up an iota of pleasure. A contract meant she'd actually have to photograph the damned blessed event.

Or maybe Mark would get cold feet or second thoughts and abandon Melinda at the altar.

That would be awful, of course. But then River wouldn't feel like the only jilted bride in the state. She could commiserate with Melinda. Curse her ex-fiancé almost-husband, a cowardly, fickle-hearted bastard. They could drown their sorrows in the champagne, meant to toast a happily-ever-after, and bemoan their sadly-never-was.

River watched as Mark encircled Melinda's waist, inwardly winced when he smiled and kissed his intended's cheek. The man was besotted.

She was going to have to shoot the damned wedding.

Twenty minutes later the contract was signed and a hefty deposit check sat on River's doodle-free desk blotter. Melinda and Mark left, and River's assistant, Ella Tucker, entered. River barely noticed. She was too busy squirting sanitizing liquid into her palms—didn't people realize how many germs were transmitted by shaking hands?—and cursing her inherited talent.

"Damn Mom's artistic streak and Grandpa's photographic eye."

"We took a vote," said Ella, her trusted sidekick of three years, "and we've decided *you* are a freak of nature."

River blinked. Normally Ella poked her head in after an appointment to ask if they'd secured the booking and what package the client had opted for. As River's assistant, she made more money when her services were required on-site. The "freak of nature" remark was out of the blue and triggered deep-rooted issues that intensified River's already fragile mood. She tried not to take offense. Not privy to the details of River's past, Ella couldn't know how keenly her observation hit home and hurt. Besides, she wasn't a spiteful woman. She was a barely-twenty nosey Nate (although well-intended) friend and associate.

Maintaining a calm facade, River forced a teasing smile. "By *we,* I assume you mean you and Ben." River's mailman. Ella's boyfriend. A guy who knew everyone's business and never shied from expressing his opinion.

Ella plopped in the chair vacated by Melinda only seconds before. "May I be blunt?"

River's mind screamed no, but it wasn't in her nature to blow people off. Besides, she could take it. At this point in her life she was fairly numb to criticism and rejection. "Consider me prepared."

"You were dumped at the altar by your fiancé, the man of your dreams, two weeks ago today. Yet you continue to operate as if nothing happened. Most women would've thrown a tantrum, retreated into a shell, hired a hit man, purchased a voodoo doll in the likeness of their ex—*something,* but you didn't even cry." Ella pumped her ever-present lip gloss tube, a sign that she was just gearing up. "You cashed in your honeymoon tickets and resumed business as usual. Which for you," she said, after swiping the shiny pink stuff over her plump lower lip, "is photographing other couples walking down the aisle, saying 'I do' and walking, or flying, into the sunset. I know you loved or at least thought you loved David. And I know you're a gentle soul, but this…restraint, this robotlike behavior is plain freaky."

River felt her calm slipping. That wouldn't do. Desperate for control, she folded the check and slid it into her wallet, then scooped up the sample albums and replaced them on the decorative shelves adjacent to her antique desk—everything in its place. "I'm not a robot," she said, careful to keep her voice light. "I'm sensible and grounded."

"You're in denial. You're also cautious and paranoid. Not your fault," Ella added as though that would ease the sting. "You're a product of your grandparents."

Better than a product of her parents—selfish and reckless. But River didn't voice that thought. She skirted talk of her parents—a free-spirited artist and an eccentric archaeologist—like the plague. Surely they were just as toxic. "Is there a point to this attack?"

"We figure it's only a matter of time before you blow."

"*We* being you and Ben."

"It would be pretty sucky if all that suppressed devastation and anger erupted during a photo shoot. How many times have you told me your reputation is everything? Ruin one happy wedding and future contracts could be at risk. You know how word travels."

Your reputation is your most valuable selling tool, River could hear her grandpa saying. She'd not only inherited Forever Photography from Grandpa Franklin, she'd adopted his work ethics. Her fractured family had also cursed her with a few assorted habits, although Ella called them quirks. Ella, though sometimes annoying, was observant and wise beyond her years. River didn't know what was more troubling. That a woman seven years her junior was analyzing her behavior, or that her concern had merit. River did feel pressure building within. A simmering mixture of disillusion and resentment. Long ago, she'd had a similar feeling and she had indeed blown. As a result she'd severed her relationship with her father.

As always, the mere thought of Professor Henry Kane whipped River's normally controlled emotions into a frenzy. She blamed him for her mother's death and for annihilating her own sense of adventure. Since David had cited her conventional and cautious ways as his reasons for dumping her, she blamed Henry for ruining her love life, too.

Chest tight, River reclaimed her seat and tucked her shoulder-length curls behind her emerald-studded ears. She bolstered her shoulders and tried not to look fragile—something else David had complained about in front of God and friends. His observation, like his rejection, had stung. Especially since she'd dedicated several years to building her strength and stamina. She couldn't help that she'd been born pale, blond and petite. Nor was it her fault that she'd been molded into a person of many quirks. Quirks David *used* to find endearing.

When had their relationship gone wrong and why hadn't he been willing to fix it?

Ella cleared her throat. "Are you thinking or ignoring me?"

River forced another smile. "Listen, Ella. I appreciate your…and Ben's concern, but I'm fine."

"Uh-huh." *Pump, pump.*

"I'm not going to have a meltdown in public."

"What about in private?"

River considered the best response while Ella swished on more lip gloss. If she forfeited control, she worried she might never get it back. She'd planned the rest of her life according to David T. Snodgrass. Happily married until they died, three children, a two-story single-family home on an acre of land, yearly vacations to Disney, a 401K plan…

River's list went on and in great detail, and now that list was in the trash bin. No plan. No map charting her way for the next fifty years. Panic had been skirting the edges of her being ever since David had said adios. In order to function, she was operating on automatic, business as usual. And she would continue to do so until she formulated a new life plan. She didn't expect Ella to understand her orderly nature and she had no desire to explain.

"Would it make you feel better if I went home now, chugged a bottle of wine and sobbed into my pillow?" River asked

"No. But *you'd* feel better."

Wrong. It was, however, a way out of this conversation.

"I'll keep that in mind." Still smiling, River pushed to her wedge-sandaled feet. "We're caught up on business. What do you say we knock off for the day? I have personal errands and you've never been one to pass up extra time at the gym." Whereas River maintained a rigid schedule that centered on jogging and moderate weight training, Ella kept fit via trendy workouts. Flavor of this month: Zumba.

"Sure, but—"

"Great." But before River could get out the door, Ben burst in. The uniformed mailman planted a quick kiss on Ella's slick lips then turned to River. "This is unorthodox," he said, looking harried, "seeing it was addressed to your home, but I couldn't imagine leaving it in your mailbox, considering its origin."

River tensed. Ben was a company man. A straight-arrow, by-the-books government employee. What would cause him to deviate from his normal route, delaying service to his regulars?

Ella rushed to River's side. "Is it bad news?"

"Maybe it's good news or promising news," said Ben. "Whatever it is, it's marked Important."

River hefted her red satchel higher on her shoulder to busy her hands. Wringing them wouldn't do. "What is it?"

Ben produced a worn eleven-by-fourteen padded envelope. "No return addressee," he pointed out, "but it's postmarked Baños, Ecuador."

River held tight to her satchel's strap, tight to her control.

"David's in South America," Ella said, excitedly pumping her gloss. "Isn't Ecuador in South America?"

"Yepper," Ben said, still holding the envelope. "That's why I rushed it right over."

Reapplying the gloss Ben had kissed off, Ella leaned in for a closer look. "Except that doesn't look like David's handwriting."

No, it didn't. But the all-capitals print *was* familiar. Although River hadn't seen it in a long, long time.

"David's on an extreme tour," Ben said, "floating down the Amazon or zip-lining across the jungle canopy. Maybe he asked someone else to send whatever it is."

Ella snatched the package from Ben and felt up the contents. "It feels like a book."

River snatched the package from Ella and slipped it into her satchel. "I'll let you know."

"You mean you're not going to open it here? Now?"

"I'd rather not." Sensitive to the couple's disappointment, River itched to make a graceful exit. "I appreciate the special delivery, Ben, but I feel a meltdown coming on and I promised Ella I'd do that in private. She'll explain." That was as graceful as it could get. River blew out of her office, through the reception area and out the front door of Forever Photography.

She anticipated dark clouds, rumbling thunder, something ominous to match her mood, but the weather was sunny and mild. A beautiful late June day. If things had gone according to her well-laid plan, she would've been a June bride. Instead she was a June reject. She shelved the thought and focused on the package. "What do you want?" she grumbled as she slid into her minivan.

It had been five years since River had last heard from her father. And that had been a lame greeting card, condolences on the passing of her maternal grandpa. As if the selfish bastard really cared.

She nosed the van toward home.

Important.

What could it be? In addition to the surprise package, she was reeling from the possibility that her estranged father and fiancé were in the same foreign region. David was actually in Peru. Wasn't that just south or east of Ecuador? The coincidence was just too weird.

Taking her usual route, River zipped through town and pulled into her designated driveway. She eyed the two-bedroom rancher she'd inherited from her grandparents, much smaller than the one she'd planned to buy with David. For a moment she marveled that she'd been willing to part with it. Though lacking in warm, fuzzy memories, it was the only place she'd ever been able to truly call home. Her grandparents, though reluctant guardians, had taken her in when she was thirteen. The same year her mom had died. The same year she'd cursed her father to hell, thereafter referring to him as Henry.

Months later, in a fit of remorse, she'd tried to mend that bridge, but her efforts had failed, driving a bigger wedge between father and daughter. River had many regrets, but mostly she was bitter. If her parents had loved her more, if they'd been less *weird,* she wouldn't have developed the eccentricities that had driven David away.

Suddenly, the tears she'd been holding at bay for two long weeks threatened to flow. River steeled her body, her mind. She would not, could not, lose control. Gulping fresh air, she plopped on the front stoop and opened the package.

Nerves jangling, she clutched the contents, seeing but not believing.

Not a book. A journal. Embossed brown leather, bulging and bound by a green elastic band. River smoothed her fingers over the worn cover. She had few memories of Henry, but she remembered him scribbling in a small, fat book that he carried in his pocket. No, not a book. A journal. *This* journal. Or at least a predecessor.

Her heart raced as the past stared her in the face. She'd wondered back then what he was writing, but when she'd asked, he'd blown her off. "Data," he'd said, as if that explained it all. Later, her mom had described *data* as documented observations and revelations about his studies. She'd likened his journal to a diary. "For his eyes only," she'd said.

Never in a million years had River dreamed she'd get a peek inside Henry's journal, let alone an invitation to peruse at will. Was this his way of reaching out, of reconnecting? Was she supposed to feel honored? Relieved? Giddy with anticipation?

The soft leather didn't comfort her as she slid off

the band, carefully, as though the journal might be ticking.

She found yellowed, stained and smudged pages. Scribbles and tiny crammed handwriting in margins—handwriting she had seen so few times—and diagrams that held no immediate meaning.

But she also found photographs. Ones she'd never seen. Photos of her. Of her mom. Of them as a family. She'd never figured Henry as sentimental. She was trying to process the notion when a trifold paper slid free and fell to the ground. Hands trembling, she unfolded the weighty stationery and found an object wrapped in tissue. It was small, but heavy. An amulet? It resembled a cross, except it had several corners and a hole in the middle. All she could tell for sure was that it was gold. And old.

Setting it aside, she read the handwriting on the stationery—the same tight, cramped writing as in the journal.

Dear River,
To prove my love—which I know you doubt—I am trusting you with a monumental secret.
 I have discovered something men would kill to possess. If you receive this package, it means I am sacrificing my life to protect a precious treasure. I'm gifting you with my journal and sweat of the sun so that you'll understand the choices I've made. Share it with no one except Professor Bovedine and beware of the hunters.

I love you,
Daddy

What the…?

Anger burned away her nerves.

Was he *kidding?* I love you? "I'm sacrificing my life"? What did *that* mean?

Frustrated, River read the note again…and again. Even when he *told* her he loved her he couldn't get it right. The tender declaration was overshadowed by his cryptic dramatics.

I am sacrificing my life.

Beware of the hunters.

Was he in mortal danger, already dead or just nuts? How like Henry to talk in riddles. He was a brilliant but odd bird who'd grown more eccentric with age. An archaeologist who'd found it increasingly difficult to secure grants to fund his expeditions due to his bull-headed, hot-dog nature. He'd refused to curb his obsession with discovering legendary treasures even when it would have meant security for his family.

She palmed the gold amulet.

Was this a portion of what he'd found in an excavation? Or, like the photos, a sentimental souvenir? It didn't surprise River that he'd choose some treasure over her, but over life? Surely, he hadn't meant that literally. Not that she cared.

Except, to her surprise and dismay, she did. Just a little. Just enough to phone Professor Bovedine, her father's oldest friend and perhaps the sole professional associate who hadn't believed Henry Kane was an inept kook. If anyone could make heads or tails out of this cryptic letter, it was Paul Bovedine. Luckily, unlike her father, Bovedine had made it a point to check in with River throughout the years, hence his number was programmed into her cell.

She gripped the phone in one hand, the journal in the other. She held her breath until someone answered.

"Professor…" *sniffle,* "Bovedine's residence. How may I…" *gulp,* "help?"

"Mrs. Robbins?"

"River?" Professor Bovedine's housekeeper burst into a sob. "River. Professor Bovedine is dead."

"Dead?" River felt the world shift away, just a little farther. "How? When?"

"Yesterday. Someone broke into the house. Professor Bovedine returned early from the university and…the police said it was a bungled burglary."

River couldn't believe her ears. Yes, Bovedine collected antiquities, but he donated or sold them to museums. He was a lifelong bachelor who traveled frequently and cared little for material possessions. From what she remembered of his rambling old house, there was little of value.

Beware of the hunters.

River stared at the letter.

I have discovered something men would kill to possess.

No. It was too bizarre. Henry's discovery and Professor Bovedine's death could *not* be connected.

Share it with no one except Professor Bovedine.

She hadn't shared the journal. She hadn't shared any news at all. She hadn't had the chance.

"We haven't heard from you in several months, River. How odd that you called today. The timing…" She hiccupped over a sob. "A package from your dad yesterday. A phone call from you today. And the professor, he… he missed them *both*."

River nearly dropped her phone. "A package? What was in it?" She regretted the insensitive question as soon as it popped out. She should've asked about Bovedine's funeral arrangements.

If Mrs. Robbins thought the inquiry rude, she didn't pause. "I don't know, dear. The mail came early yesterday. I put the package on the professor's desk and left to do my weekly shopping. I'm sure it's around here… somewhere. The burglars ransacked the house and I'm not allowed to clean until the investigation is…over. It's just so…awful."

River tried to console the sobbing woman, but her efforts were lame. Though heartsick over Professor Bovedine's senseless death, fury snaked though her system. What if Henry's mysterious package *had* somehow contributed to Bovedine's death? Just as his selfish behavior had contributed to her mom's?

Her mind exploded with a verbal rant. Her body trembled with suppressed emotions. She physically ached to have it out with Henry Kane, to address and resolve old and new issues. In the next mental bout, she blasted her ex for being a selfish, heartbreaking weasel!

Closure.

In the midst of Mrs. Robbins's teary walk down memory lane, River had an epiphany. She needed closure with her past in order to map a new future. Closure with her father *and* David. Never mind that it meant traipsing into the wild and battling deep-rooted fears. Suddenly, there was nothing more important than facing her demons. For the first time since David had dumped her, she had direction.

River clung to that thought as she tenderly ended the conversation with Mrs. Robbins. She didn't mention she'd also received a package from Henry. Why tempt questions she couldn't answer? Her father's letter had effectively sealed her lips. Except to Bovedine, and Bovedine was dead. *That* ugly truth reinforced River's decision to take action. What if Henry's ravings had merit? What if he was in genuine danger? Or in danger of going genuinely bonkers? If she didn't at least try to save him from whatever mess he'd stumbled into, she'd never be able to live with herself. For better or worse, he was her *dad*.

Rescue and closure.

Rescue and closure.

Mind racing, she tucked the amulet and journal into her satchel and squirted sanitizer into her hands. True, most tropical diseases were transmitted by insects and parasites, but just her luck, she'd be the first person in history to be infected by a malicious jungle germ clinging to the pages of a crusty journal.

That's Grandpa Franklin talking.

Cursing her germ phobia, one of David's top three complaints, River blocked out the haunting voices of her pessimistic, dysfunctional family. She could, she *would* do this.

Moving into the house, she fired up her laptop and ran a mental checklist. She had to move fast and she had no idea how long she'd be in South America. Her next booking was three weeks away—the bells-and-whistles church wedding of Kylie McGraw and Jack Reynolds. Although Kylie was a fairly new friend, she was a good friend and a kind soul. Aside from the professional obligation, River felt personally compelled to afford Kylie and Jack ample time to hire a different photographer. In addition, she'd have to give Ella some sort of explanation for her hasty departure without telling her about the contents of the journal.

Typing Cheap Airfares into her search engine with one hand and dialing her assistant with the other, River decided to stick to the generic truth. "Ella? Heads up. You'll have to handle the studio for the next couple of weeks."

"Are you having a meltdown?"

"No. I'm flying to South America to get my life back."

CHAPTER TWO

Cajamarca, Peru, South America
Altitude 8,900 feet

"WHAT DO YOU MEAN they canceled the shoot?"

"An executive decision." Spenser McGraw thumbed his cell to vibrate and placed it beside his empty beer bottle as Gordo Fish, his friend and professional side-kick, dropped into an opposing chair. The popular café buzzed with good cheer, offsetting the men's grim expressions.

They'd flown from the Scottish Highlands to South America to film an episode for the popular cable show, *Into the Wild*. Spenser was the talent. Gordo was the one-man camera/audio crew. Now instead of exploring "The Legend of El Dorado," instead of searching for a lost city of freaking *gold*, they'd been ordered to cool their heels in Cajamarca until the show's new producer and a board of equally young turks hammered out the details of a new adrenaline-charged adventure. Spenser met his friend's baffled stare. "They want to introduce an element of danger into the show."

Gordo frowned. "You're kidding."

"Nope."

"Something tells me Necktie Nate is behind this."

The nickname they'd given to Nathan Crup, their new Armani-suited producer. "Probably."

"Has that asshole watched even one episode from the past five seasons?" Gordo complained. "We've battled extreme elements and hostile people. Survived mudslides, cave-ins, avalanches and assorted injuries."

"None of them life threatening."

"Like hell. What about the time I got food poisoning in Cairo?"

Spenser found it amusing that a man who'd endured extreme temperatures, snakebites and altitude sickness would label the time he'd hugged the porcelain goddess in a ritzy hotel room as a near-death experience. "You weren't even close to dying."

"I ended up in the hospital."

"Because you called an ambulance."

"What I didn't puke up shot out the other end. For three frickin' hours. I'm telling you…" Gordo trailed off when he noticed the young woman standing next to them. "Sorry." He squinted at her name tag. "Yara."

Earlier, the sultry waitress had lingered at Spenser's table, flirting outrageously, as most women did, until he'd received the phone call from Los Angeles. Now she was back, and though she spared Gordo a glance, her focus was on Spenser. He winked, encouraging the infatuation. Yara's pretty face and voluptuous curves were a welcome distraction from Necktie's disappointing mandate.

Gordo cleared his throat. "Why, yes, I would like to order something. Thank you for asking, Yara."

Spenser smiled at the woman, then spoke in Spanish. "He'll have what I'm having."

"What are you having?" Gordo asked in English.

"Beer and tamales."

"Forget the tamales."

"They're locally famous," Spenser teased, knowing Gordo was still fixed on the Cairo incident and the "locally famous" *molokhiyya*.

"Just a beer, please," he said in Spanish. "Make that two. No, three. Two for me, one for him."

Beaming at Spenser, Yara nodded and left.

Gordo rolled his eyes. "You're hooking up with her later, aren't you?"

Never one to screw and tell, Spenser just grinned.

"Why aren't you more upset about the canceled shoot? You've been hot on exploring the possibility that El Dorado is located in Peru and not Colombia for months."

Spenser shrugged. Granted, at first he'd been royally ticked. Not just because Nate had pulled the plug on El Dorado, but because that pissant had called his Indiana Jones shtick old hat, insinuating in the next breath that Spenser was over-the-hill.

A) He didn't do *shtick*.

B) Since when was he thirty-seven years old?

Shaking off the insults, he now saw the hole in the producer's new angle. "When the board reviews Necktie's brilliant idea, they'll squelch it."

"How can you be sure?"

"Because it's been done."

Gordo narrowed his eyes. "What does Necktie want us to do exactly?"

"To canoe down the Amazon, hack through the jungle and somehow connect with a fierce tribe—preferably cannibalistic."

"You're kidding."

"Just about the cannibal part."

"Great. So we risk malaria, piranha, jaguars and make nice with hostile indigenous peoples. And then?"

"Live with them for six months. Learn and record their ways. Survive whatever shit they sling at us."

"It's been done," Gordo said with a derisive snort. "The Thrill Me, Chill Me Channel. *Spock and Parnell Live With the Kaniwa.*"

"Yup."

Gordo scratched his trimmed red beard then massaged the back of his neck, his routine when mentally reviewing a situation. "Okay," he said, waving away the chips and salsa Spenser nudged across the scarred table. "So the board nixes the living with a fierce tribe thing, but what if they still want to ratchet up the danger? We're history-buff treasure hunters, not adrenaline junkie survivalists."

Spenser didn't contradict the man, even though he was only partially right. Maybe Gordo didn't get off on adrenaline rushes, but Spenser did and he experienced one every time he suspected he was closing in on a lost treasure or legendary icon. "A hundred bucks says I get a call tomorrow green-lighting the El Dorado shoot."

"If you don't?"

"We'll proceed regardless." He wouldn't spend a minute more than necessary in Cajamarca, the city where the Inca Empire had met its end. The capture and execution of the Incan emperor Atahualpa in 1532 launched a legend that had personally haunted Spenser for fifteen years. "Trust me, Gordo. The execs at the Explorer Channel will come around whether it's tomorrow or a week from now."

"Again. How can you be sure?"

"Why mess with success?"

"What?"

Spenser brushed crumbs from his fingers and voiced optimistic thoughts instead of the dark ones dwelling in the back of his brain, thanks to the suited pissant and this haunted city. "Our ratings have slipped, but overall they're still pretty high. We've got fan clubs, websites and discussion boards. I'm in negotiations to write a book. We're still at the top of our game, my friend, and the public's curiosity regarding lost treasures and mythical icons will never die. All we have to do is Twitter about the possible changes to *Into the Wild* and I guarantee the execs will be deluged with complaints."

"We do have some pretty rabid fans," Gordo said, perking up as Yara served him *dos cervezas*. "Including influential anthropologists, archaeologists and professors of antiquities. Since you've got plans," he said, gesturing to the enamored waitress, "I'll tweet and initiate an uprising. The sooner we get the thumbs-up on El Dorado, the better. Don't forget, you're supposed to be in Indiana in less than a month. If you miss your sister's wedding, she'll never forgive you."

Not only that, Jack Reynolds, his best friend and said groom, would kick his ass. Or at least try, Spenser thought with a wry smile. Even though he already considered his sister and friend married, he wouldn't miss the official shindig for the world. "Only one thing could keep me from my little sister's wedding."

Gordo winced. "Don't say it. Don't even think it. If Necktie gets his way you'll be swimming with flesh-eating fish."

"Relax, oh voice of doom. I'm not going to die."

"You're tough and lucky," Gordo said as he turned to leave, "but you're not invincible, Spense."

Spenser watched his friend move serpentinely through the crowded café. He chugged beer to wash down a surge of old guilt. "Not invincible, Gordo, but definitely cursed."

Just then his phone vibrated. He smiled apologetically at Yara, who reluctantly moved on to her next customer. "That was a quick turnaround," Spenser said, assuming the incoming call was from Necktie. Instead it was his sister, Kylie, who only called out of the country when there was a crisis at home. A rarity since she was a problem-solver extraordinaire. He braced for bad news. "What's wrong, kitten?"

"I know you're working, but I need a favor, Spenser. A huge favor."

CHAPTER THREE

Quito, Ecuador, South America
Altitude 9,214 feet

RIVER'S HEAD POUNDED as she moved out of the Boeing 757 and into the Mariscal Sucre International Airport. Her legs and back should have ached, too. She'd been cooped up on three different planes for nearly fourteen hours. Instead, her body felt oddly numb as she walked—no, floated—into the terminal.

She dragged a rolling camera bag behind her, chalking up the zombie-like feeling to sleep deprivation. As exhausted as she was, she hadn't been able to sleep on the long journey from Indiana to Ecuador. Between the all-nighter she'd pulled preparing for her trip and the extensive travel day, she'd been awake for thirty-eight hours. Presently, she was operating on adrenaline and gallons of Pepsi.

River's first two thoughts as she navigated the bustling terminal: *I wish I spoke Spanish,* and *God, I have to pee.*

She ducked into the first bathroom she saw to take care of the second. As for the first, according to her speedy but thorough research, although the predominant language of Ecuador was Spanish, English was spoken in most major visitor centers. Quito, the capital, certainly qualified as a tourist destination, as did Baños. Situated at the base of a large volcano, the small town, some four hours south, was famous for its basilica, hot springs and its accessibility to the jungle. Although Henry had mailed his journal from Baños—also known as the gateway to the Amazon—ten to one he was in the jungle. Ten to one she'd be hiring a guide. She'd just make sure the guide doubled as a translator.

She had it all planned. Well, maybe not all, but everything within her power. She found comfort in knowing where she was and where she was going and what she was going to do. As long as she had a plan and a map, she was safe.

River exited the stall and moved to the sink. Unfortunately, she also glanced at the mirror. She looked as horrible as she felt. Pale, clammy skin, dark circles under her bloodshot eyes, limp curls escaping her stubby ponytail.

She needed a shower and sleep—maybe not in that order. She needed to get to the hotel she'd booked for the night before she dropped dead. Her head hurt and now her chest was tight. Plus, there was the whole jelly-limb, zombie-like thing going on. Not to mention she was feeling anxious about venturing into the jungle and melancholy about Professor Bovedine.

Dead.

Just like with her mom, who'd perished on one of Henry's remote expeditions, River was having a hard time accepting Bovedine's demise. Death was bad enough, but when it was senseless or could have been avoided...

If only Bovedine hadn't returned home ahead of schedule. Had Mrs. Robbins called him at the university to tell him about the arrival of Henry's package? Had he been in a hurry to view the contents? What if the package wasn't buried in the ransacked mess? What if the burglars had taken it? Although why would they, unless the contents were valuable?

The more she thought about it, the more she wanted to know what Henry had sent Bovedine. Unfortunately, Mrs. Robbins, who'd considered her employer of twenty years a friend, was an emotional basket case, and Professor Bovedine's funeral was scheduled for tomorrow. Bad enough River wasn't attending, she wasn't about to add to the housekeeper's grief by nagging her about the missing package. She knew River was keen to know the contents. The woman would call as soon as she found it. *If* she found it. And if she didn't...

River nixed the idea that whatever Henry had entrusted to Professor Bovedine was forever lost. Obsessing wouldn't do.

Shoving aside dark thoughts, she washed her hands once, twice and then splashed cool water on her face. Slightly refreshed, she used her elbow to manipulate the towel dispenser—a quirk she'd picked up from Grandma Franklin. "Public restrooms are infested with germs," the woman was fond of saying. "Never touch surfaces and never, ever sit on the toilet seat." She'd drilled the notions into River until she not only believed but practiced the rituals. If she did touch something, she attacked the germs before they attacked her. "Better safe than sorry" was almost as common a cliché in her family as, "It's for your own good."

Swear to God, the next person who said anything close to that was going to get the toe of her all-weather trekking boot up their...

Well, at the very least she'd tell them to mind their own beeswax. Playing it safe had cost her a would-be husband and saddled her with a business she wasn't even all that crazy about.

Irritated now, River powdered her face and applied tinted balm to her lips. Ridiculous, since she planned on heading straight to her hotel and dropping into bed, but what if she miraculously ran into David? Stranger things had happened. Like her father and her ex being in the same foreign region at the same time. Not that she wanted to impress David. The plan was to give him a piece of her mind. To say all the things she should have said when he'd humiliated her in front of the preacher and thirty-eight wedding guests. She had a lot of questions, too. She wanted answers. Needed closure. She didn't want to reconcile with David, although the more she thought about it, maybe she did.

She'd used that very excuse for zipping off to South America when she'd spoken to Ella. And then again with her friend Kylie. "I'm going to get back my life. I'm going to fight for the man I love."

Romantic saps, they'd believed her. Although Kylie

had insisted on hooking River up with her brother Spenser McGraw, who, as fate would have it, was also in Peru. "He knows the area," she'd said. "You don't. It's unsafe for a woman to travel in that region alone."

Maybe so. But no way, no how did she want to "hook up" with Spenser McGraw. The man hosted a treasure hunter show for the Explorer Channel.

Beware of the hunters.

She'd thanked Kylie for her thoughtfulness, but adamantly declined. "I don't want to inconvenience anyone." (True) "I know what I'm doing." (Lie)

Unfortunately, Kylie was bullheaded, insisting she had River's best interest at heart, which only irritated River more. Did *everyone* view her as fragile? The phone call had ended badly, with Kylie questioning River's state of mind and River doubting Spenser's integrity. The moment she'd realized she'd hurt Kylie's feelings, she'd apologized and hung up.

Before she made things worse.

River felt bad, but her blurted insult had come from an honest place. She'd never met Spenser, but she knew his type. If he visited his family twice a year, that was a lot. His preoccupation with legendary treasures and his career kept him in the field. McGraw was cut from the same cloth as Henry, therefore Kylie had cut him off at the knees. The man was a home-grown local celebrity, yet she was probably the only person in the county, heck, the *state*, who'd never seen his show. She had no interest whatsoever in a self-absorbed adventurer like Spenser McGraw. How Kylie worshipped her brother, even when she cursed him, was beyond River. Obviously they shared some sort of bond that River had never experienced with Henry. *Ever.*

Melancholy and angry, River freed her hair of the elastic band, fluffed her curls and reevaluated her appearance.

Lack of sleep. Jet lag. Frayed nerves.

"This is as good as it gets."

She slipped her makeup bag into the pocket of her sling travel pack, pulled out her hand sanitizer and squirted. Airport regulation had allowed her three ounces. She was almost out. Luckily, she had a few larger bottles packed in her big duffel, along with other crucial necessities, including sunscreen, bug spray and antimalarial drugs. Ella would call her paranoid. River preferred cautious. People died from tropical diseases. She'd almost been one of those people. She didn't remember anything about her battle with malaria—she'd only been two—but her family had drilled the fiasco into her head. Along with the time she'd gotten sun poisoning in Egypt, attacked by fire ants in Thailand and lost in Mexico.

Suddenly fearful about being separated from her suitcase, River hustled out of the bathroom and toward baggage claim. Thank God for the diagrams on the signs. As long as she had direction. As long as she knew where to go.

Her head throbbed, her chest ached. It couldn't be a relapse, she calmly told herself. The symptoms were wrong. *This* was exhaustion. Lack of sleep and food.

Stress. She wondered about Henry. Was he happy? Frightened? Dead?

His journal was tucked safely in her travel pack, along with her passport, wallet, handheld GPS system and other essentials. She'd reviewed his notes on the plane, but her eyes had kept blurring and her brain kept glitching. There was a lot to absorb, not all of it pertaining to his current predicament, and, though she knew she should've focused on clues about a South American treasure, she'd been mesmerized by the photographs tucked between the pages. Her mom had kept scrapbooks, but these had been in Henry's possession. The family shots intrigued her most. Why had her father kept pictures of her when he was sorry she was ever born?

I love you.

Since when?

Squashing conflicting emotions and ignoring her tight chest, River searched for the correct baggage carousel. So much luggage. So many people. Most of them speaking languages she didn't understand. She felt a little overwhelmed. No, *a lot* overwhelmed. Maybe that's why it was difficult to breathe. Maybe she was gearing up for a panic attack. She'd had them before. Whenever she felt lost. Only she wasn't lost. She was at the Mariscal Sucre International Airport. And she certainly wasn't alone. If she needed help, all she had to do was ask. Preferably someone who looked like they spoke English.

Like the man coming straight toward her.

European or American. Late thirties or early forties. Hard to tell from this distance. But his stride and posture telegraphed the confidence of a mature man. A sexy, secure man.

Wow.

Cropped sandy-brown hair and vivid green eyes contrasted greatly with his sun-bronzed skin. His mouth was…to die for. And the crinkles around his eyes suggested he smiled often, sort of like now.

Good Lord. Was he smiling at *her?*

He was still a few feet away and she was fuzzy around the edges. Even so…he looked familiar. If he wasn't a male model, an actor or a rock star, he should be. Tall, fit and rugged. Even his cargo pants and baggy layered T-shirts couldn't disguise his muscled physique. Maybe he was a sports celebrity.

She'd seen him before. Where, dammit? A magazine? A commercial?

If she could move, she'd nab her 35mm from her rolling bag. Her fingers itched to photograph male perfection.

River blushed head to toe. Or maybe she was feverish. She was definitely woozy. The visceral attraction nearly brought her to her knees.

He was the most handsome, most virile, most charismatic man she'd ever seen in the flesh.

She knew him from…somewhere….

The edges of her vision blurred as she struggled to catch her breath. Dizziness. Disorientation.

Oh, God.

Those green eyes twinkled. "River Kane?"

His deep voice both soothed and ignited her soul.

How strange. And scary. *How does he know my name?* she wondered, just before the world went black.

"SHIT." SPENSER caught the swaying woman just as her eyes rolled back in her pretty little head. Kylie hadn't been exaggerating. River Kane wouldn't make it one day in the jungle. Hell, she hadn't even gotten out of the airport without fainting. Not only that, she wasn't even in the *right* airport. If her boyfriend was in Peru, why the hell had she landed in Ecuador? He'd only learned her actual destination when he'd tried to check her arrival status. The information she'd given Kylie didn't line up with any of the incoming flights to Lima. He'd had to ask a favor of a flight attendant he'd been "friendly" with in order to track the woman.

He'd tracked her to Quito. What the hell? Bad enough he'd promised his sister he'd look out for the vulnerable photographer, but it had meant flying to fucking Ecuador, a country he'd sworn he'd never set foot in again. Not that they'd be here long. Still. *Fuck.*

Enlisting a security guard to follow him with River's rolling bag, Spenser easily carried the young woman to a row of padded seats. He guessed her at five one, weighing less than one hundred fifteen. A strong Andean wind would blow this little bit over a ledge. She wasn't bone skinny, just petite. And ghostly pale.

"Should I call a doctor, *señor?*" the guard asked in accented English.

"No need. We're fine." She was already coming around. Spenser smoothed baby-soft curls from her damp forehead as her thick lashes fluttered open. He was appreciating her flawless skin and pretty features when she nailed him with eyes as large and green as the legendary Maximilian Emerald.

His heart ricocheted off his ribs. Christ, she was beautiful, in a frail, angelic way. According to Kylie, she was also smart and sweet, though intensely private. One thing was certain. She brought out the protector in him. Hell, she probably had that effect on most men, except for the ones who took advantage of her. No doubt her waiflike aura attracted the best and worst of people.

"Who are you?" she whispered.

The question took him by surprise. Most people recognized him right away. *Into the Wild* had been a top-rated show for five years. He still couldn't believe Necktie Nate had him and Gordo, who was presently a hundred bucks richer, on ice. "Working on details," Necktie had said this morning. "Cool your heels while I do some fancy footwork. By the way, have you been immunized for yellow fever?"

Regardless of Gordo's Twitter campaign, Spenser had a bad feeling about the future of their show, similar to the feeling he was starting to get about River. Being sexually attracted *and* protective of a woman who was intent on winning back her fiancé was definitely bad.

"How do you know my name?" she asked, still gazing up at him in confusion.

"My sister told me."

River's Kewpie doll mouth curved into a dazed smile

and suddenly all Spenser could think about was kissing. Oh, hell.

"Oh, good," she said, moistening those plump lips. "You speak English." But then she frowned. "Your sister? Wait. You can't be… Please. Tell me you are *not* Spenser McGraw. You are!" she blasted before he could answer. "The billboard," she rasped.

She'd gone from pliant to rigid in his arms. Spenser was beginning to tense himself.

"I knew I'd seen you before. That stupid billboard on Route Thirty-one. The one Eden posted last year right before the Apple Festival, featuring the booked talent and highlighting a promo shot of you. As if you'd really show up," she muttered under her breath.

What the hell was that supposed to mean? "I never promised—"

"No wonder I didn't recognize you right off," she rushed on in a brittle voice. "That photo was airbrushed."

Stunned by the unprovoked insult, Spenser merely raised a brow and stared. The studio had been digitally manipulating his publicity shots for over a year now, erasing crow's feet and smile brackets, whitening his teeth, enlarging his already muscled biceps. He wasn't happy about it, but figured it went with the territory. Nature of the beast, he'd told himself. The entertainment industry obsessed on sex and youth. He got that and usually he took it in stride. However, he was still smarting from Necktie Nate's "over-the-hill" reference. And now this woman, this impossibly attractive, *young* woman, just implied he was a disappointment in the flesh. Well, hell.

Visibly mortified by his silent regard, River bolted upright and squirmed off his lap onto the adjacent seat. "I just meant…" Cheeks flushed, she looked away. "That photo didn't do you justice."

His lip twitched. "Apology accepted."

"You're not supposed to be here," she said with a weary sigh. "You're supposed to be in Peru."

"So are you."

"What? Oh, right. How did you know I was here?"

"I'm resourceful."

"I told Kylie I didn't want to impose."

"You're not." Although the sooner they got out of Ecuador, the happier he'd be.

"I'm sorry you came all this way, Mr. McGraw—"

"Spenser."

"—but, I don't need you."

A lie on multiple levels, but he admired her independence. "You sure as hell need someone, angel. You're ill."

"No, I'm not."

"You fainted."

"I'm exhausted. I haven't slept in thirty-eight…" she squinted at her watch "…thirty-nine hours. I haven't eaten much either. Then there's the jet lag."

"You're massaging your chest."

"I'm short of breath. Stress, I guess."

He got it then. "It's the altitude."

"But we're not in the mountains."

"Ecuador is a high-altitude country. You went from below one thousand feet to above nine thousand feet in less than a day. Some people bear it better than others."

"I can bear it," she said, looking annoyed. "I'll get used to it. Right?"

Why the hell was she mad? "Eventually." He snagged a bottle of water from the side pouch of his backpack. "Drink this. You need to hydrate."

She used the end of her sleeve to wipe down the nozzle. "Kylie was right about you," she said after draining a quarter of the bottle. "You're bossy."

Ah, the complexities of a big brother–little sister relationship. He grinned. "Huh. I call it helpful." He gestured to the bottle in her hand. "Drink more."

"I don't—"

"If you know what's good for you, River, you'll listen to me."

Her pale skin flushed red. Frowning, she glanced at her trekking boots, then back at him. "Good thing you're sitting down."

"What?"

Glaring, she polished off the rest of the water, then handed him back the bottle. "Thank you for your concern and the information. Feel free to return to whatever it was you were doing."

The words were polite. Her tone wasn't. She was pissed. At him. Which chafed, because, dammit, he was doing her a *huge* favor. Or rather a huge favor for his sister.

Spenser rolled back his shoulders and kept his voice light. "Kylie would ream me out if I didn't help you find your boyfriend."

"Fiancé."

"Ex-fiancé. From what I understand, *David* had second thoughts." Okay. That was cold. But, dammit, her stubborn streak was grating.

"Most relationships are not without problems, Mr. McGraw—"

"Spenser."

"It boils down to how far you're willing to go to make things work," she said, pushing unsteadily to her feet.

"And you're willing to venture into the Amazon rain forest."

She readjusted the strap of her pack. "I'm not as delicate as I look."

He raised a brow. "Maybe not. But you're in a foreign land. You don't know the language or the customs. You sure as hell don't know your way around."

She reached down and gripped the handle of her rolling bag. "I'll manage."

He stood and adjusted his own backpack. "According to Kylie, David is on an extreme tour in Peru. You're in Ecuador."

"I know where I am."

"Did you book a private puddle jumper?"

"I'm taking the bus."

"Why? If you fly, you can be in Lima in two hours. The bus will take—"

"I've never been to South America. I want to soak up

the scenery. Once again, sorry for the inconvenience. Have a safe trip back." She turned and wheeled her bag toward a horde of people pulling their luggage from the loaded carousel.

Unbelievable. Either the altitude sickness was affecting her judgment or she was a loon. He didn't know whether to shake her or scoop her up and take her to the nearest hospital. He caught up to her in three long strides. "You're not going to see much, traveling through the night," he said, pointing out the obvious.

"I'm not leaving until tomorrow."

"Where are you staying tonight?"

"I booked a hotel near the city's center. I'll taxi over, get a good night's sleep, acclimate to the altitude and set off first thing in the morning. I even know where the bus station is, and that I should take a tour bus as they're the most comfortable and have the least problems with pickpockets." She stopped at the carousel and turned to face him. "I did my research, Mr. McGraw. You don't have to worry about me. Honestly."

He almost believed her. Captivated by those earnest green eyes, he'd take her word on anything. But then she glanced away and he knew she was lying. He trusted she'd done her research. Kylie had described River as smart. A smart woman wouldn't wing a trip like this. But he didn't buy that scenic route business. Nor the part about not needing to worry about her. He realized suddenly that he'd misread River Kane. She wasn't stubborn, she was desperate. Desperate to get rid of him.

Why?

Never one to resist a mystery and a challenge, Spenser reassessed the situation.

"There's my duffel," she said.

"I'll get it."

"I can—"

"I know." He hefted the rolling duffel that doubled as a backpack off the carousel. "You can fend for yourself. Thing is, I have old-fashioned sensibilities. Sorry, angel."

The starch went out of her spine as he set the duffel at her feet. For a second, he wondered if she was going to faint again, but then he realized that she simply was no longer angry.

"Don't apologize for being courteous," she said, looking contrite. "If anyone should apologize it's me. You greeted me, revived me, stated concern for my safety…. I've been rude. I'm sorry. I'm not at my best right now. It's just…" She nailed him again with that earnest gaze, only this time she didn't look away. "I need to do this on my own."

Desperate, vulnerable and *determined*. Those three qualities added up to disaster in Spenser's book. Even if he hadn't promised his sister, no way would he let this lamb circulate in the wild without a shepherd. He wouldn't rest easy until he saw her in David's arms, and even then he wouldn't be happy. It was insane. But he was pretty sure he'd fallen in love with River Kane the moment she'd fallen into his arms.

He quirked his most persuasive smile. "Okay. Here's the deal. I won't force my company on you, but allow me to escort you to your hotel. It's late. You're exhausted. At the very least I could tell my sister that we spoke and I saw you safely into the city."

She moistened her lips and again he thought about kissing. He couldn't remember the last time he'd been this hard for a freaking *kiss*.

"So, you'd just see me to my hotel and then you'd be on your way?"

"Mmm."

She blew out a weary breath. "Okay."

He raised a brow.

"I don't want to upset Kylie any more than you do. Plus," she smiled a little, "God forbid I insult your old-fashioned sensibilities."

He grinned. "God forbid."

"Would you watch my bags for a second? I need…" She pointed to the nearby ladies' room. "All that water I drank…"

"I'll be right here." Spenser waited until she'd disappeared into the bathroom, then snagged his cell phone. He planned on hitting an Internet café after dropping River at her hotel, but it wouldn't hurt to double his efforts. Besides, Gordo was a wiz on the computer. "Feel like playing cyberdetective?"

"As opposed to sitting in Cajamarca with my thumb up my ass?"

"That bored, huh?"

His friend grunted. "What am I researching?"

"Not what. Who. I want to know everything there is to know about River Kane."

CHAPTER FOUR

NO SLEEP FOR THE WEARY. No sleep, or at least restful sleep, for those fostering sinful thoughts.

She should have been obsessed with Henry's unknown whereabouts. Or contemplating Professor Bovedine's untimely death. Or analyzing her wrecked wedding. Instead, River had spent a fitful night fixated on Spenser McGraw.

Why did he have to be so nice? So confident and capable? So...gorgeous?

When she'd spotted him on that billboard last fall, she hadn't given him a second thought. First of all, she only had eyes for David. Second, Spenser's profession was a personal turnoff. Third, driving by at fifty-five miles per hour, all she'd seen was a cocky-looking pretty boy. A less contrived photo might have made a stronger impression. Whoever had made the decision to airbrush the character and ruggedness out of Spenser McGraw was an idiot. Why mess with perfection? It wasn't just his handsome face. It was the entire package. As. Is.

The man exuded a raw sexuality that set her nerves on edge. He'd burned an indelible image into her brain. Teased her artistic nature. She ached to photograph him...naked.

He was a prime example of masculinity. A perfect gentlemen. In hindsight, even his bossiness was sexy, in a caveman me-protect-you kind of way. For some reason it was only easy to take exception in the heat of the moment. In hindsight...he'd been trying to help and she'd been overly sensitive.

She'd never met anyone like him. Or at least she'd never been affected by a man like him. He was dangerous. She didn't go for dangerous. She went for safe. Stable. Dependable. Men like David...before he'd flipped out.

Still, she couldn't remember ever looking at David and aching for him as she ached for Spenser. As much as she tried to rationalize the visceral encounter, she couldn't dispel it.

Feeling weirdly unfaithful, she'd finally dozed off after recalling a dozen special memories involving David. Their first date. The first time they'd kissed. The first time they'd made love.

Yet, she'd dreamed of Spenser.

After waking and showering, her mind was still crowded by thoughts of the six-foot hunk of walking charisma.

That wouldn't do.

She was in love with David. Yes, he'd crushed her when he'd jilted her, but he hadn't obliterated her tender feelings. They'd dated for three years and had been engaged for two. Two weeks ago, she'd almost been Mrs. Snodgrass. She didn't even mind taking his god-awful last name. *That's* how much she loved him. She was certain—when he worked through this life crisis or whatever it was that caused him to choose an old college buddy and an adrenaline-charged jungle expedition over her and their romantic honeymoon cruise—he'd realize his mistake. They were good together. They belonged together. As soon as she found Henry and sorted through this treasure mess, she'd find David and sort through their mess. This trip was about closure and new beginnings.

As for Spenser...well, it wasn't like she was ever going to see him again.

Two hours, a banana muffin and three cups of coffee later, River ventured out of the hotel and hailed a taxi for the Terminal Terrestre. She attributed her rapid breathing to the altitude and not an impending panic attack. Even though she felt like an alien in this bustling foreign city, she wasn't lost. She had her cell phone, her GPS unit, paper maps and, most importantly, a plan.

Next stop Baños.

On the trip south, she'd either study Henry's journal or catch the shut-eye that had eluded her last night. She would *not* think about Spenser McGraw.

"WHY WOULD SHE go to Baños when her boyfriend's in Peru?"

"Your guess is as good as mine, Gordo. I called Kylie hoping for a clue. She didn't have one, but said she'd contact River's assistant. I'm still waiting for the callback." Spenser popped a Tylenol and downed it with a swallow of Inca Kola, his South American soft drink of choice.

His sister's huge favor had turned into a massive pain. He still couldn't believe his shit luck.

"Are you absolutely positive the bus she got on is bound for Baños?"

"Unfortunately." He'd been waiting outside the hotel in his rented jeep when River had exited right on schedule. Last night, in her attempt to assure him she was prepared and capable, she'd mentioned she'd booked a nine a.m. bus out of town. She didn't mention her destination. He didn't figure Peru. But he didn't figure Baños. Of all the damned towns.

"You're not following her, are you?"

"I don't have a choice."

"But you haven't been in Baños since—"

"I know."

"You said you'd never—"

"Goes to show."

"Never say never. Still…"

Spenser adjusted his Bluetooth headset while passing a slow-ass car in order to keep the tour bus in sight. He'd been following at a discreet distance for the last hour. "I promised Kylie I'd look out for this woman."

"Yeah, but Baños? Are you sure about this, Spense?"

He quirked a mirthless smile. "Maybe it's time to face my demons."

"Maybe I should fly up and help."

"Hell, no."

"If I didn't know your history, I'd be insulted." After

a thoughtful pause, Gordo added, "What if I promise not to catch the fever?"

Spenser flexed his fingers on the steering wheel. Just talking about this made him uneasy. "You're a treasure hunter, Gordo. Of course you'll catch the fever."

"Not if we don't go into the Llanganatis."

The name taunted him, called to him. Instead of glancing at the formidable mountain range to his left, Spenser stared straight ahead at an exhaust-belching bus. "Did you dig up any more info on River?"

"If you don't want me to join you, just say so."

"I did."

"Right." Gordo blew out a breath. "Let me just say it's hard to dig up dirt on a squeaky-clean person who leads a low-profile life. These days most people belong to some social network—MySpace, Facebook, Bebo, Twitter, LiveJournal. Not River Kane. Aside from the website for Forever Photography, she has zilch Internet presence."

Spenser had discovered the same thing last night when he'd used a computer at an Internet café. "Kylie said she's a private person."

"Maybe she's one of those technophobes."

"Don't think so. Last night in the taxi, she checked text messages on her cell and thumbed coordinates into a Garmin Colorado."

Gordo whistled. "That's a pretty advanced GPS unit."

"Mmm." Spenser signaled to make a turn when the tour bus veered off the main highway and headed for the entrance of the Cotopaxi Volcano National Park. Miles back it had stopped at the Pasochoa Volcano reserve—another tourist hotspot. He wondered if River would disembark to stretch her legs and take a few pictures as she had before. He hoped so. He felt better seeing her, knowing she was safe and managing the altitude. Although she still looked weary and pale, at least she didn't look like she was going to faint.

Just like before, Spenser parked a safe distance away and watched several tourists stream off the bus, including—thank you, Jesus—River. After nodding to the man who handed her down, she veered off and squirted liquid sanitizer into her palms.

"So she's not a technophobe," Gordo said.

"No, but she might be a germaphobe." Between last night and today, Spenser had watched her apply that hand sanitizer at least a dozen times. "She's obsessive about washing her hands. Every time she touches something or someone."

"Maybe she's worried about catching a tropical disease. You said she'd never been to South America. Who knows what misconceptions she has about yellow fever and malaria?"

"I'm sure she did her homework." She'd made a point of letting him know she'd researched and prepped for this trip even though it had been spontaneous.

"Speaking of homework, since I couldn't find much on the Internet, I e-mailed a friend, a P.I. who has some shifty ways of obtaining background information."

"And?"

"I've been waiting to hear back and, lucky you," Gordo said, sounding distracted, "I just got an e-mail."

"What's it say?"

"Hold on. I'm reading."

Spenser massaged the back of his neck and watched as River photographed the distant slopes of the Cotopaxi Volcano. She was so intent on her subject, she didn't notice various men looking her way. Even though her attire was far from provocative—cargo pants, crew-neck T-shirt, denim jacket and a looped scarf—she was a damned beautiful sight. Ivory skin, golden curls, wide green eyes. An angelic aura that drew some devilish attention. Spenser tensed when one of the men approached. He couldn't blame the guy for wanting to make time with River, but if he laid a hand on her...

"Not a lot here," Gordo said, "but it's interesting. I'll forward it to you so—"

"Hold on," Spenser said. "I've got an incoming call." He thumbed over. "Morning, kitten. What have you got?"

"Not much. I heard back from Ella. She said River got a package the day before yesterday. It was post-marked Baños, Ecuador. Knowing River's ex was in South America, Ella assumed it was from him."

"What was in it?"

"Don't know. River wanted to open it in private. But Ella said it felt like a book. Less than an hour later, River called Ella and told her the same thing she told me. That she was flying to South America to get back the man she loved."

Spenser flexed his hands on the wheel. A decent night's sleep hadn't cured him of his infatuation. Knowing River pined for the guy who'd dumped her made his balls twitch, and not in a good way.

"If the package was from David," Kylie went on, "why did River tell me David was in Peru?"

"Don't know, hon." He watched as River sidestepped the touch of the man who'd been speaking with her for the last three minutes. When she turned to leave, the creep made a lewd gesture to his friend. Spenser reached for his door handle, then eased off. *Get a grip, McGraw.* "Listen, I gotta go, Kylie. Gordo's on the other line."

"Promise me you'll look out for River."

"I already did."

"Yes, but that was before you knew you'd end up in Ecuador. I know this can't be easy, Spenser, but—"

"I promise." Not wanting to have *the* conversation, he said goodbye and transferred over to Gordo. "What's the scoop?"

"All I can say is, this is one fricking small world."

Bothered by the surge of jealousy he'd just experienced, Spenser snapped at his friend, even as River hotfooted it back onto the bus. "Spit it out, dammit."

"River's dad."

"What about him?"

"He's Professor Henry Kane."

Spenser frowned. "*Our* Professor Henry Kane?"

"Looks like."

They'd crossed paths with the eccentric archaeologist three years ago. They'd had dinner and drinks in a desert cantina. He hadn't mentioned a daughter. Then again, Kane had talked of nothing but the Seven Cities of Cibola. The man was obsessed with legendary treasure.

Llanganatis.

Baños.

"Shit."

CHAPTER FIVE

Quito, Ecuador
Altitude 9,214 feet

"CAN'T...BREATHE."

"Don't. Care."

Gator tried to pry his employer's fingers from his throat. It was the first time he'd come face-to-face with the man known to him only as The Conquistador. It could well be his last.

"I don't care that you had to kill Bovedine," the eccentric man said. "Collateral damage. But you only brought me half of the damned map."

"All there...was."

The Conquistador tightened his grip. "Atahualpa's ransom eluded Valverde. It eluded Guzmán and Spruce and Blake. Generations of adventurers. It's inconceivable that a bleeding-heart archaeologist succeeded where they failed. That *he'll* profit from the historical find." He rammed Gator's head against the wall. "If anyone profits, it will be *me!*"

Gator knew nothing of this Atahualpa or those other three fucks. He didn't care about a historical find. He just wanted to live. "Boss," he croaked. *Asshole,* he thought. But speaking his mind would be deadly. Gator was a lot of things—most of them bad according to *good* folk—but he wasn't stupid.

With a vicious curse, The Conquistador eased his grip.

Gator slumped to the floor. He was as quick and strong as his attacker, but cold fury and a touch of insanity gave The Conquistador a powerful edge. Sucking air into his burning lungs, Gator massaged his bruised neck and watched in anxious silence as his employer snatched up the box he'd stolen from that pompous ass Bovedine.

The Conquistador sank down on the hotel suite's brown leather couch and reexamined the contents: half of a treasure map and a silver sacrificial ceremonial knife. "Tears of the moon," he'd said, when he'd first opened the package. "Proof Kane's discovered genuine Incan treasure." Then he'd gone for Gator's throat.

"Let's review your previous trip to Baños," he said, while stroking the hilt of the intricately decorated knife. "You interviewed Kane's guide."

"One of his guides," Gator rasped, wondering how he was going to get out of here with his skin intact. "Alberto."

"After some...*persuading,* Alberto admitted to mailing a package to Professor Bovedine. He said Kane had sworn him to secrecy. He assumed it had to do with the location of the treasure. You thanked Alberto by stabbing him to death."

Gator nodded, coughed. Pain ravaged his throat. Had the bastard damaged his windpipe?

"No loose ends or tongues. I appreciate that." His employer frowned. "But it seems there's more to the story. The other half of the map. Someone must have it. Who?"

How the hell would *he* know? Gator shrugged. "Maybe it's still with Professor Kane."

"Or maybe Kane mailed it to another for safekeeping. If that person knows Bovedine, if they know he's dead and suspect foul play, they may feel the need to contact Kane. Tracking Kane means tracking the treasure. *My* treasure."

"But no one knows where Kane is," Gator said, ignoring the wild look in the other man's eyes. Someone had to be the voice of reason.

"He's wherever the *X* is on the second half of the map. That old codger couldn't possibly move seven hundred and fifty tons of gold and silver single-handedly. And if my sources are correct, Kane is very much alone."

"*X* marks the spot," said Gator as he awkwardly rose to his feet. Seven hundred fifty tons of treasure? Maybe this precarious association with a madman was worth pursuing.

The Conquistador narrowed his eyes. Deep in thought? Crazy as a shithouse rat? Did it matter? Did Gator care? Hell, no. Not considering the windfall.

"I have eyes and ears in Quito, Baños and the Cotopaxi region," the other man said. "If any outsider expresses interest in Kane or Atahualpa's ransom, I'll know about it."

"I'd like a chance to redeem myself," Gator said. He didn't mind groveling. Not with a fortune at stake.

The Conquistador eyed the knife, the partial map.

Gator braced himself for another attack, but then his employer's cell phone rang.

"Talk to me," he said into the phone, then angled away as he listened. "Kane's daughter? Are you sure? Is she alone?" His shoulders tensed. "I'll be damned." He exchanged muffled words, then disconnected. He faced Gator and smiled. "This is your lucky day."

CHAPTER SIX

Baños, Ecuador
Altitude 5,905 feet

RIVER'S HEAD SPUN and it wasn't due to altitude sickness.

No one knew anything about her father's where-abouts. More accurately, no one had even heard of Professor Henry Kane. Either they were lying or she'd asked the wrong people.

Henry had mentioned Baños in his journal. He'd mailed the package containing the journal *from* Baños. Gateway to the Amazon—a prime location for stocking up on supplies before setting off on a jungle expedition. He'd definitely been in this quaint, colorful town. Yet, when River had flashed his picture at the post office, no one recognized him.

"What about a package addressed to Maple Grove, Indiana, in the USA?" she'd asked, adding the date of the postmark to give them a time frame. Ben remembered everything about the mail he carried and delivered. He'd definitely remember a package from a foreign country. It's not like Baños was a sprawling metropolitan city.

It was pretty dinky, not a whole lot larger than Maple Grove. But no one remembered the package.

Disappointed, she'd moved on to a few cheap hotels, bars and restaurants. Her father was always broke or close to it. He wouldn't hang out anywhere upscale. Even though he had his head in the clouds, Henry Kane was a down-to-earth man.

Frustrated, she grabbed a vacant seat in an outdoor café. It was late afternoon and she hadn't eaten since breakfast. She was in need of sustenance and a few moments to gather her thoughts. Although the café served Ecuadorian fare, the waiter was Italian and, luckily, spoke fluent English. That had been another problem for River in her search for her dad—a language barrier. Although there was plenty of written information available in English—maps, menus, signs—the locals she'd encountered didn't speak her native language well. Either that or they pretended not to speak it well. She'd gotten the distinct impression they'd been annoyed with her and her questions. More than once she'd wondered if Spenser would have made more headway.

Don't think about Spenser McGraw.

After Antonio took her order, River focused on the scenery rather than the hunky treasure hunter, Bovedine's funeral or Henry's well-being. She'd been in Baños, this small town tucked in a lush, humid valley, for several hours. Her breathing had eased at this lower altitude, but she'd yet to adjust to the spectacular view. She was still riding high from the bus trip down.

Ecuador, in the light of day, was captivating.

River had lied when she'd told Spenser she'd opted to travel by bus in order to soak in the scenery. She'd chosen the bus because it had been the only way to get to Baños aside from renting a car or hiring a private plane. She wasn't keen on soaring over the wild in a puddle-jumper and, even though she had her GPS unit, she preferred to leave the driving to someone who knew the area.

Still, even though safety had been her main motivator, she'd been unable to tear her gaze from the window as the tour bus had whizzed south on the Pan-American Highway.

The bustling city of Quito had soon given way to a rugged landscape, and then eventually to vivid green mountains whose peaks jutted into the clouds. An odd and arresting sight.

Then there were the volcanoes. From what she'd seen so far, Ecuador was a flipping volcanic chain. The Pan-American Highway meandered between the snowcapped wonders on a plateau that ran north to south down the middle of the country. As a photographer, River was drawn to the visual splendor. Unfortunately, she had minimal experience photographing landscapes. She photographed people. She'd felt like an amateur, snapping shot after shot, without her usual practiced forethought to lighting and composition, but she'd been unable to stop herself. She'd never seen a volcano. Today, she'd seen three. Two on the ride down. One here in Baños. The latter, Tungurahua, was the largest and most awe-inspiring because it was active and therefore potentially dangerous. Odd that she had been attracted to danger since landing in South America.

Or maybe it was simply the need to push herself beyond what anyone expected of her. Beyond what her family, and David, believed her capable of.

The longer she was in this unfamiliar region, the more intense her ingrained fears, the greater the need to slay them. Even now she ignored the creepy feeling that she was being watched. She'd had that feeling earlier today. But instead of obsessing, instead of looking over her shoulder, she chalked the sensation up to paranoia. She was out of her element and prone to old issues. She shoved them down and focused on her agenda.

Find Henry. Save Henry. Maybe salvage their relationship.

Find David...and talk.

Closure one way or another in order to move forward.

Antonio returned with her meal. River tore her gaze from the town's famous basilica and, beyond that, Tungurahua. She took advantage of the waiter's friendly smile and language skills. "I'm wondering if you can help," she said. "I'm in need of a translator and guide. Someone who knows the area. Someone who knows the jungle."

She offered as little information as possible. Just as she'd been doing all day. Henry had insisted she not share his journal with anyone except Bovedine. She assumed that meant the information inside. Not that she'd been able to dissect his cryptic notes, but she was pretty sure the treasure he spoke of was connected to a place or person named Llanganatis. The one time she'd mentioned the word today, the old woman she'd been trying to speak with had scurried away, muttering, *maldición*. River still didn't know what that meant.

Antonio flashed a smile that said he got this question a hundred times a day. "Baños is a popular starting place for expeditions into the Amazon rain forest and Andes Mountains. There are several tour companies—"

"I'm not interested in a group tour." River moistened her lips and tried not to betray the panic whispering through her veins at the thought of navigating a jungle. "I need a private guide."

The waiter raised a brow. He assessed her petite form and, as David had called them, dainty features.

River sighed. "I know. I don't look like I'm cut out for primitive situations." If she had a nickel for every time she'd heard some variation on that theme. "Regardless, I'm on a mission."

"If I may be so bold, *signorina*." Antonio looked over both shoulders before continuing in a lower voice. "In Ecuador, Americans are increasingly targeted for crimes. Robberies and assaults—"

"And worse. I know. I read the warnings on a few travel sites. I'll be careful."

"It is just that you are a woman. A very pretty, very—"

"Please don't say delicate."

He chuckled. "Ah, *sí*. Perhaps there is more to you than meets the eye."

She was counting on it.

"Check with the tourist center, two blocks down on the right," he said. "If not there, try El Dosel. It is a popular drinking hole for guides and treasure seekers."

"Treasure seekers?"

Beware of the hunters.

River forked her rice and chicken and tried her best to look nonchalant.

"Professionals and amateurs. We get them all."

"What are they looking for?"

"Inca gold. You have not heard of the Lost Treasure of Llanganatis?"

Not directly. "No." River unconsciously palmed her chest. Beneath her layered tees, she felt the amulet she'd secured on a black cord and looped around her neck. Not knowing its meaning or worth, she'd kept it hidden. Just now it burned into her breastbone.

"Google it," Antonio said. "Interesting theory. If I thought there was a chance it was true, I'd be searching, too."

She sipped juice to soothe her constricted throat. "So, you think it's a myth."

"It is safer that way."

An odd choice of words. "Wait," she called when he turned to leave. "Do you know what *maldición* means?"

He angled his head, processed. "I think so, *sí*. Cursed."

River's stomach twisted. "As in a bad word?"

"As in evil."

* * *

SPENSER'S TEMPLES throbbed. He'd been blocking memories and emotions ever since he'd pulled into Baños. He'd joked with Gordo about facing his demons, but that would require wrestling with a shitload of suppressed guilt. He wasn't sure if he could do that without getting drunk and staying drunk for a good week. Right now he needed to be sober and focused. He'd be damned if he'd lose another person to the curse and, the way things were going, River Kane was a prime candidate.

With the exception of the half hour he'd spent with Cyrus Lassiter, a crusty treasure hunter with a tarnished reputation, Spenser had been watching over the blond waif all day, albeit from a distance. He'd lost count of the times she'd washed her hands with sanitizer, doused herself with bug spray and slathered on sunscreen. Instead of being tuned in to the people—and danger—around her, she was obsessed with her skin and location. She'd constantly referred to a street map and her GPS unit, even though she'd only navigated the core of town. From what he could tell she was a mass of phobias, but that didn't stop her from trying to locate her dad.

Much to Spenser's disappointment.

Cyrus had confirmed his suspicions regarding the eccentric professor. He'd also supplied another troubling bit of information, one that had prodded Spenser into risking River's wrath by revealing his presence.

He waited until she finished her meal—God knew the woman needed fortifying—then joined her as she left the café. She was so immersed in the map, she didn't even sense his approach. *Christ.* "We need to talk, angel."

She jumped at the sound of his voice, then froze in her tracks. A dozen emotions flitted across that pale face. Surprise, relief, anger, worry and was that…?

Hell, yeah.

Desire.

He pondered that last one while she zoned in on anger.

"What are you doing here?" she snapped.

"Why did you lie to me?"

"What?"

He hadn't intended to provoke her, but damn he was pissed. Pissed he was attracted to her. Pissed she was flirting with danger. Pissed she'd put him in a shit position. Royally, irrationally *pissed.* "You said you were taking the bus to Lima."

"No, I didn't. I only said I was taking the bus. I didn't specify where."

He let that one slide. "You told Kylie and your assistant that your reason for flying to South America was to reunite with your ex."

"It's on my agenda."

Damn. "David's in Peru."

"I know where he is, relatively, and I know where I am."

"You damn well should," Spenser said, frowning at the map in her hand. "You've consulted that map or your GPS every ten feet."

"I can't believe you've been spying on me!"

"Watching over you."

"You said you'd go back to Peru."

"I said I wouldn't force my company on you."

"What do you call this?"

"An intervention."

She narrowed those mesmerizing green eyes and looked at him like *he* was crazy. "Listen, you—"

"Save it." The longer he stood here, soaking in her fragile beauty, breathing in goddamned Skin So Soft Bug Guard (he'd know that laundry-fresh scent anywhere) and coconut sunscreen, the more his temper spiked. Along with his libido. "You're in over your head, angel."

Her milky skin flushed red. "Officer!"

Spenser looked over his shoulder, spotted the uniformed *policía* standing on the corner. "Don't do it, River."

She arched a stubborn brow.

He met her obstinate glare. "I have news about your father."

She visibly faltered.

"Is this *hombre* bothering you, *señorita?*" the cop asked in broken English.

"No, I…" She tore her gaze from Spenser, smiled sweetly at the approaching lawman. "I just wanted to thank you for…keeping the streets safe."

Spenser translated for the man, added his own praise, then guided River toward his jeep.

"This better be good," she gritted out.

"Actually," he said, fighting the mystic pull of the Llanganatis, "it's bad."

CHAPTER SEVEN

RIVER BRACED HERSELF for the worst as Spenser steered his jeep toward the outskirts of town. He had news about her father. Bad news. "I never mentioned Henry to Kylie. How do you even know who he is?"

"You don't want to know. You won't like it."

She didn't press. It didn't matter. Had she risked everything for nothing? Was she too late? Had Henry truly sacrificed his life for some stupid Inca gold? She blew out a breath and blinked away tears. Losing control wouldn't do. Instead, she fostered anger. Her father had had the gall to send her his journal, to write that letter, to say he loved her…only to die?

Selfish to the end. "Bastard."

"I've been called worse."

River noted the stern-faced man behind the wheel. Today he was wearing aviator sunglasses and a variation of the clothes he'd worn last night. Brown cargo pants, trekking boots and baggy layered T-shirts. Sloppy never looked so good. She wished he had hair growing out of his ears or a fat wobbly wart on the tip of his nose. Anything to make him less attractive. She felt shallow and guilty for being so enamored with his rugged good looks. At least he was annoying today. Near as she could tell he'd left his good humor in Quito. "I wasn't talking about you. Although, if the shoe fits…"

"Guess you're still not yourself."

"What?"

"Last night at the airport, you apologized for being rude. Said you weren't yourself."

The observation chafed. She was kind and tolerant by nature. And when she had to, she could fake nice to even the nastiest people. A quality that benefited her since she was in a people-pleasing business. But with Spenser… She blamed her lack of good humor on the extraordinary circumstances, most of which she couldn't share.

"You followed me against my wishes, snooped into my history and now you're about to share bad news." River hugged herself against a chill that had nothing to do with the mild temperature. "Forgive me if I'm not feeling warm and fuzzy toward you, McGraw."

He glanced sideways. "At least you dropped the *mister*."

The chill gave way to scorching heat. This man radiated a primal aura that set her blood on fire. "This is insane," River mumbled to herself. Given her feelings for David and the impending bad news, she had no business having lusty thoughts about Spenser. Although maybe it was a defense mechanism. Something to distract her from dark thoughts. As much as she resented Henry, she didn't want him dead.

Unnerved, she looked away from Spenser and focused on the scenery. Buildings had given way to mountains covered in lush green vegetation. "Where are you taking me?"

"Someplace private."

"If you're afraid I'm going to have a meltdown when you deliver the news, don't worry, I won't. I didn't even cry when David abandoned me at the altar." Oh, hell. Why had she told him that?

"This is for me as much as you," he said, skating over talk of her wrecked wedding. "I needed to get out of town for a while."

She glanced at him. "Why?"

"Let's just say I have a love/hate relationship with Baños."

He veered off the road, taking a bumpy route through a dense copse of trees.

Where there are trees there are bugs.

She wasn't fond of any bug, especially fire ants—nasty, stinging, blister-inducing creepy crawlers—but she *feared* mosquitoes. Specifically anopheles mosquitoes. They transmitted malaria. They killed one to three million people annually. Because her mom and grandma had recounted her brush with malaria so many times, River had become obsessed with the disease. She'd researched the subject to death. Anopheles mosquitoes typically attacked in the evening and early morning.

Evening was fast approaching.

She'd taken precautions—an antimalarial drug, bug spray, protective clothing. She still felt at risk. As Spenser drove deeper into the trees, she buttoned her denim jacket and looped her extra long gauzy scarf twice more around her neck, covering as much skin as possible.

"Cold?" he asked.

"A little," she lied. Across the way, River spied a waterfall. Frothy water gushed over the craggy mountain face between and an endless variety of trees. Momentarily distracted, she gaped at the breathtaking sight. "Beautiful," she whispered, aching for the camera she'd left in her room.

"I've always thought so." After parking, he rounded the jeep and handed her out.

Old-fashioned sensibilities.

River found that quality both attractive and annoying. She really disliked the way his innocent touch incited a sensual tingling. "I asked several locals about my father. No one had ever heard of him," she blurted as they walked a narrow trail. "How is it you learned something?"

"I asked the right person. Someone who wasn't afraid to talk about him."

"Why would anyone be afraid to talk about Henry?"

"They think he's cursed."

Maldición.

River had a lot of quirks, but she wasn't superstitious. Still, she had a bad feeling about this curse business. She waited for Spenser to explain. He didn't. Maybe he wasn't one for walking and talking. Willing patience, she kept stride and kept quiet. It wasn't easy. Watching for flying blood suckers of death, she spritzed the air in front of her with insect repellent and walked through the life-saving mist.

"Have a thing about bugs, River?"

"Everyone should have a thing about bugs. Especially the kind that transmit deadly diseases."

"Won't argue with that."

"But?"

He shook his head. "Never mind."

They reached the end of the trail and he gestured toward a crude stone bench with a prime view of the waterfall. He waited until she was seated, then eased down next to her. It was all she could do not to lean into him. The man was a freaking sex magnet.

"Are you waiting for the perfect moment?" she snapped. "Searching for the right words? Whatever you know about Henry, just tell me." The suspense was killing her.

Focused on the waterfall, Spenser pushed his sunglasses on top of his head and squeezed the bridge of his nose. "I met your father three years ago by chance. Nice guy."

River didn't comment. Nice guys didn't turn their backs on loved ones. They didn't choose career over family. They didn't ignore obvious danger in order to quench their own selfish thirst.

"He's obsessed with rediscovering lost treasures," Spenser said.

"Tell me something I don't know."

"Do you know about the Lost Treasure of Llanganatis?"

"No." But her waiter had mentioned it, and she'd seen *Llanganatis* scribbled in Henry's journal. It had to be pertinent. "Let's hear it." She noted Spenser's squared shoulders, the weariness around his eyes. Was he stressed? Angry? She hated that she cared.

"I won't bog you down with historical or mythological details. Trust me, I know a lot of details."

"The condensed version is fine." She could always Google it.

He nodded, then braced his forearms on his knees.

River balled her hands in her lap, steeled her spine.

"According to legend," he said in a voice that probably mesmerized countless viewers of his show, "in the sixteenth century, the Incas buried a massive sum of gold deep within the Llanganatis mountain range, a remote and treacherous region of the Andes. People have been searching for that treasure for centuries. Many have met unfortunate ends, resulting in the belief in a vengeful curse."

He left River hanging as he stood and walked to a railed ledge overlooking the waterfall. She refrained from palming the hidden amulet, ignored the burning sensation against her skin. Trembling with frustration, she strove not to yell. "Teasing the listener with bits of information, then leaving them hanging over a commercial break might work for your viewers, but this is real life and I'm really annoyed. What's the damned curse?"

"If those mountains don't kill you, they'll make you go mad."

She blanched. "You think Henry's gone mad?"

He didn't answer.

"You think he's dead?"

"No one's seen him for three months."

She felt a little ill. "That doesn't mean anything. He could be deep in the mountains without means of communication. Alive and…"

If you receive this package, it means I am sacrificing my life to protect a precious treasure.

River massaged her pounding temples. Could the precious treasure and the Incan treasure be one and the same? Was the amulet part of that treasure or merely a talisman to protect her from a curse?

Spenser turned. "What was in the package, River?"

Her face burned. "What package?"

"The package your dad sent you. The one that led you to Baños. And before you ask, your assistant told my sister, who told me."

River thought about the amulet hidden beneath her clothes, of the journal buried in the depths of the sling pack resting against her side.

Share it with no one except Professor Bovedine and beware of the hunters.

She took a step back and answered Spenser's question with one of her own. "How much is that treasure worth?"

"Today? Around eight billion."

"Dollars?"

"Whoever discovers that treasure will be rich and

famous beyond imagining. Aside from the money itself, there's the historical significance."

This from a TV celebrity who hosted a treasure-hunting show. *I know a lot of details.*

A bell went off in River's head. "You've searched for the Lost Treasure of Llanganatis."

"Twice."

"Well, you're not dead. Or crazy. So obviously that so-called curse doesn't affect everyone."

He stepped toward her. "What was in the package?"

"Photos," she blurted. "Family photos. They were unexpected, a sentimental gift. You've probably noticed I call my father by his first name. We were never close. Then…we had a major falling out and…I came here to make amends." A partial truth, but hopefully one that would satisfy this man. Suddenly, she was as wary of Spenser as the anopheles mosquitoes.

"If you're thinking of searching for Henry, don't."

She didn't answer. She couldn't. Not without blowing her top. Not without inadvertently leaking information.

"You're not up to the journey," Spenser said in a sharper tone.

Insulted, she glared at the celebrity treasure hunter, a man who probably had a lot in common with her father. Including underestimating her guts and fortitude. "I'm tougher than I look."

"Not tough enough. And before your nose gets out of joint, let me add, few have what it takes to survive an expedition in Llanganatis. If the brutal terrain, in-hospitable weather and extreme altitude don't fell you, the curse will."

River scoffed. "Surely you're not superstitious."

"Go home, River."

"Don't tell me what to do."

"Don't be foolhardy."

"If my assistant heard you say that, she'd bust a gut. I am not, nor have I ever been, reckless. I always have a plan. I'm always prepared."

"That GPS in your sling pack won't help you find your dad."

But his journal might. Clutching her bag, she spun on her heel and stalked toward the jeep. "I want to go back to my hotel."

"To pack?"

"To think." *To read.* "Thank you for the update on Henry. Thank you for the warnings. When I speak to Kylie, I'll assure her you were attentive and protective."

She didn't protest when he helped her into the jeep. Anything to hasten their departure. But, instead of rounding to the driver's side, he leaned into her, his face mere inches from her own. She nearly swooned because of his close proximity, because of the sexy smell of his aftershave, because of the fierce expression on his outrageously gorgeous face.

"Aside from the brutal terrain and weather," Spenser said in an ominous voice, "do you know how many species of insects inhabit the Amazon and Andes?

Scorpions, spiders, centipedes and millipedes. Beetles, ticks, fleas. Mosquitoes."

Bastard. "Seventy thousand," River said in a strangled voice. "Species, that is. More or less."

He raised a brow. "I'll assume you're also aware of the associated diseases. Yellow Fever. Malaria. Dengue."

"Well aware." She fought a wave of panic. "I've taken the appropriate precautions."

He studied her with an intensity that liquefied her bones. "When you're in your hotel room, thinking about whether or not to track your dad, think on this."

His gaze moved to her mouth and her heart stilled. She dreaded a kiss, *ached* for a kiss. But he shifted and spoke close to her ear. "There is no vaccination for gold fever. And take it from one who knows, angel. It's deadly."

CHAPTER EIGHT

BAÑOS CAME ALIVE at night.

Lively voices and music filtered up from the street and floated in through the open window of Spenser's third-floor hotel room. He considered stuffing tissues in his ears. He was that desperate to avoid the memories the sounds and smells prompted. Instead, he shut the window and cranked the air. He turned up the television set. He checked his voice mail, pondered the lack of messages from Necktie Nate—what were those execs up to?

He thought about the favor he'd asked of Gordo earlier today. His partner had promised to call as soon as he tracked down the former Andean guide previously associated with Professor Kane. Spenser needed the guide to confirm or deny a story. Gordo preferred playing detective to solitaire, so he'd hopped a puddle jumper south. It had only been a few hours, still…

Spenser dialed his partner, anxious for an update.

No answer.

Ten minutes later, he tried again.

"Do you know how many Juan García's there are in Lima?" Gordo asked.

"A lot?"

"I said I'd call when I had something to report."

"Sorry I couldn't give you more to go on, Gordo."

"Remind me why I'm doing this?"

"Because it's more fun than sitting around Cajamarca with your thumb up your ass?"

Gordo grunted.

Spenser closed his eyes and willed away thoughts of River's desperate determination. "Because Cyrus Lassiter has been known to exaggerate and no one can back him up on this. Juan confided in him and him alone."

"If what Lassiter told you is true, and if Juan wasn't exaggerating, then Henry Kane's raving mad."

Spenser massaged his temples.

"Helluva thing to break to his daughter," said Gordo.

"I need verification."

Silence.

Spenser imagined his partner scratching his beard and then rubbing the back of his neck.

"I'll find Kane's guide," he finally said. "If not tonight, then tomorrow."

"I'll wait for your call."

"Sure you will." Gordo disconnected.

Spenser tossed the phone on the bed and glanced at his watch: 10:15 p.m. At this hour Gordo was trolling bars, known hangouts for guides and thrill-seekers. By 1:00 a.m. his friend would be three sheets to the wind and feeling no pain.

Sober and miserable, Spenser fell back on his rented bed and stared up at the cracked ceiling. For the umpteenth time in the last five hours, he thought about his outing with River. He'd been a bastard, but he'd wanted her to understand the danger associated with Llanganatis. He hadn't told her everything he'd learned from Cyrus about her dad's cursed expedition, because he wasn't sure how much was true. Cy was a good man, but eccentric. The treasure hunter's eccentric nature had made him the odd man out. He'd been known to embellish stories simply to garner attention. His take on Kane's expedition had been troubling. Spenser had wanted to spare River the gruesome details—real or imagined. Even though she played the tough chick, on the inside she was a wary lamb. The dichotomy was a powerful aphrodisiac. The entire time that he'd been trying to warn her away, he'd ached to hold her close. To kiss away her worries. Kissing River was fast becoming an obsessive fantasy.

He closed his eyes and groaned.

Love at first sight was a curse all its own.

The antiquated TV and ineffectual air conditioner droned in the background, along with the muffled sounds of the street. He was blocking memories, craving tequila and damning River Kane when his cell rang.

"What?"

"Nice greeting."

"What do you want, Jack?" His best friend and soon-to-be official brother-in-law. In truth, Spenser knew what the man wanted.

"I want to know you're okay."

"I'm okay."

"You're in Baños."

"So?"

"You swore off that town. Swore off that legend."

"I don't care about the legend."

"Liar."

"What do you want, Jack?"

"Your sister's on my ass. About you. About River."

"River's fine." She, too, was holed up in her room. Thinking or sleeping or watching TV, and no doubt cursing Spenser. He'd booked the room across from hers. The two times she'd stepped out, he'd stepped out, too. Both times she'd glared, done a one-eighty and slammed her door in his face. The scent of laundry-fresh bug repellent had lingered in the air, taunting him as keenly as Chanel 5.

"I spoke to Gordo," Jack said. "He told me who River's dad is and where you think he might be."

Shit.

"Are you going after Professor Kane, Spense?"

"I'm going to drive River to the nearest airport and put her on a plane bound for the States." The sooner, the better. "Then I'm going to get back to business and search for El Dorado. I've got a show to film." He hoped.

"What about Kane?"

"The authorities are aware he's missing. If they learn anything of consequence, they'll contact his daughter."

After a tense pause, Jack said, "You're an expert on

that region, that legend. If Kane used Valverde's guide or even that other guy's map—"

"Brunner."

"You could probably find him. Dead or alive. At least River wouldn't be left wondering. Also...maybe you could find closure yourself, Spense."

"Face my demons?"

"Whatever it takes to move on."

Spenser swung out of bed and nabbed a bottle of pain relievers from his backpack. "Kylie see eye to eye with you on this?"

"She wants you to let go and move on."

"But she doesn't want me to trek into the Llanganatis."

"Hell, no."

Spenser washed down the tablets with a swig of Inca Kola. He opened the window and breathed deep. Bittersweet memories swirled along with the cool air and salsa music.

He thought about River, acknowledged another kind of ache.

He wanted to move on.

"If I go," he said to Jack, "there better be a wedding to attend when I come back."

"Nothing would keep me from marrying your sister. Again."

Spenser grinned. "I'll be in touch."

He disconnected just as another call came in.

Cyrus Lassiter.

The crusty treasure hunter had promised to call if

he remembered anything more about Kane and his expedition.

"More news on the professor, Cy?"

"Not exactly," the treasure hunter shouted over lively background noise. "This is about his daughter."

Spenser tensed.

"I'm at El Dosel," Cy said. "And so is she."

CHAPTER NINE

RIVER COULDN'T DECIDE what had been riskier, climbing over her hotel balcony to the next balcony, then to the next two over, knocking on a stranger's sliding glass door and exiting into the hall through said stranger's room or…entering a bar on her own, a bar in a foreign country, a seedy bar patronized, as far as she could see, exclusively by men.

Her body vibrated with nervous adrenaline—a weird sort of high—as she assessed the boisterous, crowded room.

El Dosel was a smoky, dimly lit, testosterone-charged hole-in-the-wall. Taking in the decor, which could only politely be described as rustic, she reminded herself she wasn't here for the ambiance. Or even the drinks. She was here to find a guide. According to Antonio, the waiter she'd met earlier today, El Dosel was the local watering hole for tour operators and treasure seekers. Telling one from the other was impossible. But she was determined to find someone who would help her locate Henry.

That someone would *not* be Spenser McGraw. She'd never met a more infuriating, chauvinistic control freak.

Booking a hotel room across from hers? Following her every move? The man was practically stalking her.

Yet she was sexually attracted to him. Fiercely attracted.

Talk about twisted.

A purely shallow attraction, she assured herself. One that could be managed. Every time Spenser popped into her head, she kicked him aside with thoughts of David. Accommodating, sensible David—before his meltdown.

Dredging up the confidence and calm she used when speaking with potential clients or anal-retentive wedding planners, River skirted a few tables and moved to an open spot at the end of the bar.

The bartender, a swarthy, rail-thin man with a pencil mustache greeted her. Sort of. "American?"

River sighed. "Oh, good. You speak English."

"Are you lost?"

"No." The mere thought struck fear into her heart. She hugged her sling pack containing her GPS and map.

"I don't want any trouble. You," he said in an accented voice, "are trouble."

River practiced her superior people skills. She smiled. "I'm sorry. I didn't catch your name."

"Augusto."

"Augusto, I'm looking for a private guide. I was told I could find one here. Could you please point me toward a reliable, English-speaking, trustworthy, inexpensive guide?"

He smirked. "You ask much."

"I'll settle for someone who knows the Andes like the back of his hand, speaks broken English and won't cost me a fortune."

He pointed out a half dozen men.

After thanking him, River moved toward the least grungy and intimidating of the six. He was enthusiastic...until she mentioned Llanganatis.

"Wait," he said, his dark eyes narrowing. "Are you the woman who's been asking around about Professor Kane?"

At last! Someone who acknowledged her father's existence. She'd hoped not to bring his name into this. That supposed curse was a hindrance. Plus, Henry had warned her off treasure hunters and this place was full of them. But this was too promising to ignore. She urged the man to lower his voice and adopted a pacifying smile. "All I need—"

"I cannot help you." He jerked away as though she were diseased.

Undaunted, River moved on. She got the same response from her second and third prospects. The fourth turned her down before she finished her opening line. They all knew who she was and they all put stock in the curse. These locals were downright spooked. She got the strong sense Spenser hadn't been completely honest with her. There had to be something more to the story, worse news regarding Henry's expedition. Something that legitimized the curse.

River took a calming breath. She refused to leave

without a hired guide. Maybe if she blended in, she'd put them more at ease.

She scanned the smoky bar, snorted. Blend. Right. Who was she kidding? She looked like a Barbie doll in a room full of G.I. Joes. Her only other option was to flirt. Could she play that game? Trump fears of a curse with her own seductive charm?

Uh, no.

She wasn't that worldly. She certainly wasn't that foolish. Back to blending. At the very least she could pepper her vocabulary with a few curse words and sip on a drink. River loosened her scarf and returned to the bar. "I'll have a beer," she said, because asking for a glass of wine in a pit like this would defeat her goal.

"What kind of beer?" asked Augusto.

"What would you suggest?"

"Aside from you leaving?" Frowning, he served her a bottle of something called Pilsener.

She wanted to ask for a glass, but didn't. "Thank you." She smiled.

He didn't.

Since she didn't see a cocktail napkin, she cleaned the lip of the bottle with the sleeve of her shirt then sipped. Pilsener tasted like Miller Lite. The danger of getting tipsy on one light beer was nil, especially since she had a high tolerance for alcohol, but she did caution herself to drink slowly. She did *not* want to have to visit the bathroom in this dive.

"Heard you're looking for a private guide."

River looked to her right.

"I'm your man, lass."

"Beg to differ, mate."

She looked to her left.

"I'm your man."

She didn't figure either was her man. But either could well be her guide. The men flanking her—one dark, one light—were rugged and intimidating and probably just what she needed to survive the inhospitable and dangerous cloud forest. They were also foreigners. Scottish? Australian? Maybe they weren't skittish about regional superstitions.

"My name is River Kane. My father is Professor Henry Kane. Does that scare you?"

They both laughed.

She thought about the journal in her sling. She'd pored over that damned journal for three straight hours. Written in broken and cryptic passages, much of the contents still baffled her. But she had found a map. At least half of a map. The preceding page had been ripped out. "I need someone to take me to a certain point in the Llanganatis Mountains. Does *that* scare you?"

One man angled his head.

The other raised a brow. "No. But it'll cost you."

"How much?"

The blond man's lip twitched. "For starters…a few drinks."

SPENSER VACILLATED between worried and pissed on the fifteen-minute drive across town. How the hell had River slipped past him? How the fuck had she learned

BETH CIOTTA   93

about El Dosel? Thank God for Cy. If River got into
serious trouble, he was certain the man would step in.
But damn, Cy was pushing sixty. Sure he was in great
shape, but he was no match for several men closer to
Spenser's age and build. Men who'd spent too much time
alone on the trail, in the wild. Men juiced on booze and
intent on ravaging a pretty young woman like River. At
the very least she'd get her ass pinched or patted and
an earful of lewd invitations. His temper spiked just
thinking about it. River wasn't tough or worldly. She
wouldn't know how to handle randy, rough-and-ready
adventurers. She wasn't Jo.

Joviana Mendez.

The name conjured a rush of melancholy and shame.
Her exotic features, sharp mind and husky laugh teased
his senses. Spenser blocked the memories. He couldn't
deal with the past *and* River's present situation.

Jaw clenched, he parked his jeep in a spot he knew
well. Strode down an alley he knew well. On his previous two visits to Baños, he'd frequented El Dosel, hanging out with fellow lost-treasure enthusiasts, soaking
in the stories, the knowledge, swilling mind-bending
amounts of liquor. It's where he and Andy Burdett, an
army buddy, had fallen head over heels for Joviana,
an expert on Andean culture and legends. The closer
Spenser got to El Dosel the more the past threatened
to suck him in. The more he thought about Andy and
Jo. He experienced a moment of ball-shrinking guilt as
he crossed the threshold, but then Cy was at his side,

pointing at a huddle of cheering men, and every fiber of Spenser's being focused on River.

"Gerry and Mel roped her into a drinking game," said Cy. "If she wins, she gets her choice of one of them as a personal guide at a discounted rate."

Spenser knew both men. Gerry had settled in this area years ago. Mel came and went. They both made a decent living as private guides for thrill-seekers and treasure hunters. He wouldn't put it past either one of them to get a woman drunk, then lure her to bed.

"How many shots has she had?" Spenser asked Cy as they serpentined through abandoned chairs and tables.

"Just a couple. Won more than she's lost. Still, she's a wisp of a gal. Young, too."

Kylie had described River as being petite, fair and in her late twenties. Just now, surrounded by leathery-skinned, cynical, seasoned men, she barely looked the legal limit.

Christ.

Spenser pondered the best way to whisk that "wisp of a gal" out of here without raising hell. He noted faces. Some he recognized. Some he didn't. Some nodded in respectful greeting. Others, who recognized him as the star of *Into the Wild*, regarded him with a combination of curiosity and envy. Many would welcome a brawl. He didn't want to give them one. He didn't want to land his ass in jail or to give someone a chance to make off with River while he threw punches in her defense.

When he shouldered through the huddle, River was

knocking away Gerry's overly friendly hand. He saw red, but stayed cool. He focused on River. She looked like a lamb in the clutches of wolves. Her blond curls were tousled, halo-like, around her pale, wide-eyed face. She wore the same faded denim jacket she'd worn earlier today, but she'd changed scarves. This one was fluffy and—Christ almighty—pink. Spenser shelved the erotic image of removing that scarf and tonguing her slender neck. He also shelved the thought of wringing that lovely neck. Had she no common sense? "You made your point, baby. You win. Let's go."

He expected her to glare at him. She did.

He expected her to look drunk. She didn't.

"Spenser McGraw," said Mel. "Long time, no see. What brings you to these parts, mate?"

He gestured to River. "My girl."

She stiffened.

"We had a fight," Spenser added before she countered his claim. "I won't take her where she wants to go, so she came here looking for someone who will." He shot her a stern look. "That about nail it, angel?"

She glanced at her drinking pals, at the restless spectators. "Just about."

The fact that she played along proved she was uncomfortable with her current circumstance. Maybe she sensed, as he did, a brewing fight.

Gerry wrapped his muscular arm around River's petite shoulders. "She doesn't sound all that fond of you, Spenser, yeah?"

"She's fond of me." Spenser hauled River out of her

chair and into his arms. He kissed her. For show. For selfish reasons. For the thrill of it. To his surprise, she kissed him back. *Passionately.* Fire shot through his body, igniting lust and a fuckload of desires he'd considered ash. The fragile angel nearly brought this devil to his knees.

With a fricking *kiss*.

"Oh, aye," Gerry said through Spenser's lustful haze, "The lass *is* a wee bit fond of you."

"Damn," Mel complained.

Gerry and Mel were dogs, but they wouldn't sniff after a fellow adventurer's woman. At least that used to be their stand. He hadn't been around them in years. Hadn't been in El Dosel since…

He could feel the walls closing in. Could feel the presence of Jo and Andy.

Spenser grasped River's hand and led her out of El Dosel before he lost it. Before she came to her senses and slapped him, or kneed him, or gave him hell. Before Mel and Gerry saw through the ruse and decked Spenser in order to abscond with a beautiful, vulnerable treasure.

She tripped and lagged a little, the first sign that she hadn't been completely immune to the two shots of rum.

He was still reeling from that kiss, but she'd also stoked his temper. Once outside the bar, Spenser blew. "Do you have any idea of the danger you put yourself in?" he railed while urging her toward his jeep.

"Yes."

"And all because you're determined to find your dad."

"Yes."

"I could shake you."

"Go ahead! It'll give me good reason to sock you. Something I've been itching to do all day. How dare you stalk me!"

"I'm not stalking you. I'm protecting you. There's a difference, goddammit."

"I could've handled Gerry and Mel."

"Looked to me like they were handling you." He tossed her into the passenger seat.

"Unlike you?" she railed.

"Difference is I have no intention of bedding you."

She glared. "I don't like you, either."

"It's not a matter of like or dislike, angel. It's a matter of morals."

"Mel had morals."

Spenser choked on a laugh.

"Gerry was…frisky, but Mel didn't lay a hand on me."

"Trust me, he wanted to. And after a few more shots… *Jesus.* A goddamned drinking game? Clouding your judgment with alcohol? Putting yourself in a compromising position? What were you goddamned thinking? Strike that," he snapped as he swung into the driver's throne. "Obviously, you weren't thinking."

"Stop yelling at me!"

"Stop acting irresponsibly."

"I didn't. I had a plan!"

"Did it involve sleeping with Gerry or Mel in order to secure a guide? Because that's where that scene was headed, sweetheart."

Wide-eyed and red-faced, she squirted sanitizing liquid into her palms and rubbed her hands like she was scrubbing away vermin. "You," she gritted out, "are an ass."

He shifted into gear and left El Dosel in the dust. "Maybe. But at least I don't fog women's minds with liquor in order to screw them."

She shot him a mortified look.

"Just for the record," he added, wanting to drive his point home, "they wouldn't have fought over you or flipped a coin. They would have shared."

She gasped, then glared. "I don't believe you. They weren't like that. At least Mel wasn't like that. He even fed me the answer to one of the trivia challenges so I wouldn't have to down a shot of rum."

Spenser shook his head. "You are so freaking gullible." Christ, he was pissed. He couldn't remember the last time he'd been this angry. That in itself bothered the shit out of him.

They drove the next several minutes in tense silence, but he could hear her wheels turning. Tomorrow was a new day and she *would* find and hire a guide. She could do worse than Gerry and Mel. That thought gnawed his gut as he parked the jeep and then escorted River through the hotel lobby and up the stairs. "I'll take you."

"What?"

"If your dad followed traditional routes, I know where to lead you. If he veered off I can't make any promises, angel. Not beyond knowing the general legendary location of the lost treasure. But I can promise I won't take advantage of your pocketbook or naiveté. How old are you, anyway?"

"Old enough to take care of myself."

He lifted a brow.

"Twenty-seven," she snapped. "Are you happy now?"

Hell, yeah. He could handle a ten-year age difference.

"And I'm not naive," she added as they neared her room. "I honestly did have a handle on Gerry and Mel. They're not why I was anxious to leave the bar. I…I had this creepy feeling. Like someone was watching me."

"Everyone was watching you, angel." She was a damned beautiful sight.

"No, it was…never mind." She jammed her key in the lock, turned the knob and then paused. "Okay."

He stared at the back of her bowed head, fought the desire to run his fingers through those tousled curls.

"I don't want your help, McGraw. I really don't. But you are the safest choice and, like I said, I never act recklessly. Almost never."

She turned without warning and slammed Spenser into the opposing wall. She captured his face between her tiny hands and kissed the hell out of him. His mind and body burned as their tongues dueled. As their hands groped. She tasted like liquor. She smelled like bug repellent. She felt like heaven.

His cock grew hard and heavy.

Maybe his arousal spooked her or maybe she sobered up. But suddenly she was out of his arms and across the hall, pushing open the door to her room. "For the record," she said with her back to him, "I love David. That was just…the rum. It didn't mean anything."

Back still braced against the wall, Spenser took a steadying breath. "Look at me, River."

She cast him a reluctant glance before slamming the door in his face.

Like hell it didn't mean anything.

GATOR NEARLY BROKE his neck dropping from blondie's balcony to the street below. He'd watched her hotel for hours, waiting for her to leave, waiting for a chance to search her room. Unfortunately, his search had depended on Spenser McGraw's exodus as well. Unlike blondie, he knew McGraw by sight. He'd seen the man's show. He didn't know how the celebrity treasure hunter had gotten tied up with Professor Kane's daughter, just that he had. The Conquistador had forewarned him. The man's sources had spotted the duo in Baños and, soon after, Gator had boarded a turbine helicopter—flown by The Conquistador himself.

Gator didn't know specifics, but he sensed some sort of rivalry between The Conquistador and McGraw. At first his boss had been pissed off about the other man's involvement. Minutes later he'd been amused. Then again, The Conquistador was a fucking lunatic.

Gator speed-dialed his freak employer while slinking into the alley.

"Did you get it?"

"I searched her luggage, her room. No map," Gator rasped in a hushed voice.

"Speak up, dammit."

"I said, *no map*." Gator coughed, winced. Every time he raised his voice, he felt a ticklish burn in his throat. He'd yet to heal from The Conquistador's savage choke hold.

"Will she suspect a break-in?"

"No, I was careful, as ordered."

"Must have it with her. Pocket. Purse. *Dammit*."

"She's back now."

"What?"

"She's back!" *Cough*. "In her room. I could—"

"No. Don't touch her. Don't…" He paused and a chill went up Gator's spine. Before he could question, The Conquistador regrouped. "I've implemented another plan," he said. "It will go one of two ways. Listen close."

CHAPTER TEN

THE SUN ROSE before River settled down. Oh, she'd tried to sleep. But she was too high on rum and Spenser. She'd changed into sweats and jogged in place for thirty minutes. She'd taken a cold shower and, after spraying the sheets with disinfectant, flopped on the bed and studied Henry's journal for an hour. She'd been deliriously tired when she'd crawled under the covers, yet she'd tossed and turned with chaotic thoughts and troubled dreams.

Muscles stiff, head hazy, River stared up at the ceiling of her cheap hotel room wondering if she'd ever sleep well again. She blamed David, her father and Spenser. She blamed Mel and Gerry and a few other manipulative asses.

Men.

Talk about a curse. They plagued her existence with heartbreak and disappointment. Even Grandpa Franklin had dampened her spirit, constantly harping on her limitations and weaknesses. But at least he'd been a constant presence. He didn't send her away. He didn't abandon her. He gave her financial stability—Forever Photography—and for that she'd be forever grateful. Just as she was grateful for Spenser's offer to guide her into the Andes. Her gut said he was the safest, wisest choice. As long as she didn't listen to the rest of her body she'd be okay.

River rolled out of bed and stretched. *Don't think about kissing Spenser.*

She thought about kissing Spenser.

He'd caught her off guard in the bar. He'd manhandled her, something she hated, but instead of protesting, she'd melted in his arms. She'd opened her mouth, welcomed his tongue.

She'd lost control.

Accosting him in the hallway, catching *him* off guard, had been her way of taking back the reins. Of putting them on even ground. At least that's what she told herself this morning. Last night, she'd blamed the rum, a flimsy excuse, but reasonable. Lowered inhibitions. Compromised judgment. Hopefully, Spenser's old-fashioned sensibilities would keep him from mentioning the episode when she saw him today.

She glanced at her watch. Any sane person would still be asleep. Unless he was glued to his door, watching through the peephole, listening for her to leave her room. *Protecting* her. She didn't need a guardian, dammit, but she did need a guide.

River palmed the gold amulet hanging around her neck and absentmindedly rubbed the mysterious gift. She thought about that ridiculous curse. Thought about Spenser's knowledge of the legend and area. She thought about his trekking experience and his skillful kisses. Strike that. There would be no more kissing.

Confident she could control her traitorous desires as long as she steered clear of rum, River swung out of bed and pulled a knee-length hoodie over her T-shirt and lounging pants. She shoved her feet into a pair of flip-flops, the same rubber sandals she'd showered in last night to avoid contracting some disgusting foot fungus, brushed her hair and teeth, then moved into the hall. The sooner they made plans, the sooner they could be on their way.

Voices stopped her from knocking on his door—or at least *one* voice. Eavesdropping was rude, but curiosity bested her manners.

"Dammit, Nate," Spenser snapped. "Listen to what I'm saying. The story of a lifetime. Yes, if this pans out, we'll make CNN. We'll make fucking history. Oh, for Christ's sake. Yes. If that's what it takes. And Nate. Prepare to eat that Indiana Jones crack. He's good. I'm better. And I'm *real*."

River swallowed a curse as Spenser lapsed into silence and then laughed. Since she was only hearing one side of the conversation, she assumed he was on the phone. She also assumed the story of the lifetime had to do with the Lost Treasure of Llanganatis. A treasure that had eluded him. A treasure worth billions. *Billions.*

Beware of the hunters.

Fist balled, stomach knotted, River backed away.

Somewhere in the night she'd become a ticket to fame and fortune for Spenser McGraw. He didn't care about her. Or her father. He cared about proving a legend true and all of the perks that came with it. Typical of a celebrity type. Typical of a treasure seeker. She should've known. She *did* know…on the surface. But deep down… deep down she'd hoped, all right, fantasized, that he was different.

Idiot.

Spenser McGraw was like every man she'd ever met—a huge disappointment.

Fuming, she pushed quietly into her room and scrambled for a backup plan. As long as she had a plan, all was not lost. *She* was not lost.

Flashing back on last night, she rooted for her sling bag and located a business card. *In case you want the best,* he'd said. Another arrogant bastard. At least she wasn't attracted to him. At least he was a gentleman… of sorts. There was something to be said for "what you see is what you get."

She dialed the number.

"Yeah."

"This is River Kane. If you're still willing—"

"Willing and able, doll."

"No funny business. Just business. And just you."

"Understood," he said with a smile in his voice.

She didn't sense danger, only amusement. Committed to dodging Spenser and getting to her father, she pressed on while repacking her duffel. "I'm in a rush."

"I'm your man." He named his price.

She agreed. Thank God for the discount. She gave him the address of the hotel. "Park on the side street that runs along the north side. I'm on the third floor, fourth balcony from the...left." She had to think about that. "Be here in fifteen minutes or the deal's off."

"On my way."

Really? If he was that efficient, maybe he *was* her man. For this expedition, anyway.

River signed off, checked the time. Keeping to schedule, she downed an antimalarial tablet with a swig from a bottle of Inca Kola. She'd sipped half of it last night. The soda was warm and flat, but better than risking the drinking water. Hands trembling, she dialed Spenser's room. She anticipated a busy signal, nearly choking when he actually answered.

"Hi," she croaked. "It's me. River," she added.

"Sleep okay?"

Two meaningless words, yet his voice triggered a bone-deep sensual shiver. *Dammit.* "No," she snapped, "I did not sleep well. Too much to drink." At least the restless part was true. As for overindulging, she had a low resistance to germs but a high tolerance to alcohol. Two sips of beer and two shots of rum and all she'd felt was relaxed. "This is embarrassing, but I'm as sick as a dog," she lied. "Do you think..."

"What do you need?"

"Something to settle my stomach. Bromo-Seltzer? And while you're at it, a pain reliever. Motrin? I'm allergic to anything else." That didn't make sense, but maybe he'd chalk it up to eccentricity, or anal-retentive... whatever. She didn't care as long as it made his shopping expedition as difficult as possible. She hadn't seen a pharmacy on this street—she'd looked—so hopefully he'd be away long enough to give her a decent head start. She employed her moderate acting skills and summoned her weakest, shakiest voice. "If it's too much trouble—"

"No trouble."

Old-fashioned sensibilities. Even though he was a money-grubbing, fame-seeking bastard, he still felt compelled to look after the so-called weaker sex.

She rolled her eyes. She was stronger than any man had ever given her credit for.

After promising to hurry—*great*—Spenser disconnected.

River waited until she heard his door open and shut, until his footsteps faded down the hall, then she sprung into action. Since the front desk had her credit card information, she checked out over the phone, although she lied and said she'd leave within a couple of hours. Try a couple of minutes. She dressed quicker than a tardy bride, doused herself with insect repellent then pulled on an insulated rain slicker. The skies were overcast and the temperature would drop when they hit the mountains. Just in case, she shoved gloves into her deep pockets along with her pliable waterproof camera case. Dressed for inclement weather and a rugged expedition, she hauled her duffel and camera bag onto the same balcony she'd climbed over last night. Her heart pounded as she waited for her ride. She wasn't doing anything illegal, but it sure felt like it. The longer she waited, the greater her anxiety. She was about to embark on a journey with a stranger and who knew who'd they'd encounter along the way.

Beware of the hunters.

She flashed on a traveler's tip: *Don't keep all your important documents in one place.*

She knew that. Of all things to slip her mind!

River hurriedly rooted through her sling pack and redistributed credit cards, cash, passport and travel documents between her camera bag, duffel and sling. Her heart pounded as she nabbed Henry's journal. *So much "data" in one place.*

She heard an engine, the crunch of tires on gravel.

Although it felt like she was defacing the Bible, River ripped the remaining half of the treasure map from Henry's journal. She folded and slid it, along with his letter and her favorite family photo, into the baggy and tucked them inside her bra. She zipped the journal inside a pocket in her camera bag just as a mud-caked vehicle (was that a Hummer?) turned up her side street and parked across from her balcony. Confident she'd taken appropriate precautions, River prepared to drop her bags over the side. Her guide was a big, strapping man. He could handle it. She just hoped she could handle him.

Tall, Dark and Cocky eased out of his he-man vehicle and winked up at her. "G'day, River."

G'day? Sure. Unless Spenser caught up with her or unless Mel messed with her or unless she got bit by a mosquito. Then it would be a bad day. "Hope you're as strong as you look," she called down, then heaved her duffel over the balcony.

CHAPTER ELEVEN

RIVER SUPPRESSED THE URGE to whoop as she left Baños, and Spenser, in the dust. She'd asked her Aussie guide to haul ass. He'd complied, taking a shortcut to boot, and whisking them out of town in a heartbeat. He'd also held silent on the mad dash, which was fine by her. She wasn't in a talkative mood. She was in a foul mood. Spenser's betrayal had cut deep. Crazy, considering they barely knew each other. Crazy, considering she shouldn't have trusted him in the first place, given his obsession with treasure and fame. Still, she was fuming.

"Is that a Garmin Colorado?" Mel asked when she fished out her GPS unit.

So much for blessed silence.

"Nice," he said when she didn't answer. "Not that you need it. I know where I'm going."

"Good to know," River grumbled as she switched on the power. There was also a built-in GPS on the Hummer's dashboard, but she felt better relying on her own device. "What direction are we headed in?"

"North."

"Back toward Quito?"

"South of Quito. The Llanganatis National Park is in the Cotopaxi region."

River jerked her gaze from the Garmin to Mel. "National Park?" Henry had discovered something men would kill for in a *park?* "But Spenser said the area is dangerous."

"Parts are. Especially the part your dad disappeared in."

River's pulse spiked. Maybe Mel knew more about Henry's situation than Spenser. After all, Ecuador was his stomping ground. She hadn't questioned him or Gerry last night. She hadn't wanted to bring any more attention to Professor Kane and his potential whereabouts than necessary. Not that anyone had been willing to talk about him or Llanganatis. "What do you know about my father exactly?"

"What everyone else knows. That he was obsessed with locating Atahualpa's buried ransom."

Atahualpa. She'd seen that name scribbled in her dad's journal. She didn't know who that was, but she didn't want to ask and show her ignorance. Maybe he'd elaborate.

"The treasure doesn't exist," he said.

"You sound awfully sure."

"People have been searching for centuries. If it existed…"

"Someone would've found it by now." River focused back on the GPS unit. "You're going the wrong way."

"Alternate route. Less obvious. I assume you'd prefer Spenser didn't follow."

She didn't answer.

"Since McGraw's annoyingly honest," Mel went on,

"I'm guessing you didn't escape over the balcony to beat a room charge, but him. Otherwise, why call me?"

River fussed with her seat belt to avoid eye contact. "We're going our separate ways."

"For good?"

"For now." If Mel thought she was still attached to Spenser maybe he wouldn't make a pass. It's not that she believed her guide was immoral (as suggested by Spenser), but she wasn't an idiot. She did sense sexual interest. "Just so you know," she blurted, "I have a gun." Her biggest lie yet today. Lightning was going to strike her down any minute now—a real possibility, given the ominous skies.

His lip quirked. "Told Gerry you're gutsier than you look."

A backhanded compliment, but at least it meant he didn't consider her wholly naive and inept—unlike Spenser. She started to ask more about Henry, but her phone rang. She was surprised and relieved to know she got a signal in this remote area. Unless it was Spenser calling. She hadn't given him her number, but the man was resourceful. She glanced at the caller ID. Mrs. Robbins.

"I hope I'm not catching you at a bad time, dear," Professor Bovedine's housekeeper said.

River wasn't crazy about having this discussion in front of Mel, but she didn't want to slow their trip by asking him to pull over. Nor did she want to put off Mrs. Robbins. *Keep it vague.* "I'm sorry I couldn't be there for the professor's funeral," she said softly.

"You were here in spirit and the flowers you sent were lovely, River. As was the funeral." The older woman sniffled. "Professor Bovedine would have been touched by the overwhelming turnout."

"He was beloved and respected by many." Unlike Henry, the eccentric, selfish hot dog.

"I must be brief, but you were anxious, so I wanted to let you know. I haven't been able to locate that package, River. I fear that murdering burglar took it as part of his loot. Whatever it was, he must have thought it valuable."

If that package included the missing part of the map, and, *if* her dad really had located a lost treasure then, oh, yes, it was valuable. Except River had the second half. She didn't know where to start and the murdering burglar didn't know where to finish. That's if he went looking. Her mind raced with a dozen scenarios.

"River?"

"Sorry, I... Sorry." She snapped back to the conversation, glad to see Mel's eyes were on the road, although surely he was listening. Not that he knew what or who she was talking about. "Do the police have any leads?"

"None," the housekeeper snapped. "For a bungled burglary, the criminal was quite meticulous. I overheard one of the detectives lamenting the absence of fingerprints. Although the investigation is still ongoing."

"Yet they allowed you to search for the, um, mail?"

"The police asked me to inventory the premises and to list anything missing. As far as I could tell, the thief snatched a few small icons and your dad's package. Professor Bovedine must have interrupted him before he could steal more. Then, well, you know what happened next."

Knowing and believing that poor, kind Professor Bovedine was dead were two different things. River glanced at the passing scenery. The formidable mountains and wild terrain. Her Aussie guide. Everything seemed surreal.

"I have to run," said Mrs. Robbins, choking off new tears. "If I learn anything more, dear, I'll call."

River thanked the woman then disconnected. All she could think was, what if it wasn't a bungled burglary? What if the criminal went in looking for Henry's package? What if he killed Bovedine on purpose—one less man standing between him and a legendary fortune. Sick to her stomach, River dug through her sling pack for an antacid tablet.

"You okay?" Mel asked as she chewed the chalky pink stuff.

"A friend passed away." He'd learned at least that much from her phone conversation. "It's…upsetting."

"Sorry, doll. If you want to talk—"

Her phone rang again. River answered without looking, thinking Mrs. Robbins had had an afterthought.

"I don't appreciate being lied to."

Spenser. "I don't appreciate being used," she gritted out. The urge to punch something, preferably him, was overwhelming.

"Where are you?"

"None of your business, McGraw."

The man next to her frowned. "If you don't want him to know where you are," he said in a low voice, "hang up."

"Christ," Spenser said. "Don't tell me you're with Mel."

What the...? Did his resourcefulness include super-hearing? "I'd be lying if I told you that," she snapped, hoping to wound the celebrity's bloated ego. No doubt he couldn't believe she'd chosen Mel over him, especially after what he'd told her about Mel and Gerry's penchant to share. Only Gerry wasn't here. Just Mel, and so far, he seemed pretty nice.

"Dammit, River—"

She hung up.

Mel grunted. "McGraw's an ass."

She didn't argue. She stuffed her phone in her sling pack, undid her seat belt and wiggled around to pull her camera from her rolling bag. She needed a distraction. Something to cool her temper. Every time she thought about Spenser, his kisses, his betrayal, her blood pressure spiked. Coupled with the anxiety of finding Henry with only half of the map, of traipsing into a remote, dangerous region alongside a man she didn't know but had to trust... River shoved away her mounting fears and focused on the scenery. Capturing the right image while traveling at a high speed—Mel was still hauling ass—would be a challenge. Plus, the natural lighting was uninspiring. Not sunny, not stormy, just bleak gray. Maybe if she changed lenses and used a sepia filter...

"Fancy camera."

"I'm a professional wedding photographer. This camera is my life." Or at least her means of making a living.

"If you were my woman, you wouldn't have to work."

"No monkey business," she reminded him, not liking the direction of his thoughts.

"Just business. Got it. So, I know I'm taking you to Llanganatis," he said while she wiggled back around to get more gear. "I know you're searching for your father and that he was searching for Atahualpa's buried ransom. I know all of the conventional routes mapped out over history. But if you know something I don't, River…if you have any specific clues—coordinates, markers—I need to know."

He sounded professional and practical. He had knowledge of the area, maybe as much as Spenser. She couldn't make this trek without relying on someone and, right now, Mel was all she had. Still, she didn't trust him. After all, he'd tried to get her drunk last night. "Are you a guide or a treasure hunter?" she asked point-blank. "I never got clear on that."

"I work as a guide for people seeking treasure," he said with an easy smile. "I suppose that makes me both."

What you see is what you get. At least he wasn't trying to snow her. She grunted, then snapped two shots of a distant volcano. "I have clues," she said, knowing she'd have to give up Henry's data at some point, "although I don't know if they'll mean anything to you. I don't have a starting point."

"What have you got? If I know the marker, I can get us there. I know the Llanganatis like the back of my hand."

That was comforting. It meant they wouldn't get lost. Her phone rang. She wanted to ignore it, but what if it was Mrs. Robbins, Ella or—here was a wild thought—David. What if he'd learned she was in South America? What if he was worried about her? The notion eased her fretting, connected her to a more stable life. Her old life.

She glanced at the caller ID. "Crap." Ignoring Mel's cautionary look, she answered anyway.

"Listen, River, I don't know what went wrong, but…"

"You sold me out!" she blurted, angry that it was Spenser and not David.

"What?"

"You don't care about my father or me. You care about yourself and a story of a lifetime!"

Silence. Then, "Oh, hell. I can explain."

"Don't bother, McGraw. Don't—"

Mel nabbed the phone. "We both know you don't have the balls to go back into the Llanganatis, McGraw. Unlike you I'm not crippled by guilt. Unlike you I can get the lady in and out without catching the fever. Unlike you, I won't get her killed. Call it a day, mate. Go back to filming your pansy show and leave the challenging expeditions to the real adventurers."

He signed off and passed River her phone.

Mouth gaping, she started to ask what that was about, but instead shrieked when Mel slammed the brakes.

The Hummer skidded sideways. River fumbled her phone. Her sling pack flew to the floor. If her camera hadn't been looped around her shoulder that would have tanked, too. The seat belt cut hard into her torso as she tried to catch her breath and wits.

"Where's your gun?" Mel asked in a low voice.

"What?" She shook off the daze. "Oh, I don't… I was bluffing."

"Mine's within reach. Not that it'll have much impact against two machine guns."

Mouth dry, River looked through the dusty windows to see a dinged and muddy truck blocking the road. Two stocky men dressed in drab clothes and using caps and kerchiefs to conceal their faces, pointed big scary guns at the Hummer's windshield.

"Road bandits," said Mel.

She'd read about this type of crime, but she thought it was more rampant in Peru and Colombia. Or maybe that had been hopeful thinking. Even her waiter, Antonio, had warned her about crimes perpetrated against tourists.

Only Mel wasn't a tourist. He was a local. Sort of. At least he spoke the language.

"Maybe you can talk us out of this," River whispered.

"Stay calm and don't speak." Mel rolled down his window. A disgusting smell wafted in with the air. B.O.

and medicinal salve. The men demanded something in Spanish. Mel answered, then said to River in English, "Get out."

Heart pounding, she reached for her sling pack.

"Leave it," Mel said as the bandits opened his door. "Get out, step away and don't say a word. We may just get out of this alive."

In the midst of praying for her life, River thanked God she'd redistributed her valuables at the last minute. If they took her sling pack, which functioned as her purse, she'd still have the credit card and passport she'd hidden in her duffel. If they took that, she'd have the credit card and Xerox copy of her passport she'd slipped into her camera bag.

She backed away from the Hummer, shifting her camera so that it hung behind her—an unconscious means of protecting her precious Nikon. Beneath her layered clothing, the gold amulet burned against her breastbone and the plastic-wrapped map melded to her right boob. She bristled with anxiety and dread as Mel joined her and one of the men followed.

Bandit number two searched the interior of the Hummer. She was glad he kept his distance. Of the two criminals, he smelled the worst.

Brandishing his firearm, bandit number one barked more orders and Mel calmly replied. She didn't know what he was babbling about—she only understood the most clichéd Spanish words—but he continued to speak as he slowly emptied his pockets. His wallet. A PDA. He wiggled off a gold ring and passed that over, too. Aside from the amulet, she wasn't wearing jewelry. After reading about robbery accounts, she'd specifically left her earrings and bracelets at home. Her defunct engagement ring was back in its original box and buried in her pajama drawer.

"What do they want?" she whispered to Mel.

"Everything."

She watched in horror as he handed over his car keys. She hadn't anticipated being separated from *all* her belongings! The thought of being stranded in the middle of nowhere without her survival equipment pushed all of her panic buttons. "Wait!" she blurted. "Medicine! Insect repellent!"

Mel shot her a menacing look. She knew she sounded like a lunatic. Instead of pleading for their lives, she'd begged for bug spray. And oh, God, her phone was on the floor, her GPS in her sling pack and her road maps… "Please—"

"*¡Silencio!*" bandit number two yelled, the lapsed into a hacking cough.

"What part of keep your mouth shut didn't you understand?" Mel muttered. "For Christ's sake woman, do you want to die?"

No, she didn't want to die. Hence her pleas. She swallowed the urge to explain while bandit number one searched her coat pockets. Unimpressed with her gloves and a waterproof camera covering, he reached inside her coat and started patting her down.

Bile rose in her throat as his hands groped. Was he searching for something or just copping a feel?

Just then bandit number two yelled something from the Hummer. He sounded pleased, except for the coughing. Good Lord, was he contagious?

Bandit number one yelled something back, then barked at River. She didn't understand his order, but there was no mistaking his intention when he yanked her toward their bandit truck. At least he hadn't discovered the map hidden in her bra. For the time being, at least, her dad's secret was safe.

"We had a deal," Mel shouted. "Hummer for the woman." Catching himself, he switched to Spanish.

Apparently the deal was off. They were taking her. For what? Rape? Ransom? Petrified, River dug in her heels.

The next instant blurred. Mel morphed into some sort of ninja fighter and kicked serious bad-guy butt. *Swing, punch, swipe, kick.* He pulled a handgun as the bandits grappled for their weapons. "Run!" he shouted at River.

Was he crazy?

"Run, dammit! Hide!"

Sheer panic gave her the speed of an Olympian. River dashed for cover. Behind her she heard scuffling and gunshots. *Oh, God.*

She ran fast and hard, into dense brush and trees. She jogged every day. She had stamina, strength. She could run as though her life depended on it. Which, oh, God, it *did*.

More gunfire.

Mel. Was he injured? Dead? She felt guilty for leaving

him. She should go back and…what? It would be better if she found help. She kept running. She cut left, then right. *Don't make it easy for them to follow,* she thought wildly.

More trees, more brush.

She tripped on something, fell hard to her hands and knees.

She listened past the pounding of her own heart, the rasp of her labored breathing.

Silence.

No gunshots.

No voices.

No approaching footfalls.

Lungs burning, River rose to her shaky legs. She swiped her mud-and-guck-caked hands on her pants, mourning the loss of her liquid sanitizer—six twelve-ounce bottles of Purell. *Dammit.* She looked around, trying to get her bearings.

Her senses buzzed with a familiar panic, her precious control close to breaking.

GPS—*gone.* Detailed Ecuadorian road map—*history.*

River Kane—*lost.*

Just when she thought it couldn't get worse, the bleak, gray skies poured rain.

CHAPTER TWELVE

SPENSER NAVIGATED the rutted, muddy road, cursing the midmorning storm and contemplating the many ways a deceptively angelic spawn of Satan could die. Given the dangerous area, and River's reckless companion, he could think of several. One scenario involved Spenser himself wringing her pretty neck. He'd been nurturing his anger for an hour. When he caught up to her he'd…

His phone chirped. Maybe it was River. He glanced at the caller ID. Not recognizing the number, he traded pissed for professional. "Spenser McGraw."

"I'm in deep shit, mate."

Mel.

"Talk to me."

"Road bandits," the Aussie said in a tight voice. "Tried to take River."

Spenser's blood ran cold.

"I told her to run. Killed one bastard. The other got away in my Hummer. I copped the bandit's wheels. Tried to follow. River needed her medication, but, *dammit,* I'm wounded."

"How bad?"

"Bad enough."

"What about River?"

"Unharmed." Mel groaned and swore a pained blue streak. "I'm dumping the body and the truck and going underground for medical attention."

"Why underground?"

"Are you listening? I killed a man. I'm a foreigner in bloody South America."

"Self-defense."

"I have issues with the authorities. Not taking the chance."

Spenser wasn't in the mood or mind-set to argue. Mel could take care of himself, but the naive germaphobe? The woman who wouldn't circle the block without her GPS? "Where's River?"

Mel told him the precise whereabouts of the show-down and the direction she'd taken when she'd run off. "Don't imagine she'll venture far. Skittish about the unknown."

He'd noticed. For some reason, it chafed that Mel had noticed, too.

"Find her and take her home, mate. Locals pegged this one. Her dad's expedition is cursed."

The C-word rippled through Spenser, slowly, miserably. He signed off with Mel and relived every *cursed* moment in the Llanganatis with Jo and Andy. He refused to give in to the guilt, the regret. He couldn't afford a pity party. He was on a rescue mission.

THE DOWNPOUR had diminished to a misty drizzle by the time Spenser found her. Unfortunately, even though

Mel's coordinates had been precise, the heavy rain had made River difficult to track. Even with his extensive survival training. Two hours after Mel's initial call, Spenser spotted her, hunkered against a tree, her knees clutched to her chest.

Not wanting to spook her, he approached with care. "River, it's Spense." She didn't look up, didn't speak. Her gaze was fixed on her muddy trekking boots. Was she in shock? Injured? Kneeling, he pushed back the hood of her rain jacket and studied her pale, damp face. "Are you hurt?"

"I didn't lose it," she said in a soft choked voice

"Lose what, hon?"

"Control. This time I didn't freak out. This time I stayed in one spot. Made it easier for someone to find me." She finally met his gaze. "It worked."

He wanted to ask what she meant by *this time,* but he was momentarily transfixed by a pair of glassy green eyes. Even though tears brimmed, she refused to let them fall. Her unique blend of strength and fragility fascinated him as surely as the Holy Grail.

"I would've found my way out, but the rain washed away my path. If I'd only had a map, but those bastards took *everything.*"

Spenser blinked at the explosive anger simmering below the surface.

"My medicine, my bug spray and disinfectants. My phone and GPS. I think I made them mad when I begged them to leave my things. Like they needed a flipping road map of Ecuador? They *live* here. Bandits," she clarified.

He wrapped his hands around hers, offering comfort and heat. Her cargo pants were soaked and, even though her slicker looked thermal, she was shivering. "Come on, hon. Let's get you out of here and dried off."

She sleeved raindrops from her thick lashes. "What about Mel? We have to find Mel. He could be hurt or—"

"Mel's fine." Or at least he would be. Maybe. "He called and told me where to find you."

She scrunched her brow. "I thought the bandits took his phone."

"Guess he took it back." Probably from the one he killed.

"Why didn't *he* find me?"

"He said he's searching for your medicine." Another half truth. He worried she'd fall apart if she knew he'd been shot. "What kind of medicine, River?"

"Primaquine. You had him wrong, you know. Mel's a nice guy."

He didn't know about nice but Mel had elephant-size balls and a strong sense of chivalry—at least where River was concerned.

"If anything happens to him—"

"Mel can take care of himself."

"But they had guns. He was outnumbered and—"

"Stop." Spenser hated that she was torturing herself and despised the jealously she stoked with talk of Mel.

It was petty and conjured memories of another rivalry. He couldn't go there. Wouldn't go there.

"I'm a wedding photographer, not a photojournalist. I don't do war zones. I don't do...this. I wouldn't even be here if it wasn't for...Henry. Selfish bastard. This is his fault. When I find him..." She choked back a sob. "He better be alive, dammit."

Chest tight, Spenser scooped River into his arms. "Time to fly home, angel."

"No! Have to press on," she said in a shaky but determined voice. "Need closure. Need direction. Need—"

"Shh." He backtracked through the thicket, conscious of her petite form and vulnerability, her uncontrollable shivering. He cursed the bandits who would've harmed her and mentally praised the man who'd saved her skin. Looks like he owed Mel Sutherland.

"We should call the police," River croaked.

"Mel's handling that end." Since he owed the man, Spenser wouldn't complicate Mel's life by alerting the authorities. Hell, between internal corruption and a significant increase in violent crimes, the Ecuadorean police had their hands full. Chances of catching a rural bandit and retrieving an American tourist's luggage were slim to none. As soon as she was calm, he'd explain the situation. Until then he was handling this fragile package with kid gloves.

Spenser placed River in the passenger seat.

"I'm filthy," she said.

At first he thought she was worried about getting

his leather seats dirty, then realized she was gawking helplessly at her muddy hands.

"Mold, bacteria, decaying animal parts. Who knows what was in that jungle slime? It's even under my fingernails."

He remembered her penchant for obsessively sanitizing her hands. She wasn't merely concerned about cleanliness, she was paranoid about germs.

"I hope those bandits choke on my Purell, not that they'd drink it," she rambled on, "but you know what I mean."

Again, he was surprised by the fire in her voice, albeit a controlled fire. He almost wished she'd burst into tears. Tears he could handle, but this volatile repression…he was at a loss. He nabbed his water bottle, soaked his kerchief and pressed it into her hands. "I have soap in my gear. Hang on." He hustled around and opened the hatchback, located his toiletries and hurried back.

She looked at him as though he'd handed her a bar of gold. "Thank you," she whispered, then started scrubbing.

Meanwhile, Spenser unzipped her jacket to make certain she was fairly dry from the waist up, raising a brow at the plastic-wrapped camera hidden beneath. "Looks like they didn't steal *everything*."

"Only my means of survival," she grumbled, as he tugged off her sodden boots and thick socks. "And knowledge men would kill for."

Spenser slowly straightened and braced his hands on the jeep's roof.

"They didn't understand English. Maybe they won't be able to read it," she said, still scrubbing. "I have to get it back. I have to tell Mel where to look." She looked at him wild-eyed. "Give me your phone."

He didn't budge. "What knowledge, River? What does Mel have to get back?" Was this about her father? His expedition? The treasure?

She focused on him, blinked, and suddenly she was less shocky. She passed him back the kerchief and soap. They were back to square one—her not wanting his help. "Thank you for finding me, but…I can't do this with you. I need…someone else. Someone I can trust."

She trusted Mel, but not him? That was one hell of an insult. Then he remembered. "For what it's worth, that phone conversation you eavesdropped on? My partner and I have been at odds with the studio on the next episode of *Into the Wild*. That phone call was a power play. I have other things to save aside from you."

Her cheeks flushed.

"Shit. Sorry. I didn't mean it like that. I'm just—" Screwed. She was under his skin, in his blood. Just like, Jo. Only she wasn't anything *like* Jo. "Shit."

"I wasn't eavesdropping. I came over to talk to you and overheard…I didn't listen to the whole conversation." She frowned. "What do you mean a power play?"

"The show's producer wanted to send me to the end of the world. Ushuaia," he clarified. "To explore Argentinean cuisine on the Southern Fuegian Railway. Like viewers need another Anthony Bourdain or Michael Palin."

River blinked.

"Never mind. Bottom line—Nate wanted me to be somewhere and I'd promised to be with you. I had to give him something."

"Something big, you mean. Like the Lost Treasure of Llanganatis. Like I said," she snapped. "You sold me out."

"Do you see Gordo?"

"Who?"

"Gordo Fish. My cameraman."

She bit her lower lip, glanced over his shoulder. "He could be hiding in the brush."

"He's not." The drizzle had subsided, the sky was beginning to clear, but Spenser's mood grew darker by the second. Usually women showered him with flattery and sexy come-ons. This one blasted him with insults and shoved him to arm's length. "Do you know how worried I was when I discovered you'd checked out of your room? In the midst of my packing, my sister called. She didn't want you to feel pestered so she pestered me. Had to lie my freaking ass off. *River's fine. I'm fine. Everything's good.* Then I find out you've taken off with Mel Sutherland, a man with a reputation for being a hound and a hothead."

"And you're a serene monk?"

"I don't like how it makes me feel when I think you're in danger, angel."

"I don't like how it makes me feel when you look at me like that," she whispered.

He wanted to pull her into his arms, to cherish and protect. More than anything, he wanted to kiss her. Deeply. Intensely. "Then stop being so damned... intriguing."

"You think I'm intriguing?"

"Like an ancient puzzle. I could work you for a life-time and never grow bored."

He'd shocked her. Hell, he'd shocked himself. Knowing he was head over heels and admitting it out loud were two different animals. Just now he felt like a jackass.

"David thought I was boring."

"David's an idiot."

"And controlling. Not David. Me. He accused me of being controlling. On our wedding day. At the altar."

"Then he's a bastard."

"I'm not controlling. I just need order. I need—"

He kissed her—deeply, intensely—satisfying his own needs. At first she surrendered—pliant, willing—and he swore he tasted heaven. But then he felt her palms on his chest—resistance. His senses crashed back. She was vulnerable and he'd taken advantage. He eased off. "Bad timing."

She averted her gaze, licked her kiss-swollen lips. "I don't trust this."

"You mean you don't trust me."

"I'm in love with David."

"So you keep saying." Spenser pushed out of the

jeep, breathed deep, seeking serenity or at least one goddamned clear thought.

God knew what thoughts raced through River's head. After a moment, she cast him an enigmatic look. "Mel said you don't have the balls to go back into the Llanganatis."

The Aussie had taunted Spenser with even more, things he wished River hadn't overheard. Things he loathed talking about. "Unfortunately, I have the balls to do whatever you ask of me, angel."

"Do you use lines like these on every woman you're trying to…impress?"

"No. I usually fall back on clichés. Those don't come with you."

She hugged her middle and shivered. "How far are we from Triunfo?"

His mind shifted from sex to another kind of thrill altogether. Anyone following Brunner's map in search of the lost Incan gold started their quest in Triunfo, a small village high in the Andes. "Was it Mel's idea to take Brunner's route?"

"Who's Brunner?"

Spenser raised a brow. "Why Triunfo?"

"How far?"

Christ, she was evasive. "Two hours. Roughly."

She scanned the area. "Which direction?"

The anxious hitch in her voice had him digging in his backpack. "Here." He thumbed in coordinates, then placed his personal GPS unit in her hands.

"This is a lot fancier than mine," she said, staring down at the backlit screen.

He heard awe and relief in her voice. More than ever he was curious about her obsession with maps. He was curious about a lot of things.

"Henry mentioned Triunfo in his journal." She met his gaze. "That's what the bandits stole. Part of what they stole. I need it back."

She'd been in possession of the professor's journal? Spenser had watched the old guy jot notes in a worn leather book when they were talking about the Seven Cities of Cibola. Had he recorded notes about Atahualpa's ransom? Penciled his route? His theories and conclusions?

Of course he had.

Spenser's senses buzzed with the familiar anticipation of unraveling an ancient mystery. He had a hundred burning questions. He also had concerns. "Take off your pants."

"I beg your pardon?"

"They're soaked, River. Take them off or I'll do it for you." He turned away, resisting the temptation and allowing her privacy. "Catch pneumonia and you won't be going anywhere. You can wear something of mine for now."

Mind racing, he returned to the hatchback and rooted through his gear. He counted to twenty, giving her ample time to shuck her pants, while bracing himself for the sight of a half-naked angel.

He should've counted to fifty. He wasn't amply

prepared for the sight of her bare legs. The fragile angel had killer legs, runner's legs. Toned, shapely. He imagined kissing his way up those milky smooth thighs. Imagined parting her legs and...

He jerked his gaze to her feet. *Get a grip, McGraw.* "You'll swim in these," he said, thrusting a pair of his sweatpants and socks into her lap, "but they're dry."

Instead of standing there, ogling while she wiggled into his pants, he rounded to the driver's side and climbed in.

"Thank you," she said in a small voice.

"You're welcome." He harnessed X-rated thoughts while she shimmied into his pants. Somehow, someway he had to smother this infatuation with River Kane—otherwise it could be the death of her. Or him. Or both.

Fuck.

"I'm sorry I eavesdropped," she said. "Sorry I assumed—"

"Forget it." He keyed the ignition and hit the road.

"If we're going to do this, we should keep things professional."

"Agreed."

"No kissing."

"Got it."

She fell silent then cleared her throat. "About Mel—"

"What about him?"

"We should tell him where we're going. In case he finds my stuff."

"Mel won't find your stuff. Consider your stuff lost. How much do you remember of your dad's journal?"

"Bits. Pieces. I reviewed it a lot over the last two days. What do you mean, Mel won't find my stuff?"

Too aggravated to sugarcoat it, Spenser opted for the truth. "Mel was shot. He's seeking medical help."

"Oh, *no.*"

"He'll be fine."

"But what if—"

"What-ifs are a waste of time and energy." He'd what-iffed his expedition with Jo and Andy to death.

"But what if—"

"Fine." He redialed the last incoming call, frowned when it rolled over to voice mail. "It's Spenser," he said. "Call me." He glanced at River, who'd turned an even whiter shade of pale. "Don't think the worst. He's probably with a doctor."

"Maybe he couldn't make it to a doctor. I can't believe this. I endangered Mel, my father." Still clutching the GPS, she drew her knees to her chest, dropped her forehead and shuddered.

"River—"

"Just take me to Triunfo."

As much as he wanted to pick her brain about the contents of the journal, River's battered body and spirit gave him pause.

Triunfo would have to wait.

CHAPTER THIRTEEN

Diablo Jungle Lodge
Province of Cotopaxi
Altitude 9,300 feet

A SHOWER HAD NEVER felt so good.

Face raised to the low-pressure drizzle, River allowed the water to wash away the grime, to warm her chilled bones. She didn't even care that she didn't have her flip-flops to protect her bare feet. The shower stall, though small, was pristine. Everything about her private thatch-roofed bungalow, though rustic, was pristine. Yes, it was in the middle of the jungle. Yes, it was elevated on wooden stilts, reminding her of a treehouse, but it was equipped with anti-insect window screens, electricity and hot water. The queen-size bed sported fresh linens and mosquito netting. As paranoid as she could be, she doubted she was susceptible to athlete's foot, bedbugs or malaria at the Diablo Jungle Lodge. According to the pamphlet on the simple plank desk, this was an all-inclusive, four-star resort.

When Spenser had pulled up to the main building of the sprawling eco-resort, she'd balked. According to his GPS unit they were only forty minutes from Triunfo.

She didn't want to waste another day, plus she couldn't afford this place.

"You can't afford anything," he'd reminded her.

Rude, but true.

For the first time, she'd focused less on her stolen supplies and more on her lost funds. No cash. No credit or debit cards. She was at Spenser's mercy. At least until she arranged for her bank to wire her some money.

She thought about the terrible men who'd robbed her at gunpoint, the criminals who'd tried to rob Mel of his life. Each moment played out in vivid color, just as if she'd snapped individual frames with her Nikon.

Fighting tears, River shampooed her hair twice, then used the complimentary conditioner. She soaped her body, rinsed, then soaped up again. "You're being ridiculous," she told herself. "You can't wash away memories."

The image of Mel fighting those bandits, the sounds of gunfire, riddled her with guilt. If she hadn't enlisted the Aussie guide, he'd still be in Baños swilling rum with his pal Gerry. Instead, he was gunshot, having narrowly escaped death.

Because it was easier than accepting full responsibility, she blamed Henry Kane and his stinking obsession with Atahualpa's ransom. Maybe there was something to that curse. First Professor Bovedine. Now Mel Sutherland. She couldn't help connecting the two incidents, even though it wasn't logical. *Random violence,* she told herself. *Different countries.* Plus, Spenser said Mel would be all right. Why think the worst?

Because it was how she'd been raised.

"Your delicate constitution makes you a lightning rod for disaster, River."

Or so she'd been told—again and again…

River turned off the water and nabbed a thick towel. "Pull it together," she told herself. Not that she'd fallen apart. Not completely. Not like in Mexico. Still, Spenser had seen a glimpse of her delicate side. The side she'd worked hard to overcome. He'd been so kind…until she'd pissed him off.

Seconds later, he'd flustered her by looking at her like…like a man besotted. He'd likened her to an ancient puzzle. *"I could work you for a lifetime and never grow bored."* Who said stuff like that? Not any man she'd ever dated. Certainly not David, although he had bought her a couple of mushy Hallmark cards. But those were someone else's words, not his.

Worse though, David had never kissed her like…a man besotted. Spenser's lips transported her to another dimension. His tongue incited new sensations, unleashed unknown desires. His intoxicating kisses made her ache for things she'd only read about in an erotica novel she'd received at her bachelorette party. No doubt Spenser was just as skilled in the bedroom (and various other locations) as the book's fictional hero.

Spenser *oozed* sex. He also oozed a fair amount of bull. He'd gazed into her eyes and intimated a lifetime. She doubted he was capable of much beyond a one-night stand.

Spenser McGraw. International treasure hunter and hunky star of *Into the Wild*.

He was the kind of man women flocked to. The kind of guy who had groupies.

Was he intrigued with River because she wasn't impressed with his celebrity status? Or, in spite of his vehement protest, was he using her as a means of landing the story of a lifetime? It had to be one or the other. Maybe it was both. Or maybe he had a different motive altogether. It didn't matter. Bottom line: He didn't want her for her. He didn't even know her. They'd been acquainted for what, three days? She didn't believe in love at first sight. Didn't trust spontaneous lust. Maybe if she called his bluff… What would *he* do if *she* intimated she'd fallen madly, deeply in love?

Damn him for screwing with her mind.

River towel-dried her hair then slathered her body with herbal lotion. She nurtured her frustration with Spenser and the feelings he invoked because it was better than obsessing on Mel's fate. She prayed Spenser was right and that he'd made it to a doctor. She prayed he was healing. Being responsible for a man's death was beyond her coping abilities, and her coping abilities were damned impressive.

Head throbbing, chest tight, River shrugged into the complimentary bathrobe. The hem dragged the floor. The sleeves were too long and the sash almost wrapped around her waist twice. She hated that it made her feel small, adding to her fragile mood, but anything was better than slipping back into Spenser's sweats. There'd been something uncomfortably intimate about wearing his clothes. Uncomfortable, because she had no business having intimate feelings for another man when she was in love with David.

David who didn't have the balls to stick around and work out their problems.

Unlike Spenser, who had the balls to do anything she asked of him (so he claimed), including taking her to a place where something bad had happened, something that had left him *crippled with guilt*. Thinking back, Mel's words had been somewhat ominous. More than ever she pondered the wisdom of enlisting Spenser as her guide. Was he somehow incompetent? What did she really know about the man?

About as much as he knows about you.

A knock startled River out of her musings. Pulling the sash tight, she checked to make sure the amulet and treasure map were still hidden where she'd stashed them, then moved to the door. She expected Spenser. Instead, an attractive middle-aged woman stood on the bungalow's private terrace bearing gifts.

"Spenser purchased these in the gift shop and asked if someone could deliver them to your room," she said. "We're short-staffed so as soon as I was able I brought them over myself."

River stared. Spenser had bought her clothes?

The woman, who sounded and looked American, glided in like she owned the place. "Something to wear to dinner," she said, flaunting a silky purple dress. "And something to relax in." Striped drawstring pants and a green long-sleeved tee. "He was right," she said as she hung the clothes in the closet. "You are petite. But I think these will fit. If not," she turned and smiled, "you can return them."

"I...thank you." River's cheeks burned. "I don't have any money. For a tip, I mean. I'm so embarrassed."

"Don't be. I wouldn't take a tip if you offered. Lana Campbell," she said, offering her hand in greeting. "My husband, Duke, and I own this place."

"I'm doubly embarrassed."

"Spenser's an old and good friend."

"Mortified, then."

Lana's smile never faltered. "I'm just glad he's put the past behind him. Can I get you anything else? A snack to hold you over until dinner? No telling when Spense will be back from Ambato."

He'd escorted her to the bungalow, told her to shower and catch a nap. Said he'd be back in a while. He hadn't said anything about Ambato, wherever that was. And what did Lana mean about Spenser's *past?* Was her observation tied to Mel's taunts?

River's head spun. "Thank you but I'm not hungry. I'm..." She massaged her throbbing temples, her tight chest. "What's the elevation here?"

Lana eyed River and frowned. "Hell's bells. Altitude sickness? Why didn't Spense just say so? I'll be back in ten minutes with coca tea. Ah-ah," she said, cutting River off. "I insist. It will help."

River wanted to say that she wasn't as frail as she looked. But this instant, that probably wasn't true. She felt physically and emotionally raw for a dozen different reasons. She needed to recover before Spenser returned. He'd want to talk about the journey ahead. Which meant she needed to decide how much to tell him. The bandits had robbed her of the journal, but not of her means of locating her dad. They had the cryptic written clues and observations, but she had the map. Or at least a portion of it. Still, she had to be careful. Had to think smart. If coca tea would relieve at least some of what ailed her, then she wasn't about to turn it down. She ached to ask about antimalarial tablets, but didn't figure that was something the eco-lodge stocked in their gift shop.

"Are you sure I can't bring you some food?" Lana asked as she backed over the threshold.

"I'm sure," River said, forcing a smile. "But I'd kill for some insect repellent."

CHAPTER FOURTEEN

Hotel Coronado
Ambato, Ecuador
Altitude 8,455 feet

"I SHOULD SQUASH YOU like the bug you are."

Gator, who'd been slumped in a cushioned chair, re-covering from an unexpected tussle with a crazy-ass Australian, stiffened.

The Conquistador had been in his own world for the last fifteen minutes, carefully skimming every page of the worn journal. Suddenly, he was across the room and yanking Gator to his feet.

Bam!

Gator flew backward from the force of the other man's blow. His skull cracked against the marble floor. "Shit!" Blood gushed from his throbbing nose. "Fuck!" Nauseous, he pushed into a sitting position, loosened the bandanna around his neck and stemmed the bleeding. "What the hell?" *Cough. Hack.*

"The map's missing."

"What?"

"The second half of the map." His employer waved the open journal in front of Gator's face, but all he saw was stars. "She ripped it out," he growled. "Did you search her?"

"No, but, Pablo did." Gator swallowed a wave of bile. "Or at least he started to." He'd stopped when Gator found the journal and shouted, "Mission accomplished." Gator had ordered Pablo to the truck. It should have been a clean getaway, but the stupid prick had tried to take blondie, and the Australian had gone ballistic.

"I gave you specific orders."

"I followed them."

"But you didn't get the map."

Gator burned with anger and frustration. The roadside robbery had been a goatfuck, but at least he'd raced away with the goods.

So he'd thought.

He'd searched River's camera bag and purse while Pablo had detained her and Sutherland. He'd found the journal, recognized the writing—same as on the partial map he'd stolen from Bovedine. He'd seen notations and drawings. He'd been so certain and he'd been *right,* except...Blondie had torn out a vital page. Not his fault, but by God he was suffering the consequence.

"If that map's not in my hands by tomorrow, you," The Conquistador growled, "are dead meat."

"I don't know where she is."

"I'll find out." The man had endless sources and deep pockets, yet nobody knew anything about him. *More ghost than conquistador,* Gator thought as the crazy bastard placed a call.

Tired of addressing his employer by his pretentious

alias (*The* Conquistador? Why not just Conquistador? Or—if he insisted on formality—Mr. Somebody or Another?), *the* Gator decided to think of his outlaw boss as Con. He wouldn't say it out loud—with his luck it would earn him a thrashing—but he'd think it.

Nose throbbing, Gator pushed to his feet and headed for the ice bucket. While he'd been doing the dirty work, Con had flown ahead and retreated to this posh suite. Gator noted bottles of quality booze, a box of cigars, a laptop computer and a table strewn with charts and maps. He'd seen those maps when he'd first come in, recognized the names scripted in the headers. Valverde, Guzmán, Spruce and Blake. The adventurers Con had mentioned before. Apparently they'd all charted maps or guides. There was another map by someone named Brunner. Con had been drinking whiskey and comparing those maps with the partial map Gator had stolen from Professor Bovedine.

If anyone could find that treasure, Gator thought, it was the mysterious, devious, intensely focused man who'd hired him. By his own bragging, Con had been studying the legend and region for years. He was determined. *Obsessed.*

Again, that partial map, Kane's map, caught Gator's bleary eyes. No doubt about it. It had been ripped from the journal that was now—thanks to him—in Con's possession. All his employer had to do was crack Kane's code. All Gator had to do was get the *other* half of the map—the half on blondie's person—and he'd, *they'd,* have the means to locate a king's ransom.

"I should have Miss Kane's location within the hour," Con said as he snapped shut his cell and poured himself another drink.

Gator pressed a makeshift ice pack to his busted nose, envisioned a confrontation with blondie. All her belongings—her duffel, camera bag and purse—were in this suite. He'd concentrate this search on her person. "Could get rough."

Con toyed with the silver sacrificial knife—more booty from Bovedine—before stabbing it into the table. "Harm River Kane and I'll slice off your dick," he said, then returned his attention to the whiskey and journal.

Dead or dickless. Gator was tired of the threats, the physical and verbal abuse. He should collect payment for services rendered and walk away, but something told him he was in too deep. Con wouldn't let him walk. He'd have to slip away and run…without payment.

Fuck that.

"Pour yourself a drink, then order in some food. You look like you're going to pass out. I need you fit and alert."

Said the man who just broke my fucking nose. Gator poured three fingers of straight whiskey, contemplated the motivation and mind-set of the man currently skimming a cryptic journal while fondling a pair of satin panties he'd pulled from blondie's duffel.

Motivation: Eight billion dollars.

Mind-set: *Cra-zee.*

Gator downed the liquor and poured another glass.

He helped himself to a Cuban cigar, then eyed the most expensive item on the room service menu. One way or another, The Conquistador would pay.

CHAPTER FIFTEEN

EVEN WITH HIS EXTENSIVE shopping list, Spenser was in and out of Ambato in less than two hours. He knew exactly what he wanted and what River needed. Or at least what she thought she needed. He wouldn't have found three-quarters of the supplies in Triunfo.

Midway through his shopping excursion, he'd gotten a call from Mel. River would be relieved to know the man was alive and recovering, although he'd be out of commission for a week or more. Partly because of the wound. Partly because of the dead bandit. Spenser had assured him he hadn't contacted the police. He'd also assured him River was fine, his temper flaring the more Mel asked for details.

"In case you've forgotten," Spenser lied, "River's mine." To which Mel responded, "Didn't see a ring on her finger."

The Aussie's interest bothered him more than it should have. It's not like he had a chance of seducing River. As soon as she found her dad, she'd be heading off to patch things up with David. That bothered Spenser, too. Why would she want a man who'd made it clear he didn't want her?

Joviana slammed into his heart and mind. *"Why did you want me, Spenser?"*

At the time, he could've listed a hundred reasons.

Desperate to avoid morbid thoughts, Spenser cranked up his MP3 player, listening to Green Day and mentally reviewing the route he'd taken on his second expedition into the Llanganatis—Brunner's route.

Twenty minutes from Lana and Duke's jungle lodge, Spenser got a call from the person he'd been itching to hear from all day.

"Found him," Gordo said.

"You're a miracle worker."

"Won't argue that. Your Andean guide didn't want to be found. He fled Ecuador to escape the curse. Said every other guide associated with Professor Kane's expedition died a grisly death."

So Cy had gotten that much right. "Go on."

"Juan swore he'd be taunting fate if he even talked about the expedition."

"But you swayed him."

"Like you said, I'm a miracle worker. Also helps that he's a fan of *Into the Wild*."

"No shit."

"Still cost us."

"I owe you, Gordo."

"Get away from the Llanganatis and we'll be square."

Spenser focused on the one-lane dirt road chiseled into the thousand-foot cliffs as he drove higher into the cloud forest, deeper into the mists. He thought about

River, who'd find her way into the "beard of the world" (as Brunner had called the forsaken region), even if Spenser turned back. "Consider me in your debt."

Gordo sighed. "Short version. Your man Cyrus didn't exaggerate."

Damn.

"Kane's a whack job, Spense."

"Eccentric." Though they'd only met once, Spenser liked the man. Plus, he understood the powerful pull of Atahualpa's ransom. "Delusional maybe. Obsession screws with a man's mind. So do the Llanganatis. The professor's been in and out of those mountains for almost a year straight."

"Yeah," Gordo said. "And the last person to see him alive, the guide who tried to follow the professor back to wherever he kept disappearing, got a poisoned arrow through the heart. Juan said—"

"I know. Cy told me. I don't believe it. You met Kane. The man's a marshmallow."

"Even marshmallows are capable of murder if they're loco."

"That image doesn't compute."

"Neither does Professor Kane's farfetched claim." Gordo blew out a breath. "The professor's been missing for what, three months? How long can a crazy man survive in the wild alone?"

"Depends on the man."

"After what you told me about that cursed region, considering Juan's story and all I've read…Kane's probably dead."

"Probably."

"You have to tell River."

"I know."

"No reason to go into the Llanganatis."

"I know."

"You say *I know*, but you don't sound convinced."

"River's determined to find her dad." He flashed back on her panicked rambling about closure. "Even if I share every gruesome detail of Juan's story, she'll insist on tracking him."

"Let her hire another guide."

"She did. Mel Sutherland."

"She's with Mel?"

"Was." Spenser relayed the road bandit account.

"Another victim of the curse."

"Mel's not dead."

"The day's young."

"Meaning?"

"He's gun shot! Infection? Complications?"

Spenser grunted. "Sometimes you're such a girl."

"This is about facing your demons, isn't it?"

"Partly."

"And because of the promise to your sister."

"Partly."

"There's a third part? Oh, hell. Don't tell me you think Professor Kane's ravings have merit?"

Considering, Spenser pulled into the small parking area of the Diablo Jungle Lodge. "What if he made contact with the Sambellas?" They were a lost tribe.

The last survivors of a people never conquered by the Spaniards.

"Another legend, Spense."

"But it could account for his claim. A mix-up in translation, maybe."

"You're grasping at straws."

"I'm…" Spenser trailed off at the sound of a man shouting. Dressed in brown cargo shorts and a green "Diablo" T-shirt, the lodge employee ran into the main lobby, then blew back out with Lana and Duke in tow. Lana spied Spenser and sprinted toward the jeep while Duke and the harried employee continued into the jungle. "I'll call you back, Gordo."

"But—"

Spenser disconnected and left the jeep just as Lana skidded to his toes. "I'm sorry, Spenser. I had no idea she was so susceptible. Then she showed up in the kitchen, asking for a refill and the cook complied. Three cups later, she asked about our most adventurous activities and he hooked her up with Nick." Lana palmed her forehead, glanced toward the thick tangle of trees. "We've never had anything like this happen."

"Where's River?"

"Zip-lining through the canopy, high as a kite on coca tea."

BY THE TIME SPENSER and Lana caught up to Duke, he and Nick (a college kid working as a seasonal guide) were three-quarters up the side of a capirona tree. Capironas typically grew to over one hundred feet, high enough to jut out of the main canopy.

"The initial platform is up there," Lana said. "River's swinging between landing platforms two and three. Not sure if the mechanism malfunctioned or if she used the brake and then froze. Nick—"

Spenser didn't wait for details. He climbed the wooden rungs bolted into the tree trunk. When he reached the man-made platform, Duke was strapping into a harness.

They traded a look.

"Right," Duke said, easing out of the gear. "You go."

Spenser had zip-lined in Costa Rica, Peru and Belize. Duke knew and trusted his expertise, plus if any one could reason with River, he could. Or so his friend assumed, just like he must have assumed Spenser and River were an item.

Nick rambled as Spenser suited up. "I didn't know she was high," he said. "I just thought she was energetic. A free spirit. I got her to wear the leather gloves but she refused a helmet. I know," he said when Spenser shot him a fiery look. "But she was so damned pretty and... determined."

"You thought if you let her have her way, you'd get laid," Spenser said.

"It wasn't like that. Okay. I admit I wanted her to like me. But it didn't seem like a big deal," the kid went on. "She said she'd zip-lined before, but then she stopped midair and I couldn't get her to move on. She was hanging there for, I don't know, fifteen minutes? I kept shouting from the platform but she didn't budge. The system's designed for one person at a time. I didn't know what to do. I—"

"Shut up, Nick." Duke latched Spenser's rig to the cable. "There are four platforms total," he said. "Then you're out of the canopy and zip-lining over the river. Lana and I will meet you on the other side and drive you back. Do me a favor, Spense, and don't let River charm you into anything stupid," he said with a disgusted glance at Nick. "Get her down as quickly as possible, but take it slow."

"Good luck with that," Nick said to Spenser. "She's a speed demon. Oh, and prepare yourself. Pretty as hell, but she smells like she took a bath in deet."

Spenser almost smiled. He pushed off, strapped into a rappeller's harness, attached by carabiner to a zip line of stainless steel aircraft cable, and soared to River's rescue. Spenser flew through the treetops, marveling that River had had the nerve to soar like a bird. She didn't strike him as a thrill seeker. Then again, thanks to an overdose of coca, her judgment and senses were skewed. Now she was stuck between platforms, suspended eighty feet above the ground, surrounded by trees and various canopy wildlife. That had to be sobering. He expected to find her in hysterics or, like this morning, in a repressed zombie state.

He touched down on the second platform, checked his gear and peered down the cable. There she was, hanging in the distance, a bright speck of turquoise amidst the vivid green jungle. His heart lodged in his throat. Even though he knew Duke's system was top of the line and that the safety equipment was top notch, he didn't trust the man who'd allowed her to zip-line without a helmet, a man who'd panicked and left her dangling out here alone. What if Nick hadn't buckled her properly into the harness? What if she started flailing around, trying to force free her jammed pulley? That's if it *was* jammed. Maybe Lana was right. Maybe she'd frozen in fear.

Instead of wasting time shouting out or running for help like Nick, he reattached his cable and slowly descended. The added weight caused the cable to sag and bounce. Not a lot, but enough to rouse a reaction from River. She turned and he could see now she'd been taking pictures.

"Dammit, McGraw," she shouted, "you screwed up my shot!"

She didn't sound scared, just annoyed. That was good. "There'll be others!"

"Not like that. And I can't get a steady shot when you're...dammit," she said after a glance back at a specific tree. "You scared away the monkeys. Go back!"

"This is a one-way ride, angel."

"Then stop!"

Spenser manipulated his gear, slowing, but not stopping. "Is your brake jammed?"

"What? No. I locked it down because I saw—"

"Release it and continue to the next platform."

"But—"

"You're not only playing loose with your safety,

but mine. This cable system is designed to handle one person at a time."

"You're the one who put us at risk," she shot back. "Couldn't you just wait on the platform until I was done—"

"You're done. Session over." He was close enough now to reach out and touch her. His heart hammered in his chest, his adrenaline spiked. He had a vision of her falling, of Andy falling. Of reaching out and... "Strap down your camera, put your glove back on and zip to the next platform. Slowly."

She started to argue, then thought better of it. "You are a spoilsport."

"I can honestly say, you're the first to think so." He watched as she followed his instructions. Seconds later, she was in motion. "Slow," he shouted.

"Spoilsport!"

He gave her some lead time then followed. She didn't look like a pro, but you didn't need special athletic abilities to navigate this zip-line. Gravity did most of the work. What worried him was there was no guide waiting on the landing platform to help her decrease her speed. Fortunately, she descended at a reasonable pace and touched down without incident.

He stepped in behind her, tempered his actions. He wanted to haul her into his arms, to crush her against his body and somehow transport her to safety without letting her go. He ached to kiss her, out of relief, out of need, but they had that damned agreement.

She was also buzzed.

He could see it in her eyes now, in the way she shifted from foot to foot. Pumped up on adrenaline and coca. Christ. "Well done," he said while checking over her gear.

"It's not like it's hard. Nick showed me what to do."

"Plus you've zip-lined before."

"Never." She giggled. "What a rush!"

He frowned. "You told Nick—"

"He was being a drip. Said he'd never done a solo run with a newbie, so I eased his mind."

"With a lie."

"I *had* to do this."

"Why?"

"Because David picked an adventure in Peru over a life with me. Because when I find him I'm going to prove I'm not fragile or overly cautious. That I'm capable of taking spontaneous risks."

"Like zip-lining."

She shoved her curls out of her eyes with the back of her gloved hand and smiled. "I was feeling exceptionally motivated."

"Hmm." That smile could light up Finland's sunless winters. It certainly warmed the dark corners of his heart. "Just how much coca tea did you drink?" he asked while tightening her shoulder straps.

She shrugged. "Four, five cups? Lana said it would cure my altitude sickness and, boy, did it." She pumped a fist in the air. "I feel great!"

"I'll bet."

"My heart feels really fluttery, but that's probably

from soaring though the jungle like a flipping toucan! *Or,*" she said, leaning in and batting her thick lashes at him, "maybe it's because I'm standing so close to the hunky star of *Into the Wild.*"

He'd never seen this side of River—flirtatious, carefree, bold. He wondered if anyone, aside from the horny college guide, ever had. Sure, she smelled like mosquito repellent, but she hadn't whipped out a bottle of sanitizer or asked what direction they were traveling. Her normally pale skin glowed and her green eyes sparkled. This moment she didn't appear fragile at all, but hearty and full of life. She looked goddamned beautiful, even in her goofy getup. The baggy striped pants he'd bought in the gift shop, her turquoise slicker, the pumpkin-orange scarf, the thick leather work gloves and diaper-like harness. There wasn't a single sexy thing about her attire, yet every fiber of his body hummed with desire. Part of him cut college boy some slack. The other part damned the horny kid to hell.

Spenser gripped River's shoulders. His gaze locked on those lush pink lips. "Keep flirting like that, angel, and you're going to get more than you bargained for."

"I bet you know a lot of tricks," she said in a breathless voice. "In bed, I mean."

"I know what you mean."

"Ever done it in a tree?"

"You're confusing me with those monkeys you photographed."

"There's always a first time."

This would be the "charming him into doing

something stupid" part of the program. "Not this time." He maneuvered her to the opposite side of the platform.

She snickered and glanced over her shoulder. "Get more than you bargained for?"

Touché. "You're lucky I'm a gentleman."

"Old-fashioned sensibilities."

"Mmm."

"Ever get tired of doing the right thing?"

"Trust me. I have lapses." He clipped her rig to the next cable. "Here's the deal. Lana and Duke are waiting for us at the end of the line. The longer we take, the more worried they'll be."

"Why are they worried?"

"Because zip-lining under the influence is dangerous."

Her brow furrowed. "You're drunk?"

"I wish." He had a painful hard-on and a knot in his gut. Unrelated to each other. Both related to River. Dulled senses sounded pretty good just now. He pointed to landing number four. "Think you can get there without stopping in the middle or giving me a heart attack?"

"No promises," she said, then pushed off.

Spenser held his breath as she zip-lined to the next point, a little too fast for his comfort, but at least she didn't stop for pictures or hang upside down, arms stretched wide. How long did a coca tea high last? A natural stimulant, he'd known people who'd gotten a slight buzz from the leaf, but River's reaction was extreme. Would the effect slowly wear off or would she crash? Either way, he wanted her on the ground as quickly as possible.

He soared to her side.

"Hey, why do you get to go really fast?" she asked as he finessed her to the next take-off position.

"Because I'm a trained professional."

"As a trained professional, have you ever zip-lined across something like that?"

He looked to where she pointed. Didn't blame her for sounding nervous. A wide river and a nearby waterfall. "Something similar." The expanse and decline were the most intense segment of this canopy tour. Normally, he'd be psyched, but he kept imagining the woman in front of him freaking out and falling down. He secured her rig then squeezed her shoulders. "Nothing to it, hon."

"Then why do you sound worried?"

He didn't say.

She turned with a sweet smile and patted his arm. "Don't be scared. Just take it slow and don't look down." And with that, she pushed off.

Spenser died a thousand deaths as she zoomed down the cable, full out, forty to fifty miles an hour, blonde hair whipping and voice screaming, *"Woo-hoooooooooooooooo!!"*

The little devil was having the time of her life.

He should've been pissed, but, dammit, he was impressed. Relief flooded through him as she slowed at the appropriate time and landed on the other side. Lana and Duke moved in and Spenser zoomed down—full out, fifty to sixty miles an hour. Heart lighter than it had been since he'd entered Ecuador, he soared over one river with eyes on another.

His feet touched down, but he was still floating. Crazy. He pulled the laughing green-eyed angel into his arms and poured his soul into a kiss. Her response was passionate and he swore he'd died and gone to heaven.

His euphoria was short-lived.

With only a groan and a sigh as warning, River crashed in his arms.

CHAPTER SIXTEEN

"PLEASE DON'T REPRIMAND Nick" was River's parting plea to Lana and Duke as Spenser helped her out of the lodge's Suburban.

She'd awoken mid-ride feeling exhausted and slightly disoriented, but there was nothing wrong with her memory. She'd acted recklessly. Worried her hosts, Spenser's friends. She'd apologized to Lana and Duke at least a dozen times. They didn't blame her, but Nick…

Duke grunted.

Lana told her to get some rest.

River peered up at Spenser as he guided her up the wooden walkway to her bungalow. "They won't fire him, will they?"

"He broke company rules and put a life at risk."

"I bullied him into it."

"You charmed him into it."

Her cheeks heated. She remembered manipulating that kid into doing something against his better judgment. She remembered flirting. With him. With Spenser.

"That stuff I said in the tree, intimating we should…"

"Do it like monkeys?"

She was beyond mortified. "I'm sorry."

His sexy smile melted her already wobbly limbs. And he wasn't even *looking* at her. He was focused on the walkway. Good thing, since she was focused on him and dusk was fast approaching. One of them needed to see where they were going.

"I'm not usually like that. I'm not a tease."

"I know."

"I don't have indiscriminate sex."

"I know."

She frowned. "No, you don't. How could you? Maybe I'm a faithless sex fiend."

"Are you?"

"No. But I'm not an angel, either. I know some tricks in the bedroom."

That earned her a glance. "Really?"

Damn. "No." She looked away. A thousand self-doubts welled. "Maybe that contributed to David leaving me. Maybe he couldn't imagine a lifetime of *doing it*—lights off, missionary-style."

"Is that how it was?" Spenser asked. "Every time?"

She felt compelled to defend her fiancé. Strike that. *Ex*-fiancé. She didn't know why. Wait. Yes, she did. Because it wasn't wholly his fault. "I like knowing what to expect. I thrive on routine."

Or at least she used to. She'd been out of her comfort zone the last few days and, though she was battling deep-rooted fears, at least she wasn't hiding from them. It was surprisingly empowering.

"Did he ever try to spice things up? Ever suggest—"

"No. He was always a gentleman. Always mindful and respectful and…" She blew out a frustrated breath. "It's not like I tried to spice things up, either. I felt uncomfortable taking the lead. Some men would find that, well, according to *Traditional Bride Magazine,* most men like to be in charge."

"Most men like variety."

"Meaning?"

"I like being dominant, but it's also a turn-on when the woman takes control."

His words stoked erotic images and an intimate ache. "Really?" They'd reached her bungalow. End of the line. She thought about the bed inside. Thought about how sexy and vibrant and alive Spenser had looked zip-lining through the jungle canopy. "Never mind. Don't elaborate. I can't believe we're even having this discussion. I know. I started it. I'm not myself. I haven't been myself since…"

"David abandoned you?"

She flushed head to toe, burning with embarrassment and…anger. "Yes." She turned away and braced her hands on the terrace railing. She stared out at the darkening jungle, flashed on painful memories.

"I had my life mapped out. I knew where David and I were going to live. Our combined income. What we could afford and what we should save for. I even planned ahead for family vacations, invested in a Disney time-share. By the time we had kids, we'd own a house in the best school district. We'd live there forever.

"A kid should have roots," she plowed on. "A place, one place to call home. They should go to one school so they can develop solid, lasting friendships. Kids need stability. They need to know they can count on their parents—as providers and nurturers. The more stable the parent, the more confident the child."

"So you want for your kids what you didn't have."

Her stomach knotted. "Very perceptive."

"Not really. Just working the puzzle."

She turned, her anger simmering toward boil. "Stop saying things like that. Stop *looking* at me like that!"

"I wish I could. I don't want this, River."

"There is no *this*. You keep intimating there's some-thing between us. Something…special."

"There is."

"We just *met*."

"Sometimes the heart knows at a glance."

He looked so sincere. So…besotted. *He's a treasure hunter. A celebrity. An actor.* "What do you want from me?"

"More than I should."

Why hadn't David ever said anything like that? Her heart pounded. With frustration. Anticipation. Or maybe it was the remnants of that coca tea buzz. She tucked her trembling hands beneath her armpits and rooted her feet. Pacing wouldn't do. "For the sake of argument," she said, in a controlled voice, "*we* would never work. You're a globe-trotter, a risk-taker. I'm a…"

"What?"

She grappled for the words and snagged Ella's observation from a few days before. "A freak of nature."

Now he looked annoyed. "Who told you that?"

"My parents, my grandparents, the assorted distant relatives and ragtag friends my mom used to leave me with after my father barred me from traveling with him anymore. Okay, none of them called me a freak of nature, specifically. But it was implied. I'm a lightning rod for disaster. *That* they said."

"Then your family did you a disservice, angel. Tell someone something enough times and they start to believe it. Especially a kid."

"But I *am* prone to mishaps. Every time I travel somewhere remote or exotic. Every time I let down my guard. Every time I try something the least bit adventurous. I've only been in Ecuador three days and I've already suffered altitude sickness, been robbed, gotten lost, caused one man to get shot and another to lose his job."

Spenser rubbed his hands over his celebrity-gorgeous face. "Let's take this in order. In these parts, lots of people get altitude sickness. Plenty of people get robbed, especially tourists. Trust me, it could have been worse. As for getting lost, there are methods to find your way without the aid of a map or GPS and I'm going to teach you. And as for Mel, he called. He's laid up but on the mend. That leaves Nick. Duke will give him hell, rightfully so, but I don't think he'll fire him for one mistake."

River nearly wilted with relief knowing Mel was mending and she appreciated Spenser's rational take on her recent calamities. But he didn't know her history. "What about the coca tea? I got whacked on medicinal tea, something people down here drink in abundance, according to Lana. She's never known anyone to have such an intense reaction. Have you?"

"No. But, for what it's worth, coca tea's illegal in the U.S. It's a stimulant, River. Coca leaves contain cocaine. A small amount, but according to Lana you drank the equivalent of two pots in less than an hour. By your own admission you went for almost two days with no sleep. You overindulged in alcohol the night before and had a harrowing experience this morning. Your system's off, that's all."

He had an answer for everything. He had a way of making her feel normal. It was disconcerting and...a major turn-on. She backed away. "I'm in love with David." She wasn't sure why she'd blurted that just now. Wasn't sure she even believed it anymore. How could she love one man yet be so fiercely attracted to another?

Your system's off, that's all.

Spenser opened the door to the bungalow and waved her inside. "You should get some rest. I'll have dinner sent over later."

He didn't sound or look angry, but she knew she'd touched a nerve. She realized now that she'd brought up David to push away Spenser, except...she didn't want to be alone. Night was closing in and so were her troubled thoughts. Thoughts about Bovedine, her dad, the curse and whatever had plagued Spenser's last trek into the Llanganatis. "Don't you want to talk about my dad's journal?"

"Later."

She hadn't expected that. Given his interest in the lost treasure, she was sure he'd be anxious to pick her brain regarding Professor Henry Kane's *data*. "Just so you know, I won't let my phobias deter me from my goal to find my dad. I won't let you talk me into turning back, and if you abandon me—"

"I won't abandon you."

Between the implied promise, his intense gaze and the testosterone-charged air, River's knees fairly buckled. She swallowed hard and licked her dry lips. "I've never known anyone like you."

His gaze drifted to her mouth. "Just so you know, angel, next time you offer up sex, sober or buzzed, I won't say no."

Her heart thundered in her ears as he turned to leave. "Where are you going?"

"To get drunk."

CHAPTER SEVENTEEN

"TROUBLE IN PARADISE?"

Spenser glanced up from his tequila and saw Duke.

Backlit by a citronella tiki torch, his old friend, a former army buddy like Andy, flashed a full bottle of Cuervo and an empty glass.

Spenser was happy to see the liquor. Not so much Duke he preferred to be alone. "Shouldn't you be inside, regaling your dinner guests with stories about the history of the Diablo Jungle Lodge?"

"Dinner was over an hour ago. I was fascinating, as always, but now guests are trading stories about their own backgrounds over complimentary bottles of wine. Lana sent me to check on you. She said you've been out here by the pool for three hours."

"I like it out here." Everyone else was in the communal dining area or hanging in the bar. Or, like River, tucked in their bungalow for the night. He appreciated the silence, the privacy. He had a lot to sort through. He'd even shut down his satellite phone. He wasn't in the mood to speak with his sister or Jack or Gordo or, God help him, Necktie Nate. He wasn't in the mood to speak with Duke, either, but booting the man from his own property seemed rude.

"Let me rephrase. You've been out here *alone* for three hours. Drinking."

Spenser raised a brow. "Here to lecture?"

"Here to join you." Duke dropped into the chair across from Spenser. He poured himself a drink. "Good thing I brought my own bottle. Yours is close to empty."

"Lecturing."

"Wondering."

"About why I came back to a place I swore off?"

"We hoped it was a sign that you'd put the past behind you. We assumed you were preparing for another crack at the treasure. Maybe for the show. But Gordo's not here. And River…she's not like Jo. She's out of her element. What's the deal, Spense?"

"Heard of Professor Henry Kane?"

"Who in these parts hasn't? Locals buzzed about him for months. He was good for the economy, especially in Triunfo, where he hired help and purchased supplies. Now no one will utter his name."

"Because they think he's cursed."

Duke nodded. "People connected with the expedition started dropping like flies. A few illnesses. Typical accidents associated with the Llanganatis. You know how dicey it gets when the fog rolls in."

Spenser drained his glass, wishing the liquor would burn away memories like it burned the back of his throat.

"But then there were out-and-out murders," Duke went on. "One of Kane's most trusted guides was stabbed to death in Baños. Another, the last one to

deliver provisions to a designated drop-off point, followed the professor back up Cerro Hermoso and got a
spear through the heart. Though no one witnessed the
attack, they say Kane himself chucked that spear."

All of this was old news to Spenser, yet it still made
him uneasy. "Kane's not a killer."

"In that last month, he slipped away, alone, for days
at a time. He warned his guides not to follow him—at
the risk of death."

"I still don't buy it."

Duke shrugged and poured them both a drink. "I
assume you knew him."

"Mostly by reputation but, yeah, we met." Spenser
flashed on their animated and extensive talk about the
Seven Cities of Cibola. The man was eccentric and obsessed, but fascinating. And kind. At least that had been
his impression and Spenser's instincts were top notch.

"The Llanganatis lure explorers from all over the
world. Every man, every team has a story. *You* have a
story. Two of them, for Christ's sake. Why the pointed
interest in Professor Kane?" Duke asked.

"He's River's dad."

"Damn."

Everything happens for a reason, one of Spenser's
favorite clichés, whispered through his brain. Along
with, *Nothing ventured, nothing gained.* He was sick to
death of the guilt. If this was some sort of cosmic shot
at redemption, he'd be a cowardly ass not to take it.

"You know," said Duke, "rumor has it Kane's loco
or dead."

"I know. River suspects. She's still committed to finding him."

Duke sipped his drink.

Spenser tensed. "She's tougher than she looks."

"I didn't say anything."

"You didn't have to."

"You're in love with her."

He was. But given his history and these circumstances, he feared the admission would be as good as a death sentence. "I don't even know her. We only met three days ago."

"I was head over heels for Lana the moment I laid eyes on her."

"That was different. She wasn't hung up on some other guy."

Duke paused mid-sip. "Déjà vu."

Spenser suppressed a surge of panic. "River isn't anything like Jo."

"No, she's not. But you were in love with Jo and Jo was in love with Andy."

"And I was convinced I could win her over." Shameful memories battered Spenser. He drank more tequila to dull the pain.

"The other guy—"

"River's ex-fiancé."

"Any chance he'll show on the scene?"

Spenser hadn't considered that. "I don't think so. He dumped her at the altar. Joined an extreme tour. Doubt he even knows or cares where she is."

"You don't know that for sure." Duke drummed his

fingers on the wicker table. "What if he has second thoughts? Gets drunk one night and calls River, hoping to reconcile? What if he learns she's having a family crisis and races to her aid?"

Spenser said nothing.

"Where's the tour?"

"Peru."

Duke stared. "Fuck sake, Spense."

If so inclined and if fate was a truly cruel cocksucker, David could be in the Llanganatis in a matter of hours. Then it would be Spenser, River and David. A triangle of old and wannabe lovers.

Déjà vu.

Almost.

"Difference is," Spenser said mid-thought, "we're not searching for Atahualpa's ransom. We're searching for River's father."

"Who was searching for Atahualpa's ransom."

Again, Spenser held silent.

"Facing your demons and hoping to dodge the curse. Tough assignment."

"You're not a superstitious man, Duke."

"No, but you are. At least where Atahualpa's ransom is concerned. No wonder you're getting shitfaced."

Spenser topped off his glass. He wasn't drunk, but he was getting there. It wasn't solely about numbing himself to the past, but to River. Even though he'd sensed and felt her desire, she kept throwing up roadblocks. Namely David. It was too close to his dealings with Jo for comfort.

Duke sighed. "Tough is relative. River won't be able to heft the supplies for a three-day journey. And that's if the weather cooperates. Which it usually doesn't. You should allow for a week or two. You need help."

"She won't like it."

"Do you care?"

Spenser grunted. What he cared about was River's safety. His mind ticked ahead.

"Normally I'd suggest a few reliable guides, but as soon as you mention Kane's name—"

"I have someone in mind."

Duke angled his head. "Gordo?"

"If I invited Gordo, River would assume he was here on business. To film the journey."

"You have to admit it would make a hell of an episode for *Into the Wild*."

"I know, but I can't go there."

"Okay. Not Gordo. Who then?"

"Cyrus Lassiter. He's made more trips into Llanganatis than anyone I know."

"Can't argue that. Still—"

"Like you said, no one else will do it. Plus, I like Cy."

"Don't see how that figures as a credential, but you would."

"What's that supposed to mean?"

"Means I saw Andy's faults. You didn't. When you're ready to have that discussion, let me know." Duke stood. "The lodge is booked solid, but if you need somewhere to crash, Lana and I have a pullout sofa—"

"I'm good. Thanks." He'd already resigned himself to the hammock on River's terrace. He just needed some time. Some space. If he was lucky, he'd pass out from the booze instead of lying there, pondering ways to seduce her or obsessing on the challenge ahead.

"Would it help if I told you, *again,* that you weren't at fault for Andy's death?"

"No. But thanks." Heart heavy, Spenser watched his old friend go. He blocked welling memories of his army days, the good times, the bad times, the times spent with Duke and Andy. He especially didn't want to think about Andy. He drank more tequila and focused on his current dilemma. Any definitive clues to finding Henry Kane had been stolen by those scumbag bandits, along with any notes about the treasure or his so-called contact with General Rumiñahui—a man who'd been dead for centuries.

Had the professor smoked toad venom, hoping to connect with the spirits, specifically Rumiñahui? Had he made contact with a lost tribe and misinterpreted something they'd said? What was the real story behind Kane and his botched expedition? Had he made a unique discovery or had he lost his mind? Spenser would give a year's salary to read that journal. Although if it were in his hands just now, he doubted he'd be able to decipher the contents.

Vision blurring, he pushed out of his seat before he ended up under the table. Numb was one thing, comatose another. He thumbed on his satellite phone, dialed Cy midway to the bungalow.

"No, I don't have any more info on Kane or his dead guides," Cy grumbled, sounding distracted.

"The problem with cell phones and incoming call display," Spenser said, "is that it negates an automatic courteous greeting."

Cy grunted. "When have you ever known me to be formal? What do you want, boy? Be warned, my mood's foul. Sorting through monthly bills and coming up short on funds."

"I can help you with that."

"How so?"

"Need your services."

"For what?"

Spenser rolled his eyes as he navigated the board-walk. "What do you think? I'm going into the Llanganatis. Going after Kane."

"And the gold."

Spenser hedged. He couldn't think about that aspect. Every time he envisioned the lost treasure his temperature spiked.

"You know those mountains," Cy said, sounding suspicious. "What do you need me for?"

"River's coming along."

"She's crazy for trying. You're crazy for letting her."

"She won't take no for an answer. I need your help, Cy."

"And I could use the cash." He sniffed, then chuckled. "Hell, I was bored, anyway. Starting point? Time?"

"Triunfo. Tomorrow morning."

"See you around nine," Cy said, then signed off.

Spenser eyed the bungalow ahead of him, thought about the woman sleeping inside. How he'd like to curl up next to her and kiss her into oblivion. He stumbled up the steps and frowned at the damned hammock that would serve as his bed. Drunk, but not drunk enough to pass out, he was in for a long night.

CHAPTER EIGHTEEN

She was walking down the aisle. He was standing at the altar. He looked nervous. Her own stomach fluttered.

Butterflies.

She was nervous, too. A lifetime of stability. A lifetime with David. She should be giddy with excitement. Brimming with love. Burning with lust. Instead she felt queasy. Fretful.

More butterflies.

She could hear their wings beating. No, that was her heart. Racing. Zooming.

Buzzing.

Ears buzzing. Something buzzing. Something creeping. Crawling.

Bugs!

River's eyes flew open. Her sluggish mind fought through the panicked daze. She'd been sleeping. Dreaming. Where was she?

Ecuador.

Jungle.

Lodge.

Heart thudding, she clutched the cool sheet to her chest. She was locked in her bungalow. Tucked into bed.

Safe.

So, why did she feel at risk?

She breathed deep as her eyes adjusted to the moonlit room.

She listened to the foreign sounds coming from outside. Monkeys? Birds? In the branches? On her roof? Closer still, a faint buzz. What—

Bugs!

Sweating buckets, River squinted up at the mosquito netting draped over her bed. It was moving. Oh, no. Oh, hell. Ninety percent of the animal species in the Amazon were insects. Not all of them flew, but by God they crawled. Spiders, beetles, ants…

That couldn't be right. What about the insect screens over the windows?

Mosquitoes.

She couldn't see them, but she sensed them.

And something else. Someone else.

The floor creaked.

Spenser?

Then she smelled the stink. A familiar stink. Road-bandit stink.

Oh. God.

She tried to scream, but nothing came out. What did he want?

The map.

Don't give it up! Don't give in!

Chest tight, River's right hand balled beneath the covers. Her knuckles brushed against something cool and hard.

Her camera.

Before drifting off, she'd scrolled through the pictures just as someone would skim the pages of a book.

She grasped the Nikon, aimed at the stink...and shot.

Flash!

A bright explosion of light in a mostly dark room.

The intruder flinched and faltered. He thudded to the floor, yelped in pain, then *coughed*. Bandit number two!

River reached for the bedside lamp, meaning to throw it at him, got tangled in the netting.

Bugs!

The netting broke from the ceiling and covered her like a bug-infested shroud.

Shrieeeeeeek!

She squeezed her eyes shut, frightened and repulsed by the countless insects. Would they sting? Bite?

She felt hands, human hands. *The intruder.* She fought for all she was worth. "Get off. Get. *Off!*"

"Shit!" he hissed when her fist connected with his face. "Calm down, angel."

Spenser? She opened her eyes. He'd turned on the lights. Suddenly she was eye to antenna with a big-as-a-Buick beetle! "Bugs! Get them off! Get them—"

"Stop fighting me, dammit. You're making it worse."

River forced herself to be still, even though her heart galloped and her skin crawled. Spenser freed her and immediately flung the bug-laden netting outside and over the terrace. "How did those things get in here?" he asked as he moved back inside.

Another man burst through the door. *Duke.* "What the hell?"

"River got tangled in her mosquito netting," Spenser said. "Goddamned thing was covered with beetles and moths."

Butterflies.

He stooped to help her to her feet. She saw the concern in his eyes, saw the annoyance on Duke's face. She'd freaked out. Over bugs. But it wasn't just the bugs.

"No wonder," Duke said as he strode to one of the windows. "Where's the screen?"

"He must've taken it off," River said, cursing the nervous hitch in her voice. "Guess that's how he got in…and out."

"Who?" both men asked.

"The bandit. I woke up and he was…here."

"Someone was in this room?" Spenser grasped her shoulders. "Did he touch you? Hurt you?"

She shook her head. "I shot him. With my camera," she clarified. "Blinded him. Then I screamed. I guess I scared him off. I'm not sure. It happened so fast and I was…disoriented."

"Disoriented from a nightmare, maybe?" Duke asked. "This is an exclusive resort, River. The property's secure—"

"But not a fortress, right?" She glared at the man

doubting her word. "I'm telling you someone was in here!"

Spenser threw his friend a look.

Duke cursed. "Fine. Stay with River. I'll check outside."

"Wait!" she called. "What if he has a gun? What if—"

"Duke can handle himself," Spenser said as the man disappeared into the night.

"The way Mel handled himself? The way Professor Bovedine—" She broke off, fought tears.

"Who's Professor Bovedine?"

Desperate to gather her wits, River pushed away from Spenser and bolted for the bathroom. She craved a hot shower, but settled for the sink. She soaped up a washcloth and scrubbed her face, hands and arms. She could still feel the netting, those bugs. Still worried that the coughing bandit was contagious. Common cold? Bronchitis? Tuberculosis?

Scrub. Scrub.

She glanced up and saw Spenser standing on the threshold, filling the doorway with his big body. His chest was heaving. His eyes were bloodshot. He smelled of liquor. She remembered then. "Are you drunk?"

"I was. Apparently a rush of adrenaline is as sobering as a cold shower."

"I'm sorry I scared you. I'm sorry I freaked. Between the bandit and the bugs—"

"You mean the road bandit from this morning?"

"Yes."

"That's impossible, River. How would he know you were here unless he somehow followed us? And to what purpose? Aside from your camera and the clothes on your back, he stole everything—"

"Not everything."

"What—"

"No one's out there," Duke called. "Except for a couple of concerned guests and employees. Roused a lot of people with that scream."

Blushing, River followed Spenser back into the bedroom.

"Found the screen, though," Duke said as he moved to the open window. "Damn monkeys."

"You think a monkey pulled off that screen?" Spenser asked.

"Happened before. Once. Some are more curious than others. More bold."

River shook her head. "It was a man."

"Twelve-foot drop outside this window, sweet-heart."

"He could've climbed up the side of the bungalow," River said. "Or swung over from a tree branch."

"Like a monkey?" Duke asked as he refitted the screen.

She bristled. "He stank."

"Monkeys stink."

"Do monkeys slather themselves with some sort of strong-smelling herbal salve?"

"I caught a whiff of that," Spenser said to River. "Thought maybe you were sore from zip-lining."

"I'm hunky-dory," River snapped. "More than I can say for the bandit. He has an awful cough. An *unmistakable* cough," she said, driving home the point that her intruder had indeed been the road bandit from this afternoon.

Duke raised a skeptical brow.

River grabbed her Nikon from the bed. "I took a picture." She scrolled back one frame. "Damn." The shot was distorted. A wash of light. An indistinguishable shadow. It proved nothing.

Spenser looked over her shoulder. "You said you were disoriented. Maybe…"

"I could swear." River sank onto the edge of the mattress. Had she dreamed it? Imagined it?

"I'll walk around the grounds," Duke said. "Put the staff on alert as a precaution." He eyed River and Spenser. "Want me to send over some coffee? Cola?"

Maybe he thought she was still high on coca tea. Or maybe he smelled the liquor on Spenser. Maybe they'd been drinking *together*. Had she been the topic of conversation? Had Spenser mentioned her "quirks"? The run-in with the road bandits? How she'd gotten lost? Combined with the coca tea/zip-line incident and now *this,* Duke no doubt thought she was a nut.

"We're fine. Thanks, Duke." Spenser walked the man out, then locked the door. He turned and regarded River with an enigmatic look. "I'm staying."

"I'm glad."

"All night."

After that scare, he expected her to argue? "Good."

"I'm in no mood to sleep on the floor or in a chair."

"It's a queen-size bed," River said. "We're adults." They could keep their hands to themselves. They could honor that no-kissing pact. Right?

She sat. He stood. They stared.

Her mind rewound and replayed the past few days. Spenser had saved her from one crisis or another, no less than five times. "I know what you're thinking."

"I doubt it."

"You're thinking I'm not cut out for a trek into the Llanganatis. You think I'll wimp out."

"I think you'll tough it out."

She blinked. "You do?"

Spenser crossed his arms and leaned back against the door. He looked a little drunk, a lot frustrated and unbelievably gorgeous. She tried to imagine David, here, now. Tried shifting her lustful thoughts and desires to the man she supposedly loved.

She couldn't.

"I have it on good authority that your dad kept disappearing up Cerro Hermoso," Spenser said. "That's a fifteen-thousand-foot volcano in the Llanganatis, the rumored burial grounds of that legendary treasure we talked about. We'll have to hike for two or three days to get there. You'll have to endure altitude sickness, rain, sleet, earthquakes and fog so thick you won't know up from down, let alone left from right. Parts of the cloud forest are so dense and gnarled, we'll need a machete to cut through. There are bugs. Lots of bugs. At fourteen thousand feet we'll hit high Andean plateau country.

The *páramo* is famous for its quaking bogs." He lifted a brow. "Marsh and mud. Andean quicksand. Still want me to take you?"

In more ways than one.

Good Lord. She'd just had a hair-raising fright and all she could think about was jumping Spenser's bones. She didn't trust herself to speak. Babbling wouldn't do. She nodded.

"Just as I thought." He pushed off the door and rubbed the back of his neck. "You're riddled with phobias, yet you're willing to face your fears to find a man you don't even like!"

River tensed. David lurked in the back of her brain, lamenting her quirks. "I'm sorry if that's annoying."

"It's not annoying, dammit. It's impressive. Christ."

His warped compliment warmed River more than the mushiest Hallmark card on the planet. She didn't protest when Spenser shot forward and pulled her into his arms. Didn't struggle when he kissed her—hard, deep and much too brief.

He backed away, jammed a hand through his hair. "Shit."

"The agreement," she rasped, her mind whirling from the taste of him, the feel of him. She wanted to take back that no-kissing pledge. She wanted another kiss, a longer kiss. She wanted…

"I know. I slipped. I'm not perfect, but I'm honorable." He blew out a breath. "Won't happen again."

The disappointment was crushing. In the split second that River mentally scrambled, wondering how to address her sudden and crushing need for intimacy, Spenser pulled farther away.

"We'll leave at dawn," he said, double-checking the door and windows. "It's late and today was relentless. We should turn in."

She wanted nothing more than to crawl into bed with this man, to rip off his clothes, to ravage his mouth, to… "Spenser—"

"Forget what I said before. I'll take the floor."

She grappled for a way to ease the tension, a safe topic that would keep him from shutting down. The map. She needed to show him the map. The map hidden in her pillowcase along with the letter and amulet. They could lie in bed and discuss a plan. "I need to tell you what I remember of Henry's journal."

"And I need to hear it. But with a clear head. I need to sleep off this fucking buzz. Right now all I can think about is stripping you naked and kissing every inch of your sweet body."

River's mouth fell open.

"I know. You're in love with David." He untied and toed off his hiking boots. "I'm going to take a long shower. Go to bed, angel, and don't worry. Remember." He quirked a self-deprecating smile. "Old-fashioned sensibilities."

She stood there dumbstruck, lust-struck. She glanced at the bed, thought about joining him on the floor. How was she going to control her erotic urges?

"Don't worry about the lack of netting," he said,

misinterpreting her anxiety. "You've been taking pri-maquine tablets, right?"

"Yes, but, they're in the hands of the bandits now. I took one this morning as scheduled, but tomorrow…" Why had he reminded her?

He moved to the four boxes stacked by the door. Someone had brought them up earlier, but she figured they were Spenser's personal hiking supplies. She was surprised when he rooted through and handed her a month's supply of antimalarial medicine and… "You bought me Skin So Soft Bug Guard?"

"Also a few bottles of the local version of Purell and some other supplies—clothes, toiletries."

Tears burned her eyes. Instead of making fun of her obsessions, he'd supplied her with the means to ease them. Earlier today he'd loaned her his GPS. "That was really thoughtful, Spenser. Thank you."

"You're welcome." He brushed her curls from her face, focused on her mouth, then turned abruptly and disappeared into the bathroom.

"He bought me bug spray and hand sanitizer," she whispered, in dreamy-eyed awe. She'd never been more touched or turned on in her life.

CHAPTER NINETEEN

GATOR HATED THAT WOMAN.

She'd woken up before he'd been able to knock her out with chloroform. She'd blinded him with some damned flash, causing him to bash his forehead when he'd fallen. Dizzy and seeing spots, he'd slipped while escaping out the window, twisted his ankle in a second fall and intensified his injuries while running for his fucking life.

If he'd had his way, he would've lunged and killed her before she'd screamed. Permanently silenced, he could've searched her room at length. Searched *her*. He could've found the second half of the map. But Gator was fond of his Johnson, and The Conquistador's threat to cut it off still rang in his ears. Gator cursed the crazy-ass bastard as he limped toward his hidden truck. "Like he needed another obsession."

Con had first laid eyes on River Kane the night before in Baños. He'd been lurking in the shadows of that dive bar while Gator had been searching her hotel room. He'd fallen instantly in love or in lust, some sort of morbid fascination. *"When the time is right,"* he'd said, *"River Kane is mine."* Gator didn't get the attraction. The woman was a loon. Maybe that was it. Like attracts like. Or maybe it was the rivalry Gator had sensed between Con and McGraw. Maybe Con wanted her only because McGraw *had* her. All Gator knew for certain was that blondie was a pain in his head, neck, ankle and ass.

Hurting all over, he sat in his truck, surrounded by darkness and his own black thoughts. Sutherland had given him a black eye. The Conquistador had bruised his throat and broken his nose. Now, thanks to blondie, he had a deep gash in his forehead and a sprained ankle. Swearing, he found his blessed tube of muscle-easing salve and coated his neck and ankle. Then he pulled a first-aid kit from under the battered seat and dug out the gauze and tape. At this rate he'd look like a friggin' mummy by week's end. That was if he was alive by week's end.

Minutes later he ditched the medical kit and snagged his satellite phone. He dreaded making this call, but it was safer than admitting failure face-to-face.

"Did you get it?"

He was beginning to hate that question. He detested his answer even more. "No, boss." Gator explained what had gone down. He half expected Con to reach across the miles and strangle him.

Instead of cursing or yelling, Con spoke in a quiet, deliberate voice—which was somehow worse. "I want the second half of that map."

"I don't understand why we can't just use the clues in that journal," Gator blurted out in frustration. Con had scoured that old book for an hour while waiting for his source to call back with River's whereabouts. "You said there were clues."

"I also pointed out they're written in code, you fuck-wit. Only helps if I can decipher them. I'm working on that. Meanwhile, McGraw has the lead."

"But *you* have the first half of the map."

"McGraw won't need the first half. *I* don't need the first half. It's merely a shortcut."

"Alberto said whatever the professor found was on Cerro Hermoso. Can't we—"

"Do you know how fucking big that fucking vol-cano is? Do you want a slice of eight fucking billion U.S. dollars? Get me the fucking *map*." The man disconnected.

Gator's head throbbed, his ankle screamed. He un-screwed the quart of whiskey he'd taken from Con's stash and drank from the bottle. He didn't want just a slice of the treasure, he wanted the whole pie.

He'd get the fucking map.

CHAPTER TWENTY

SPENSER WAS IN THE SHOWER stall, hands braced on the slick tiles, head dipped, wishing the hot water could wash away his sins—those committed and those in his soul—when the glass door slid open.

"I can't go to sleep with bug cooties. I have to shower."

He glanced over his shoulder, saw River—naked, arms crossed self-consciously over her bare breasts.

Oh, hell.

Send her away.

His hesitation caused her to blush. She'd put herself out there, risked rejection, humiliation. She wanted to act on the attraction she'd been fighting since the moment they'd met. She was torn about a lot of things, but not this. He could read her every thought in those expressive green eyes. This second she was feeling exposed in more ways than one.

He grasped her wrist and pulled her inside the cramped stall. A dozen pornographic thoughts crossed his mind. A hundred romantic thoughts tortured his soul.

She raised her face to the spigot, soaked her golden hair.

He could stare at her for eons. So pale. So pretty. Usually he went for the buxom, voluptuous type, but River's delicately boned body was a smoking hot turn-on.

Spenser's mind raced, his conscience twinged. He wanted this, but he didn't. He squeezed liquid soap into his palms, admiring her toned curves before pressing his front to her back. The sensation of skin on skin intensified his already burning need. Surely she felt his hard-on pulsing against her lush ass, but she didn't flinch. Didn't bolt.

Oh, hell.

His heart pounded as he soaped her arms, her breasts. Small. Round. Firm. *Perfect.* His thumbs grazed her pebbled nipples.

She gasped. "I've never done anything like this before," she whispered as he soaped her taut belly.

His fingers ached to slide south, but he heard the hesitation in her voice, felt the tension in her body. She wanted this, but she didn't. Spenser stilled. "In spite of what I said this afternoon, about not refusing sex the next time you offered—"

She turned in his arms, wet, naked and so goddamned pretty it made his chest hurt. She slaked water from her face and nailed him with those earnest green eyes. "I know what you're thinking."

He was thinking he wanted to bury himself between her beautiful legs for a month.

"You're thinking I was jilted. I'm vulnerable. You're thinking I'm sheltered. Conservative. You're thinking I had a roller coaster day, that I'm not myself and that I'll regret this in the morning."

"There is that."

"I'm thinking of this as a damage control."

His lip twitched. "How so?"

"You were right. There *is* something between us," she said. "Some spark. I've never felt anything like it. You don't want it. I don't want it. Maybe if we act on it, it'll go away."

"Scratch the itch?"

"Sort of. If we don't act, the itch will only get worse. Instead of concentrating on the rugged terrain we'll be distracted by sexual tension. If we're distracted, there's a chance one of us will mess up and get hurt."

He smiled down at that angelic face. "Logical, but..." He trailed off as she squirted soap into her palms then lathered his shoulders, his chest, his stomach. The feel of her hands—caressing, exploring—ignited his blood. He groaned when she wrapped her soapy fingers around his rock-hard shaft. "What are you doing?"

"Taking the lead." She was staring at his cock like shiny new bling, or maybe she was simply avoiding his gaze. "You said you like being dominant, but that it's a turn-on when the woman takes control," she rambled as she stroked. "You said—"

"You talk too much when you're nervous."

She glanced up, desire sparking hot in her eyes. "Then shut me up."

He kissed her with the passion of a star-crossed lover.

One hand cradled her face while the other slid over her slick back, the swell of her hip, the curve of her ass.

She let go of his cock in order to press her length against him. She grabbed two fistfuls of his hair, infused their kiss with a torrid passion that torched his brain cells.

The water pounded. The steam swirled.

He broke the kiss, desperate to suckle her breasts, to taste her folds.

"Show me some of your tricks," she whispered.

"Looking to spice things up, angel?"

"Yes."

"Ever made love in the shower?"

"Never."

He was so hot for this woman, he couldn't think straight. He'd blame the tequila, but this was lust. Lust infused with love. He kissed her again, then maneuvered her around. He wanted to obliterate that bastard ex-fiancé from her mind. He wanted to give her sex like she'd never had it before. He placed her hands on the tiles, kissed the back of her neck, then nipped her earlobe. "Do you want it slow or fast?"

"I…I don't know."

He squeezed her nipples, rolled and plucked. "Sweet torturous foreplay?" He abandoned her breasts, slid his hand between her legs and probed her wetness. "Or instant gratification?"

She moaned. "Fast," she said. "This time."

Implying this was going to be a long night or maybe the first of many. "You're killing me, hon."

"Please don't bite the dust before I get my instant gratification."

He smiled at that. Angel and devil rolled into one. He angled her body and thrust deep from behind.

He absorbed her lusty groan, savored her tightness.

Oh, *hell*.

His body pulsed with a heady rush. Being inside River was more thrilling than discovering an ancient relic. Blindsided, he spoke close to her ear before taking her fast and furious. "This one's for you, River. Slow will be for me."

CHAPTER TWENTY-ONE

She was walking down the aisle. He was standing at the altar. He looked besotted. Her own heart fluttered.

She was smitten, too. A lifetime of incredible sex. A lifetime with Spenser. She was giddy with excitement. Brimming with love. Burning with lust.

But then he was gone. He had a show to shoot. Myths to debunk. Treasures to discover.

"If those mountains don't kill you, they'll make you go mad."

The curse.

Bovedine gone. Mel gone. Henry gone. Spenser...

"No!" River's eyes flew open. Her heart pounded.

"Easy." Spenser pulled her into his arms. He pushed damp curls from her face and kissed her forehead.

She clawed through the mental cobwebs, willed her pulse steady.

"Bad dream?"

"Didn't start off that way," she whispered against his chest.

"Want to talk about it?"

"No." She thought about how thrilled she'd been at the prospect of marrying him. As if that could or would ever happen. "Sorry I woke you."

"I never drifted off. Not completely. You, on the other hand—"

"I was exhausted. Between the roller coaster day and our nocturnal gymnastics…"

He laughed.

"I had no idea I could bend into so many positions."

"A pleasant discovery on both our parts."

She flushed thinking about all the ways they'd made love. And with the lights on! After making her come in the shower, he'd toweled her dry, laid her on the bed then kissed, licked and savored every inch of her body. Sweet torturous foreplay. She'd lost count of her orgasms, but she remembered all the positions. She remembered all his sexy, dirty talk and the besotted expression on his face when he'd finally allowed himself to peak. She remembered falling asleep in his arms and dreading the morning.

Now the first streaks of dawn permeated the bungalow. The last vestiges of sleep faded away.

As if reading her mind, Spenser smoothed a calloused palm down her bare arm. "Regrets?"

"No." It was strange. She thought she'd feel guilty for betraying David. Even though he'd left her, he still owned her heart. Or so she'd thought. "But I am confused."

"Want to talk about it?"

"No." She needed to sort through her feelings, her relationship with David. She needed to get a handle on what she felt for Spenser. Anything more meaningful than friendship or lust was dangerous. Even now, lying like this, talking like this, she was treading in risky territory.

Conscious of Spenser's weighted stare, she eased back and met his gaze. "What?"

"Kylie said you were intensely private."

She shrugged. She equated expressing her feelings with being shut out or shut down. There always seemed to be some adverse effect.

"I want to know what makes you tick, angel. How you developed so many phobias. I want to hear about your childhood. Your relationship with your parents."

"I don't talk about those things."

"Why not?"

Her insides froze. "Because they make me feel bad. Do you like discussing things that make you feel bad? What happened on your last trek into the Llanganatis? Mel said you were crippled with guilt. Why? What did Lana mean when she said she's glad you've put the past behind you? What's behind your love-hate relationship with Baños?"

Spenser dragged a hand over his face. "You're right. No thrill in discussing painful topics. On the other hand, keeping all that angst inside sucks, too. The hurt, the regret, frustration, bitterness, guilt, shame—whatever— it just…festers. I've been living with a mountain of angst for a long time, River. I want to move on."

She rose up on one elbow and stared down at the insanely bewildering man beside her. "Are you for real?"

"What do you mean?"

"It's just that you're this macho, thrill-seeking adventurer. A textbook alpha male. The provider. The protector. Yet you say the mushiest things. Mr. Sensitive. Mr. Insightful. I don't get you, Spenser McGraw. You're an enigma."

"You mean, like you?" He winked. "Makes us an interesting match."

She flashed on her good-dream-turned-nightmare. "We're an awful match."

"Why?"

"I could name a dozen reasons."

"Name one."

"I can't live your life." She blew out a frustrated breath. "I need stability. I need order. I need—"

"Show me the shots."

"What?"

"Yesterday in the canopy. I was worried about your safety and you were snapping pictures of monkeys."

"It wasn't just the monkeys. That high up, beyond the canopy, I could see what I thought was a snow-topped volcano."

"Cerro Hermoso"

"I just…I was mesmerized. It looked so far, but near. So forbidding, yet surreal. Henry's there, I thought. *There.* But where? It's so…"

"Massive."

"Yes. And—"

"We'll find him."

"You can't know that for sure."

He stroked her cheek. "We'll give it our best shot. Speaking of shots..."

"Oh, all right." Heart pounding, River nabbed her Nikon from the bedside table. She dreaded sharing those photos with Spenser. Silly, since she shared her work with people all the time. Silly, because she was used to her work being judged. Except this wasn't her normal work. Monkeys versus people. Volcanoes versus wedding cakes. Photographing in the wild...she was out of her element, her comfort zone.

"I promise I won't break it."

River started. "What?"

Spenser grinned. "You've got a death grip on that camera. Hard for me to see the three-inch screen when you've got it pressed to your chest."

"It's just that they're crude, untouched, I mean. I haven't had a chance to—"

Spenser pried the Nikon from her grip, powered on. Obviously, he had some knowledge of digital cameras.

"Use this button to scroll forward and back. And this one to zoom in and out." River scooted closer so she could see what he saw. Lying on their backs, shoulder to shoulder, heads angled together...naked. She'd certainly never viewed photos like this with Ella. "I should have framed that one differently," she said, frowning at the shot of four... "What kind of monkeys are those anyway? Do you know?"

"Squirrel monkeys. Unusual to see an isolated few. They usually roam the treetops in troops of twenty to a hundred. Interesting shot. Intimate. And you framed it just fine."

He scrolled back, an action shot of zip-lining from her point of view, the jungle canopy a green blur, the tips of her trekking boots… Criminy. "I was trying to capture the feeling of well, flying, only I didn't set the shutter speed right and…"

"Shhh."

River lay still, pulse racing as Spenser studied the pictures she'd taken over the last two days. Pictures she'd snapped through the window of the speeding bus, shots of volcanoes, waterfalls and tropical birds. Shots of Baños—the architecture and the surrounding mountains. As a professional, she found fault with each picture, but that didn't diminish the wonder every scenic photo inspired. With a little tweaking, some retouching and…

"Whoa."

River blinked at the monitor, smiled. "Oh. That's Carla Aubry. Or rather her thigh. She and her husband were bawdy newlyweds, a lot of fun, actually. I thought they'd appreciate a close-up of Richard sliding the garter, well…you can see."

"Uh-huh." Spenser grinned. "Sexy." He scrolled through a few more of the wedding shots she'd yet to delete. "I can see why my sister and Jack hired you to shoot their wedding. Kylie didn't want you just because you're a friend." He glanced at her with bald appreciation. "You're a skilled photographer, River."

Her cheeks burned, her heart fluttered. "Thank you."

"You have an artistic flair with people, but…"

"What?"

He set the camera on his bedside table. "I like the nature shots even better."

She blinked. "I don't know whether to be flattered or insulted."

He brushed a thumb over her red-hot cheeks. "You're right. Those jungle shots are crude, as in raw, as in *passionate*. Are you happy being a wedding photographer?"

Another uncomfortable subject because, no, she wasn't. Not completely. But it offered stability and she was good at it. "I'm good with people. I tune in to their personalities and that enables me to recognize the perfect photo op. Take now, for instance. You."

She reached over Spenser, grabbed her camera, then scooted to the edge of the bed.

He rolled on his side, propped up on one elbow, and raised a questioning, sexy brow. His heated gaze slid over her body.

She didn't care that she was naked. The point was Spenser was naked. And he looked…incredible. Yes, she wanted to distract him from a conversation she didn't want to have, but also… She looked through the viewfinder and focused…. "I've ached to do this ever since I first saw you at the airport in Quito."

He cocked an ornery grin. "I'm not going to find these posted on the Internet, am I?" he asked as she snapped a shot of his ripped torso.

"Don't insult me." River continued to snap away,

various angles and compositions. Her artistic eye skimmed the hard planes and contours of his chiseled abdomen and chest, his broad shoulders, smooth back and muscled arms. His stubbled jaw, mussed hair, the twinkle in his beautiful green eyes. She felt a sensual pulse between her legs and, *geez,* he was only exposed from the hips up. Inspired, she flung away the sheets, revealing his sculpted thighs and... "Oh."

"Mmm."

He had a hard-on. A *massive* hard-on.

Her stomach coiled tight. Her inner thighs tingled. River licked dry lips and snapped a fully nude shot of an incredibly virile man.

Click. Click. Click.

"You could probably fetch a pretty penny for these from *Playgirl*," Spenser teased in a gruff, low voice. "I'm a celebrity, you know."

"So I hear."

"I can't believe you've never seen my show."

"Don't take it personally."

He smiled. "By my estimation you've taken two dozen shots in less than three minutes."

"I'll delete them if you want," she said, feeling a little guilty and a lot horny.

"No. I like the idea of you ogling naked pictures of me." He winked then and relieved her of the camera. "Are you as turned on as me?"

"Incredibly turned on."

Spenser rolled on top of her and covered her mouth with his own. His tongue swept inside, igniting her passion. His hands caressed her naked curves, stoking intimate desires. His kisses were intoxicating. His touch lethal. She could easily imagine becoming addicted to this man, his macho antics and sensitive musings.

She could easily imagine him breaking her heart.

Take control!

River bent her leg, used leverage to flip their position. She took the lead, nabbed a condom packet from the nightstand and tore it open. They'd slipped up the first time last night, in the shower. Unprotected sex in the heat of the moment. Spenser had been quick to address that, and luckily he had an ample supply of Trojans.

"Sweet torturous foreplay?" he asked as she dallied.

She gave him the exact opposite. She straddled his erection and rode him hard. He gripped her waist, groaned his pleasure. Her muscles tensed and quivered. She was flying, soaring, in control, out of control. He rose up, rammed deep and she screamed her release. Limbs melting, lungs burning, River slumped on top of the thrill-seeking treasure hunter.

Beware of the hunters.

Dammit.

Spenser stroked a hand down her back and then, again, reversed their position. "My turn."

She expected one of those explosive episodes, like in the shower. Like what she'd just done to him. But Spenser took it slow and deep. By the time he brought her to her second orgasm, she couldn't form a coherent thought. By the time he climaxed, she was nearly comatose. He kissed her sweetly, tenderly, and she nearly wept for the beauty of the moment. "Damn you," she whispered.

"You're an adventurer, River."

"Maybe a long time ago."

"It's still there. The fire. The curiosity."

He said things she longed to hear, but the timing...the timing was terribly wrong. She framed his face with her hands. "Listen to me. I have a plan, a mission. Rescue Henry from whatever mess he's in, then hash out our past issues. Closure. I'm here for closure. With Henry. With David. I want to move on, too, Spenser. But I have to do it in my world. I have a business. A...house." She started to say a life, but she wasn't all that nuts about what she'd be going back to. *At least it's stable. Safe.*

He raised a brow. "So you're telling me I'm moving too fast? Crank it down a notch?"

She gawked, then laughed. "Don't you ever give up?"

"That's right. You've never watched my show."

"That really bugs you, doesn't it?"

"Actually...no." He flashed a devastating smile. "But it does put you at a disadvantage."

"How so?"

"Hundreds of thousands, no, millions of viewers, unlike you, know what makes me tick."

She smirked. "Enlighten me. Short version, please."

"I've searched for the Holy Grail, Excalibur, Montezuma's treasure, Black Beard's treasure, the Ark of the Covenant and the Seven Cities of Cibola. Some of them twice. One of these days I'll shout, *eureka!* It's all in working the puzzle, unraveling the mystery. You're looking at a man who believes in infinite possibilities, angel."

River stared up in him in awe, grappled for a response and failed.

"I'll make you a deal. You tell me about your past and I'll reciprocate. We'll be trekking through the wilderness for a few days. It'll help pass the time and maybe help us both in our quest to move on."

She wanted very badly to know what haunted this man, enough to share her own baggage. Maybe it would help to uncork all the angst she'd bottled up over the years and, besides, it would keep her from obsessing on her phobias and Henry's well-being. She skimmed a thumb over Spenser's stubbled jaw, smiled. "You'll stop me if it gets boring, right?"

Green eyes dancing, he planted a quick kiss to her lips then hustled into the bathroom. "Time to attack the day," he called out. "I need to question you about your dad's journal. It would've contained clues to his exact location. Without it—"

"It's okay. I have a map. Or at least half of one."

That brought him back bedside.

She didn't know what to make of his expression, but the full frontal she liked. As for her own nudity… She reached over the bed and grabbed the first piece of clothing she could find. One of Spenser's T-shirts. Awfully assuming to pull it on, but at least it would cover a good portion of her body. Having a drawn-out business conversation in the buff was beyond her comfort zone.

"I ripped it out of Henry's journal," she explained. "Yesterday morning, after I heard you on the phone, before Mel picked me up. I had trust issues. I was anxious about the journey ahead. I thought it might be best to redistribute my valuables. Most everything was in my sling pack. Money, credit cards, travel documents, the journal. What if I lost my sling? What if someone stole it? So I divided everything between the sling, my camera bag and my duffel. Fat lot of good that did. I didn't anticipate bandits stealing *all* my belongings."

His silence made her nervous. Instead of biting her fingernails or pacing, she bolted to the bathroom to brush her teeth. *Instead of panicking,* she could hear Grandpa Franklin say, *do something constructive.* "I know what you're thinking," she called. "It's sacrilegious, tearing a page out of an archaeologist's documented studies."

"I'm thinking you're full of surprises."

Mouth foaming with toothpaste, she glanced up and saw Spenser standing on the threshold in all his naked glory. The man didn't have a self-conscious bone in his glorious, muscle-ripped body. Tearing her eyes from his most impressive physical attribute, she rinsed and spit. "It's just…I thought, what if I lost the journal or someone stole it? Then I'd have no hope of finding Henry. It was a spontaneous decision. I tore out the map and hid it on my person."

"Half the map," he said, moving in beside her and nabbing his own toothbrush.

"That's all there was. The preceding page was torn out. I think maybe, I have reason to believe, Henry mailed that portion to Professor Bovedine."

Spenser rinsed and spit, then reached in the shower and turned it on. "Who's Professor Bovedine?"

"He's… What are you doing?" she asked as he tugged his T-shirt up and over her head.

"We smell like sex, angel. You want to say goodbye to Lana and Duke and hello to Cyrus Lassiter smelling like—"

"Point taken." Cheeks burning, she stepped into the shower ahead of him. "Who's Cyrus Lassiter?"

"Tell me about Bovedine."

"Professor Paul Bovedine. Archaeologist and staff member at Cornell University," River said as they soaped each other's bodies. "He was one of Henry's oldest friends."

"Was?"

She swallowed an emotional lump. "He died five… or was it six days ago? I've lost track of time. Victim of a random botched burglary, although I'm not sure it was random *or* botched."

"What do you mean?"

River scratched shampoo through her hair, marveling that they were having this conversation while showering together. It was weird in a wonderful sort of way. She'd never been this casually intimate with David. "Professor Bovedine received a package from my father the day before I received mine. The package, and whatever was inside, is missing. I know it's crazy, but I can't shake the feeling that whoever broke into Bovedine's house specifically wanted that package. Bad enough to kill for it." She glanced over her shoulder at Spenser. "Crazy, huh? How would they know the contents? How would they trace the package from South America to upstate New York?"

"Lots of people, particularly in this region, knew about your dad's expedition," Spenser said as he helped her rinse away the suds. "He'd hired several local guides. Over the course of a few months, most got ill or had accidents. All died but one." He shut off the faucet. "Two were murdered."

River shivered. *What have you gotten yourself into, Henry?*

Helping her from the shower, Spenser wrapped her in a towel, then gave her a detailed account as they both dried and dressed.

Her mind reeled. "The guide that Gordo talked to…"

"Juan."

"He said Henry gave him one package to mail. A package addressed to me. But there were *two* packages," she said as she laced up her trekking boots. "That means Henry entrusted Bovedine's package to someone else." She glanced at Spenser. "Alberto?"

"The timing makes sense. Possible someone beat or bribed the information out of him then killed him to keep him quiet."

"Then flew to America, stole the package and killed Professor Bovedine to keep *him* quiet."

"All supposition, angel." Spenser pulled a short-sleeve black tee over a long-sleeved gray one.

River tugged on a pair of brown cargo pants. "But suppose it's true? He said he'd discovered something men would kill to possess."

"Who? Henry? When did he tell you that?"

"He wrote it in a letter. It was tucked inside the journal."

Spenser moved to answer a knock at the door.

Heart pounding, River moved to the bed and rooted her treasure baggy from the pillow. Two days ago, she wouldn't have shared this information with Spenser for the life of her. But now…she knew now that she couldn't do this alone, and after the debacle with Mel… It was almost as if Spenser was fated to help her find Henry, yet she couldn't let him go into this without showing him what he was possibly up against.

Beware of the hunters.

Were they dealing with one murdering maniac? Two? Three? Were they working together? Separately?

Hunters.

Plural.

Stomach knotting, River sank into a chair, the baggy clutched in her lap.

"Duke said you'd be cutting out early," she heard Lana say. "Brought you and River some coffee and a light breakfast. You'll stop over and say goodbye, right?"

"You bet. Thanks, Lana."

"Sure you're up for this trek, Spense?"

"As fit as I've ever been."

"You know what I mean."

River looked over and saw his shoulders tense. "I've got good reason to face my demons."

"That reason named River?"

"See you in a bit," he said with a smile in his voice. He shut the door and River squirmed in her seat. He set the tray on the table—a pot of coffee, scrambled eggs, bacon and toast.

"That was nice of her," River said.

Spenser claimed the chair across from her. "Lana and Duke are good people." He poured coffee. "Tell me about the letter."

She hesitated a second, then passed him the folded stationery. "He said he's sacrificing his life to protect a precious treasure. What if that precious treasure is Atahualpa's ransom? What if he actually found it, Spenser? Eight billion dollars. Sadly, I bet there are a lot of men who would kill for that kind of windfall."

He cast her a fleeting look, a pained look, then focused back on the letter.

Her leg bounced. That wouldn't do. But then she thought, what the hell, she had good reason to be nervous.

"No wonder you worked so hard to get rid of me," he finally said. "Kane swore you to secrecy."

"Plus the hunter thing," River said. *Bounce, bounce.*

"So you assumed hunter meant treasure hunter."

"Isn't it obvious? And typically treasure hunters are amoral, obsessively driven, untrustworthy…"

"Ouch."

"Sorry. I just…never mind."

Smiling a little, he drank coffee and read the letter a second time. "I doubt Henry meant every word literally."

"He always did talk in riddles," River grumbled. "Plus the journal… It's like it was written in some kind of code."

"Probably was." Spenser shook his head as if stumped or blindsided by something in the letter. More code? "Sweat of the sun."

She sensed a shift in his mood, a suppressed intensity. "Does that mean something to you?"

"Sweat of the Sun, Tears of the Moon."

Yeah? And? River bit her thumbnail, her anxiety spiking with each passing second.

He indicated the platter of bacon and eggs. "Fuel up, angel." Then leaned back in his chair and stared into space.

"Not hungry."

"Once we get into the mountains we'll be existing on basics."

His manner was calm but his tone was gruff. His mind was a million miles away, or at least as far as the Llanganatis. River bristled. "I shared Henry's letter hoping for enlightenment, yet you're holding back. Tell me about sweat of the sun, dammit."

"Eat something."

She'd eat dirt if it would get him to spill his guts. Eyes narrowed, she tore into a butter-slathered piece of toast.

He quirked a halfhearted smile, then focused back on the letter. "Incas valued precious metals not as money, but as religious symbols. Gold represented 'sweat of the sun.' They molded it into golden plates, goblets, ornaments—"

"Jewelry?"

He nodded, drank coffee. "The gold treasures were in honor of the Incan sun god. Silver stood for tears of the moon and was molded into objects in honor of the moon god, sister of the sun." He paused, flashed the letter. "Says here: 'I'm gifting you with my journal and sweat of the sun.'"

God, let him be trustworthy. Heart pounding, River dipped into the baggy and passed Spenser the small gold amulet.

He held it in his palm and regarded it in quiet awe. "Chakana."

"Meaning?"

"Inca cross. An Andean symbol of Incan civilization. Known in other mythologies as world tree, tree of life... I've seen my share of chakanas, but this one..." He stood suddenly and walked to the window, studied the amulet in the stark sunlight. "*This* is an ancient work of art. Superb craftsmanship. Pure gold."

Ancient gold.

Gold fever.

River's skin prickled with goose bumps. Pulse racing, she stood and joined Spenser. "Could it be part of the treasure? Could it be..." She trailed off, rattled by the intense look in his eyes, an intensity directed at the chakana. The man was mesmerized. She snatched back the amulet, looped it around her neck and returned to her seat.

He cleared his throat. "Sorry," he said, and joined her at the table. "Map?"

Part of her balked. If he was that transfixed by the ancient amulet, what would happen when he got a look at the possible location of its origin? On the other hand, if anyone could figure out Henry's markings and whereabouts, it was an obsessed treasure hunter. Leg bouncing, River passed Spenser the yellowed page she'd torn from her father's journal...and hoped for the best.

"Cerro Hermoso," he said at first glance.

"The volcano."

"I recognize the sketch, and the name is scribbled in the margin, but everything else..." He shook his head. "I've studied maps and notes by Valverde, Guzmán, Spruce, Blake, Chapman, Brunner . This is all new."

Those names meant nothing to her, but she was absolutely riveted by the wonderment on Spenser's face, the infectious energy rolling off his body in waves. Riveted and worried. "There's an *X*."

"*X* marks the spot."

Desperate to break his fierce trance, River snatched back the map. "Can you get us there?"

"I'll get us there." He pushed out of his chair and surprised her with a deep, tender kiss.

Heat snaked through River's body. Thoughts whipped in her brain. Between last night and this morning they'd made love several times, several ways, showered together, slept together and had a couple of heart-to-hearts—sort of. They barely knew each other, yet they connected in ways that baffled River. Why wasn't Spenser more rattled?

"We need to haul ass," he said as he moved to the door. "I'll pack the jeep. You eat. You're going to need all your strength and then some."

Fork poised, she flashed back on a name he'd mentioned earlier. A man he'd said they'd be meeting. "Who's Cyrus Lassiter?"

He quirked a wry grin before moving outside. "An amoral, obsessively driven, untrustworthy treasure hunter."

CHAPTER TWENTY-TWO

El Triunfo, Ecuador
Altitude 10,000 feet

THE VILLAGE WAS MOSTLY as he remembered it from nine years ago. Crowing roosters. Mangy dogs. Women riding donkeys and men carrying machetes. Barefoot children in ankle-deep mud.

But this time, instead of stopping, instead of mingling with the locals and soaking up lore about the lost Inca treasure, Spenser drove straight through. He'd heard all the stories. He didn't need supplies. Nor guides. Nor directions. He knew how to get to Cerro Hermoso. After that, he had Kane's map.

Strike that. River had the map. She'd confiscated her dad's things before they'd left the Diablo Jungle Lodge. The map and letter were inside a baggy, tucked inside her bra. The Chakana was dangling from a black cord hanging around her neck.

She didn't trust him.

He didn't blame her.

There'd been a split second when he'd burned with gold fever. When he'd coveted Atahualpa's ransom.

Not for the wealth, but for the discovery, the historical significance, for the chance to shout, *eureka!*

And she'd sensed it.

He couldn't help being dazzled by the ancient cha-kana or by Kane's detailed, although somewhat cryptic, map. But he could manage the intensity of his enthusiasm. He was nine years older. Nine years wiser. This time, instead of trying to impress the woman at his side, he only wanted to protect her. This time he'd lead with his head and heart, instead of his dick and pride.

Spenser ignored the curious looks of the locals as he maneuvered the jeep over the muddy, rutted road. River, on the other hand, was paying the locals rapt attention, snapping photos as they slowly rolled through the village. The woman was a talented photographer, but it was more than technical skill that made her pictures special. It was her tender heart and adventurous soul. Maybe she'd led a cautious personal life, but where her work was concerned, she took chances. The risqué garter photo, shooting the canopy while zip-lining at high speed.

Taking photos of Spenser in the raw.

He smiled to himself, hoping to hell that "private sitting" wouldn't bite him in the ass.

"Wait," she said. *Snap. Snap.* "Aren't we stopping?"

"We wouldn't be welcome."

"Why not?"

"Maldición."

She glanced over her shoulder, speared his heart

with her worried gaze. "Do you believe in that ancient curse?"

"Yes." He'd felt it. Lived it. "But I also think it can be avoided with pure intentions." An optimistic, and only recent, hypothesis.

"I guess you didn't have pure intentions first time around?"

"Two times around. No. I didn't."

"Do you want to talk about it?"

"No. Not now. Not yet." He squeezed the steering wheel, noted his white knuckles and rolled back his shoulders. "We'll meet up with Cy just around that bend."

"Oh, joy."

"River—"

"You don't have to rehash your reasons." She settled back in her seat, massaged her chest. "I get it. Cyrus Lassiter is an asset. He knows the mountains. He can heft more weight than I can and, considering we need to tote two weeks of supplies on our backs...I get it, Spenser. I just...I had to adjust to the idea. Henry said tell no one but Professor Bovedine. But I realize now, Henry never imagined I'd make this trek. He wouldn't have credited me with the nerve or motivation."

Spenser heard the hurt in her voice, saw the anguish in her expression, however slight. "I don't know what happened between you and your dad, River, but he loves you."

She snorted.

"That letter—"

"Actions speak louder than words. Or rather, lack of words…never mind."

"Want to talk about it?"

"No. Not now. Not yet." She pointed through the windshield. "Is that your friend?"

Spenser nodded and pulled his rental jeep alongside Cy's battered form of transportation. The seasoned treasure hunter was leaning against the hood—arms crossed over chest, ankle over ankle, his long salt-and-pepper hair pulled into a scraggly ponytail. Cy gave them a two-fingered salute.

"He sort of looks like Sean Connery in that movie *Medicine Man*."

"Didn't see the movie, but I sort of see the resemblance. Like I said before, River, Cy's eccentric, but he knows his stuff."

"Sounds like Henry. Aren't there any normal people in your field?"

Spenser didn't comment. But he did wonder what Kane had done to sour River on his world. She was staring out at the daunting landscape, clearly wondering what sane person willingly trudged through gnarled jungle and quaking bogs as a lifestyle. Gearing up for the challenge, she'd already slathered her face with sunscreen and doused herself in bug guard. And though she'd probably die before admitting it, she was struggling with the increasing altitude.

Spenser reached for her hand and squeezed. "You don't have to do this. You could wait with Lana and Duke, while Cy and I—"

"Henry entrusted me with his secret, his journal. I've already lost the journal, I can't risk… I have to tell him about Professor Bovedine. I need to see what treasure he chose over me."

"There's no guarantee he's alive, River."

"There's no guarantee he's dead." She pushed open the door and greeted Cy.

Spenser joined her and shook the man's hand. "Thanks for doing this."

"Heard there's gold in them thar hills," Cy said with a wink.

"We're not looking for gold," River snapped. "We're looking for Professor Henry Kane."

Cy raised calloused palms in surrender. "I know, sweetheart. Relax."

"They say he's cursed. That everyone connected to his expedition is cursed. Are you sure you want to do this?"

"Legend has it anyone who enters those mountains in search of Atahualpa's ransom is cursed." Cy tugged a blue plaid fedora over his wind-ravaged ponytail and shoved on a pair of tortoiseshell sunglasses held together at the nose with black electrical tape. "I've been in and out of the Llanganatis over one hundred and forty times. Do I look dead? Or crazy?"

"You might want to rephrase that last question," Spenser said while glancing at the incoming call on his phone. "I need to take this. Cy, our backpacks and provisions are in the jeep. Can you redistribute the weight?"

"Sure."

Spenser could feel River's curious stare as he moved out of earshot. "Took you long enough to return my call."

"Sorry," Gordo said. "Had a few too many last night and tussled with a loudmouthed hunter who trashed our show. Spent the night in jail."

"You all right?"

"Aside from the black eye and bruised pride? Spiffy."

"You've got too much time on your hands."

"Whose fault is that?"

Spenser brought his partner up to speed.

"Holy shit. Do you think… Is it possible?"

"Anything's possible."

"I should be with you, not Cyrus Lassiter."

"Cy's knowledge trumps yours in this instance. No offense."

"Yeah, but…using one kook to find another? Not to mention dragging an inexperienced woman into dangerous territory. She's a wedding photographer, Spense, not an explorer. This has disaster written all over it."

"I don't think River will make it to the *páramo*," Spenser said in a low voice. "Aside from the rigorous hiking, she's struggling to breathe easy at ten thousand feet. How will she manage fourteen thousand? That's why I asked Cy along. If anyone can get her safely back to Triunfo, it's him."

"You suggested he's not trustworthy."

"He is when it comes to a woman's safety. *Chivalry*

is Cy's middle name. I used to think he had some sort of Sir Lancelot complex. Always rescuing damsels in distress. Plus, like I said, he knows these mountains—a hundred shortcuts and hiding places."

"So they backtrack while you go on alone?" Gordo asked. "That's insane! Oh, wait. Oh, shit. You've got the fever. You're not even in the mountains yet and you're possessed."

"I've never had a clearer head." It was true. At least without that chakana and map in hand.

"Then why take River at all? Spare her the physical anguish. Charm her out of the map and sweet-talk her into staying behind. If anyone's capable of casting a spell over a woman, it's you."

"Gee, thanks. But I won't manipulate her, Gordo."

"Worried about fumbling the discovery of your career?"

He was worried about losing River's affections. "I need you up here."

"About time."

He filled Gordo in on specifics, then hightailed it back to the parked vehicles. Cy was adjusting the straps of the backpack Spenser had purchased for River in Ambato. Aside from her turquoise jacket and orange scarf, everything River was wearing, down to the flowery cotton bra and panties, he'd purchased. She'd insisted on paying him back. He'd said they'd fight about that later. He figured they'd fight about a lot of things later. Why that made him smile he had no idea.

"Good news?" River asked with a suspicious frown.

"Just thinking about how cute you look in those boots." He'd managed to find her a pair of pink knee-high Muck Boots, whereas his and Cy's were standard black.

"One thing's for sure," Cy told her, "all those bright colors will make you easier to spot when you lag behind."

"I won't lag."

Cy raised a bushy gray brow. "We'll see about that."

Clearly perturbed, River nabbed Spenser's phone. "May I borrow this? I need to check in with Ella. I don't want her to worry."

Spenser eyed the mid-morning sun, a hazy ball in a dreary sky. If they were lucky it wouldn't rain, but they had a lot of territory to cover before dark, and time was ticking. "Make it quick, angel." She trudged off and he looked to Cy. "You armed?"

"You have to ask?"

Spenser checked his own sidearm, then holstered it beneath his coat.

"Expecting trouble, boy?"

"Possibly more than usual. Just make sure one of us has River in our sight at all times."

"Expect you'll fill me in when you can," Cy said as River turned back their way. "Feisty thing. That'll serve her well, but did you notice her labored breathing?"

"I noticed." Spenser shouldered on his own backpack,

containing fifty pounds of gear. Cy's looked to weigh about the same. River's pack weighed far less but he anticipated she'd tire within the first couple of hours.

"Guess we should take it slow."

Spenser shook his head. "Let's try to reach Brunner's first camp by nightfall."

"She'll never make it," Cy said.

"That's the plan."

Frowning, River approached and passed Spenser his phone.

"Bad news?" he asked.

"No news," she said, avoiding his gaze. "Let's get this show on the road." She pulled her new GPS unit from her pocket. "Which way is north?"

Brows raised, Cy pointed.

She thumbed in coordinates. "Great. Let's go."

Chuckling, Cy took the lead.

Spenser pulled River into his arms. "I'll find your dad, angel."

"You mean *we*."

He brushed a kiss over irresistible lips. "Let's go."

FOR THE FIRST HOUR, River easily kept up with the men. They were navigating a valley, skirting a river at a very brisk clip, but she was a runner. She had strength, stamina. Yes, she was a little out of breath, but deep thoughts and churning emotions fueled her footsteps.

David hadn't called.

Not even to casually ask how she was weathering their breakup. Ella had checked her phone messages both at home and work. He hadn't written. Ben had kept track of River's mail. In order to get that information out of her assistant, River had lied. It couldn't be helped. Ella had been under the impression River had flown straight to Peru, to David, to patch up their relationship.

"I decided to treat myself to a spa experience at a four-star resort before seeking out David," she'd said. *"I'm gearing up. Physically and spiritually."*

"Uh-huh."

"It's been great, except my purse got stolen. I need you to cancel my credit cards."

"Okay."

"I'll get the bank to wire me some money. And I'll pick up a phone card and check in with you when I can. I just don't want you to worry if you don't hear from me for a week or so."

"I'm not worried."

"You're not?"

"River, Kylie McGraw called here a few times. She said she asked her brother to see you around. Told me not to worry. I watch Into the Wild *all the time. Spenser McGraw's a hottie and a flirt. Too old for me, but probably in the 'sexy older man' zone for you. I'm thinking you're shacked up in that four-star resort having your own kind of extreme adventure."*

River blushed head to toe. *"I'm not—"*

"So is Spenser as sexy in person as on TV?"

"I haven't seen him on TV."

"Drool worthy?"

River sighed. "You have no idea."

Ella squealed. "This is so cool! Wait until I tell Ben!"

"No! Don't tell Ben. Don't tell anyone. There's nothing to tell!"

"Uh-huh."

"Ella—"

"*Everything's fine at Forever Photography. Don't give us a second thought. Call me when you come up for air. Spenser McGraw.*" She whistled low. "*Talk about the ultimate revenge. Take that David.*"

Ella's parting statement slammed River like a nervous bride's tirade. She hadn't slept with Spenser out of spite, had she? She wasn't capable of such a thing, was she? When she'd handed Spenser back his phone she hadn't been able to look him in the eyes. The mere possibility that she'd slept with him just to hurt David struck her with shame. Within the first half hour of the hike she'd gone though a quarter bottle of her pocket sanitizer to wash away the icky feeling.

Thirty minutes later the trail turned muddy, knee-deep in a few places, and even as she fought not to slip, she still obsessed on her motivation. She wasn't the vengeful type. If she were, she could've stuck it to David financially. She could have bad-mouthed him all over Maple Grove. Or as Ella had mentioned, bought a voodoo doll or hired a hitman. But then the thought niggled, what if she'd slept with Spenser to fill some insecure need? Reassurance that she was indeed desirable, even with her quirks? That possibility made her feel pathetic.

Two thoughts dogged her as they left the clearing and broke into dense forest.

One, I don't have indiscriminant sex.

Two, I don't want to die.

Certain there was an anopheles mosquito with her name on it, she doused her body, clothes and all, with a cloud of bug guard.

"What's that stink?" Cy asked, then sneezed three times in succession.

"It doesn't stink." The first words River had spoken aloud in over an hour. "It's laundry-fresh Skin So Soft Bug Guard."

Cy stopped in his muddy tracks, sneezed again. "Did you have to pollute the air with the entire bottle?"

"I didn't—"

He pulled a machete from his belt.

River stumbled back. Alberto had been stabbed to death. In Baños. Cy lived in Baños.

The older man rolled his eyes, "Christ almighty," then turned and hacked through thick vegetation.

Spenser thumbed up the brim of his hat, regarded her with a tender gaze. "River, there are no malarial mosquitoes here."

"What?"

"Unlike the lower rain forest, the higher jungle is slightly safer. No anopheles mosquitoes. No deadly snakes. The biggest threat is the damp cold."

Good news, sort of. Two thoughts dogged River.

One, Spenser's cowboy hat was incredibly sexy (unlike Cy's dorky fedora).

Two, at least she wouldn't die of malaria.

"Ready to talk about it?" he asked as he followed Cy's hacked path.

"What?" Her childhood? Her parents? Her vengeful, pathetic use of sex?

"There are dozens of antimalarial medicines. You're cautious, methodical even. You would have consulted a physician, researched. Primaquine's not a preventative as much as a treatment. You've had malaria. You're worried about a relapse."

River's pulse accelerated as they pushed through the sun-deprived forest. "Working the puzzle?"

"How am I doing?"

"Your deductive skills are amazing."

"You provided ample clues."

Which meant she hadn't been as private about her past with this man as was her norm. She couldn't contemplate that. Not now. Brain full. "It was a long time ago. Back when we traveled as a family. An expedition in Africa. I don't remember any of it. I was only two. But my parents brought it up several times over the years, as did my grandparents and assorted friends in my mom's artistic circle."

"Your mom was an artist? What medium?"

"She specialized in charcoal sketches and watercolors, although she often experimented with primitive paints. Whatever was available. She traveled with Henry. Visually documented his expeditions."

River followed Spenser as he wielded his own machete, widening Cy's path. He seemed intent on protecting her from the lash and sting of branches and pricklers. She was intent on avoiding his gaze. Even though she'd agreed to talk about the "bad stuff," it was far from her comfort zone. "I almost died, or so I've been told. The beginning of my 'lightning rod for disaster' life."

"Calculating the years," Spenser said, "even then there would have been reliable preventative measures against malaria."

"Are you suggesting my parents were irresponsible?"

"Just working the puzzle, angel."

"According to Henry it was a tribal shaman's fault."

Spenser stopped cold, turned.

"You know. A witch doctor."

"You're kidding."

River died a thousand deaths. "This is why I don't talk about my past. It's embarrassing. My father, a highly educated man, believes I, his only child, was cursed with a delicate constitution. Low tolerance to germs, prone to infection. An inability to function in primitive conditions."

Still Spenser stared.

"According to my grandpa, who got it from my mom, Henry got carried away on one of his expeditions, stepped on a shaman's toes and that shaman retaliated by cursing his unborn child. That would be me."

"Losing time!" Cy bellowed from ahead.

"You're not cursed, River."

"Over the next five years, I developed countless viruses."

"Most kids do. Hell, I contracted measles, chicken pox and mumps, all before I was seven."

"I got severe sun poisoning in Egypt and was attacked by fire ants in Thailand. The fire ants I remember. The pain. The blisters."

Spenser gripped her shoulder. "Those things could've happened to anyone."

"But they happened to me. They wanted a boy, a scrappy boy suited to their adventurous lifestyle. Instead they got a wimpy girl who proved a heartache and a hindrance."

"I'm sure they didn't—"

"They did." She cringed at the sympathy in his eyes, looked around his strong and capable body. "I can't see Cy anymore. We need to catch up." She'd told Spenser more than she'd ever told anyone about her childhood. If she kept going, she'd be telling him how they'd decided she'd be safer in the States. How Henry refused to give up his travels and how her mom refused to give up Henry. Spenser was wrong. She didn't feel better for spilling her guts. She felt like an idiot. Exposed. Raw. She felt like a freaking freak of nature!

When Spenser didn't move, she grabbed his machete and whacked a tangle of vines. It felt good. Like punching something. She whacked again, exerting energy, expelling anger.

Not a wimp.

Not cursed.
Whack!
Rescue and closure.
Whack, whack, WHACK!

CHAPTER TWENTY-THREE

Somewhere in the Cloud Forest
Altitude 12,000 feet

"SHE'S LAGGING, but she's not giving up."

"I know." Spenser stood at the face of a steep incline alongside Cy. River was coming toward them, moving at a snail's pace, but moving. Surprising, given they'd been hard at it for close to four hours.

Navigating the dense forest was no cakewalk. Even though Spenser was experienced and fit, he still felt a burn in his thighs, a tightness in his chest. At times he'd had to stoop, hunch or angle to squeeze through thick jungle and narrow tunnels of vegetation. Although the incline was sometimes subtle, they were constantly gaining altitude.

More than once Cy had thrown him a look that said, *let's stop.* Not that he or Spenser needed a lengthy breather, but River would've benefited. Spenser didn't want her to benefit. Didn't want her to rejuvenate. Call him an ass, but he wanted her to cry *uncle.*

River, damn her, was not only tougher than she looked, but stronger. Spenser expected her arms to give out after five minutes of swinging his heavy machete.

She'd brutalized gnarled vegetation for close to thirty. She wasn't nearly as effective as Spenser would have been, but he recognized the need to burn off anger.

While she'd hacked, he'd reflected on her story. He'd be resentful, too, if his dad had drummed it into his head that he was somehow inferior. Even though Spenser had disappointed Dewy McGraw by not following tradition and running the shoe store that had been in the family for four generations, the old man had been his staunchest supporter. Obviously, River felt unloved and unwanted by her dad. He didn't know about her mom, but he knew there was more to the story. As much as he wanted to press, he'd held silent. Asking River to speak at length would have been cruel. She was struggling to keep up, struggling to breathe. He kept waiting for her to ask him about his "bad stuff." Kept waiting for her to succumb to her phobias, to admit defeat, ordering them to stop or turn back. But she'd yet to utter even one request or complaint.

"I've had a bad feeling the last mile or so," Cy said.

Spenser nodded. "Like we're being watched, only I haven't seen or heard anyone."

"Could be the altitude messing with our heads."

"Could be we're being watched."

Cy shoved his fedora back on his head. "Still waiting to hear what I've gotten myself into, aside from the obvious treasure hunt and associated curse. We're looking for River's dad, but who's on our tail? And why?"

Spenser offered select details.

"So you're attributing a couple of loosely linked

deaths and near-death incidents to the map in River's possession."

Spenser had only studied the partial map for three minutes tops, but the damned thing was branded on his brain as distinctly as Valverde's guide or Brunner's map—charts he'd studied for years. His pulse spiked as he envisioned the discovery of a lifetime. A secret hidey-hole crammed with gold and silver Inca and pre-Inca handicrafts. Sculpted birds, animals and life-size human figures. Pots of jewelry and the sacred Indian corn.

A king's ransom.

"I'm just saying, Cy, what if?"

"Then I'd say, holy freaking miracle, and quickly add that River would be safer if you or I had that map."

"She'd be safer out of the equation, period."

"Almost forgot," Cy said. "You want her to peter out and turn back. Guess you expect me to return her to Triunfo while you track down Professor Kane and the treasure."

"That's the preferred plan."

"She won't like it and neither do I. I'd tick off a half dozen reasons, but here comes your gal."

Spenser's heart hitched as River lumbered toward them, muddy from the knees down, hair mussed beneath her rolled-brim hat, face flushed and sweaty.

"Why did you stop?" she wheezed.

"We have to go up," said Cy.

"Up where?"

The older man pointed to the jungle-carpeted cliff.

A seventy-degree incline with roots, stubby plants and dwarf trees sticking out of the muddy face. "The only way to get to the *páramo* and beyond."

Spenser held silent as she accessed the challenge. *Come on, angel. Fold.*

"You've done this before?" she asked Spenser, eyes trained on the climb.

"Both times kicked my ass."

"Any tips?"

For Christ's... He'd expected her to tough it out—for a while—but this was ridiculous. If looking at the formidable terrain ahead didn't scare her off, what would? "It'll take three hours."

She bent forward, rested her hands on her thighs and gulped air. "It might take me twice that, and given that incline, I'll probably have to crawl on all fours, but," *gulp, gasp,* "nothing worth having comes easy, right?"

A cliché he'd used more than once on Gordo. Just now it irritated the hell out of him. "There are prickle bushes, arrow plants with spikes and a shitload of branches and bushes that'll poke your eye out if you're careless."

"I'll be sure to avoid them."

"Those are the things you need to grab hold of for stability!"

"You don't have to yell."

"I'm not yelling!"

Cy shot Spenser a look that said otherwise.

River reached into her jacket pockets and traded her insulated gloves for the leather work gloves Spenser had provided. "These should protect my hands from the worst of it, right?" she asked Cy.

He eyed her up and down, frowned. "We're not going anywhere until you rest."

"No time," Spenser said.

"I'm fine," River snapped, even as she massaged her temples and gasped for air.

"A pain in my ass. Both of you." The treasure hunter reached down and scooped a handful of select green seeds from the jungle floor. He poured a few into River's palm. "Squash these between your fingers and suck out the milky fluid."

"What is it?"

"A natural drug," Spenser said, remembering how Jo had encouraged him and Andy to partake. Liberally.

"A miracle drug." Cy squashed several between his own fingers. "You'll breathe easier and reduce the risk of muscle cramps. Plus there's the bonus energy boost."

River's already flushed cheeks burned a deeper shade of red. Probably reflecting on her experience with coca tea. "No, thanks."

"But—"

"Let's do this." She dug in for the climb.

Spenser hauled her back. "A minute," he said to Cy. Hands raised in surrender, the senior adventurer backed away while Spenser tugged River close. "Is this another stunt to prove something to David?"

"No."

"Your dad?"

"No."

Spenser frowned. "Me?"

"Get over yourself, McGraw. This is for me."

Back to an arm's-length attitude. "What happened between this morning and now?"

"What do you mean?"

"You won't look me in the eye. Not for any length of time."

"Really?"

"Just now you're staring a hole in the tree behind me."

"I'm not—"

"You are."

She tried to shrug him off. "We're wasting time."

Spenser grasped her stubborn chin. "Look at me, dammit." She did and his heart skipped. Not in a good way. "What's wrong, angel?"

She stonewalled for five seconds then blurted, "I didn't like the way you looked at the chakana this morning. Like it was…the Holy Grail."

Spenser flashed back on the charge he'd felt when he'd held and admired that ancient relic. "In a way it is." If she possessed one tenth of his fascination with legendary treasures and lost civilizations, she'd obsess on that amulet as well.

"I don't like how you're trying to get rid of me."

"I'm not—"

"You purposely set a brutal pace today and now you're trying to scare me off this climb."

"It's dangerous!"

"And I'm a lightning rod for disaster."

Fury shot through his body. "Don't put words in my mouth, River." Rather than shake her, he spun away. "God*dammit*."

"You want me to chicken out. To poop out. You want me to give you the map, and entrust you, oh, Mr. Macho, Mr. Celebrity Treasure Hunter, with finding my dad while Cy escorts me back to the Jungle Lodge or some other safe haven. Deny it."

He couldn't. Fists clenched, he turned and saw her leaning against a tree, fighting for balance and breath.

"You said you wouldn't abandon me," she said in a raspy voice.

Empathy tempered his anger. "I won't refuse to take you and I won't leave you alone. But I *wish* you'd volunteer to go back with Cy. Aside from the risky terrain, River, there's the possibility that someone's trailing us or maybe waiting up ahead, looking for a prime moment to jump you for that map."

"All the more reason for you to keep me close. To protect me."

"That's the point. If you'd give me the map, if you'd turn back, I wouldn't have to protect you. I'd be absorbing full risk."

She shook her head. "I need to be there. I need to do this."

"You don't trust me."

River unzipped her jacket and pushed off the tree. "Tell me you're not considering the possibility that Henry discovered the legendary lost treasure." She produced the chakana, holding it in front of her as if taunting the devil. "Tell me you're not wondering if this is part of Atahualpa's ransom."

Spenser burned with familiar desires. His fingertips tingled. He gravitated toward her, toward the amulet, wanting to examine the craftsmanship, to ponder the origin. He stopped cold.

"Just as I thought." She shoved the necklace back under her shirt.

"River—"

"This isn't about me or my dad. It's about you."

"You're not being fair."

"You're not being honest." She looked away. "Cy! How much juice do I need to get me to the top?" she asked, squashing seeds between her fingers.

Spenser watched as the older man approached and advised. He watched as River complied and then ordered Cy to take the lead.

His head throbbed with two scenarios. Either she'd fly to the top or plummet to the jungle floor.

Without looking at Spenser, she sucked back more of the tasteless white fluid then launched herself at the daunting jungle wall. "Are you coming or not?"

Heart pounding, he gathered up a supply of the *droga*. She was going to be the death of him. Fuck it. Better that than the other way around. "Let's fly, angel."

CHAPTER TWENTY-FOUR

GATOR'S STOMACH LURCHED as The Conquistador piloted his helicopter through a turbulent patch of sky. So many clouds. Some of them black. He worried that his employer was insane enough to fly into the storm dead ahead, but at the last second, the man made a sharp turn and dip and suddenly they were skimming the top of the jungle.

Holy shit.

Con laughed and Gator realized the man was fucking with him. "Few have the balls to fly into the Llanganatis," he yelled over the engine's roar.

In other words, few were crazy enough.

"Commercial airliners steer clear," Con added as they gained altitude and sped toward a cloud-covered mountain. "This area is known as South America's Bermuda Triangle."

Great.

Gator was beginning to doubt his own sanity. Instead of calling The Conquistador from Triunfo, he should've driven to the nearest airport and skipped the country. But self-preservation had taken a backseat to greed. He could taste that Inca treasure. Eight billion dollars. The closer he got to the legendary mountains, the greater his hunger. He'd already killed two men, risked his own skin and freedom, and suffered bodily injury. Looking through high-powered binoculars, he'd watched McGraw and blondie suit up and disappear into the jungle with a treasure hunter that he recognized from Baños. That's when he'd had one of Con's obsessive thoughts. "They're after *my* treasure."

Now he was flying into an Andean Bermuda Triangle with a fucking lunatic.

They buzzed into a cloud bank and Gator tightened his seat belt. "Hope to hell you know where you're going," he muttered.

"I know where McGraw is headed. We'll be waiting. You'll get the second half of the map, and then I'll know *exactly* where I'm going."

Gator frowned. "You mean *we*."

Instead of answering, Con bobbed and weaved, maneuvering the helicopter through a sudden hailstorm while Gator fought not to puke.

CHAPTER TWENTY-FIVE

RIVER IGNORED the disgusting muck, the threatening plants and the potential bugs and germs. She ignored the excruciating burn in her muscles and the eye-crossing lack of oxygen.

She climbed.

And climbed.

She grabbed hold, dug in and focused on reaching the *páramo*. Anger fueled her every labored move. Anger directed at Henry, Spenser and herself.

The climb was so steep and she was so weak that she did indeed keep to her hands and knees. Spenser and Cy seemed tireless, damn them. Although Cy was focused, whereas Spenser seemed distracted. What was he thinking about? She would've asked had she the spare breath.

Miraculously, about an hour into the climb, she started feeling better. Then, soon after, she was feeling no pain. It had to be the seeds. She'd had a double dose thus far, and if she needed more she had no qualms about asking. Anything to get her to the top. Closer to Henry. Closer to closure…and returning home.

Spenser had pegged it back in Baños. She was out of her element. She thrived on order and there was no order in the wild. Everything was up to chance. Everything was chaos. She couldn't think straight. She'd fallen into bed with a man she barely knew. She'd entrusted Henry's fate to not one, but two treasure hunters. She was flirting with hypobaropathy and jungle rot. She was high on seed juice.

She was a mess.

But a determined mess.

River clawed soggy dirt and toed spiked branches in order to move inches closer to regaining control of her life. She couldn't shake the worry that she'd used Spenser to fill a need. She couldn't shake the suspicion that he'd used her to locate a treasure. She didn't trust what they'd shared. She didn't trust anything or anyone...including herself.

The ground shimmied, jolting River out of her mental monologue. "What's that?"

"Earth tremor," Spenser said, moving in next to her.

"Some call the Llanganatis 'the mountains of electricity and earthquakes,'" Cy shouted down.

"Electricity?"

"Electrical storms," Spenser clarified.

The sky rumbled.

River frowned. "Great."

"Rain's coming," Cy shouted. He was several feet ahead of her. "Going to get messy."

"We need to climb faster," River said, even though she was moving as fast as she could without poking out her eye. She had *not* come this far to fry. She could just as easily get struck by lightning at home.

"If I hurry," Cy bellowed over a distant crack of thunder, "I can reach Brunner's camp and have at least one shelter ready by the time you get there."

"Do it," Spenser said, giving River a boost when her foot slipped off a branch. He'd been shadowing her all day. Catching her when she bobbled. She appreciated the gesture, even though it dented her pride.

Cy held his position until River caught up. "Give me your pack," he said.

"Why?"

"The lighter your load, the faster you'll climb."

"But it'll burden your load."

"No burden," he said, tugging at her straps.

She glanced at Spenser. It was the first time she'd really looked at him since they'd started the climb. His complexion was off and he was sweating profusely. "You don't look so good."

"I'm fine."

"You don't look fine."

"So you said. Give Cy your pack."

"But—"

"Just do it, dammit."

Another shimmy and rumble. A gust of cool, then humid wind.

Adrenaline and dread surged through River's fatigued but oddly charged body. Her brain felt weirdly disengaged. *Can't think straight.* She didn't want to give up her backpack, although she couldn't reason why.

"Torrential downpour equals poor visibility and the possibility of a mudslide," Cy said.

Suddenly she wished her feet had wings. She relinquished her backpack and watched in awe as Cy scrambled up the tricky cliff face and disappeared from view. "Wow. What is he? Man or mountain goat?"

"Keep going, angel."

"*You're* a grouch."

"Keep going!"

She crawled upward, smiling when she realized she did indeed feel lighter. She moved faster, but she wanted to fly. "How many seeds do you think Cy sucked to get *that* kind of energy boost?"

"Don't know. Don't care. God*damn*."

River flinched at the sound of Spenser's pained curse. She looked back and saw him shrugging off his cumbersome pack while clutching one knee to his chest. Pulse racing, she backed carefully to his side. "What is it? What's wrong?"

"Nothing. Just give me a minute."

She glanced at the darkening sky. Lightning flashed behind ominous clouds. Those clouds could burst any second. "Sure you need a whole minute?" she nervously teased.

He shot her an annoyed look, tried to stretch his leg, wiggle his foot and muttered a curse.

River tried to focus on the moment, on Spenser. She felt as though someone had injected her brain with Mexican jumping beans. "Did you twist your ankle?"

"No."

"Wrench your knee?"

"Cramp."

"What?"

"Muscle cramp. A goddamn charley horse. Get it?"

She got it. She just didn't understand. Her muscles hadn't cramped and he was far more fit and experienced. Then she realized… "You're not breathing right."

"We're at thirteen and a half thousand feet, River."

"But I'm not having nearly as much trouble as you. Didn't you suck the seed juice?"

"No."

"But you had a whole pouch."

"For you."

"I'm sure there was enough—"

"I needed a clear head."

River frowned. "I have a clear…okay, not totally clear, but—"

"Exactly."

Perplexed and anxious, River looked at the angry sky, then back at Spenser. His expression warned of another kind of storm. Male pride no doubt figured in, but it went deeper, touched on his past.

The bad stuff.

"Where's the cramp?" she asked. "Foot, calf or thigh?"

"Thigh. What… *Fuck!*"

"I'm sorry," River said as she kneaded the knotted muscle, "but sometimes you have to hurt to help. Try to stretch your leg again, but slowly. And don't pump your foot. Stretch. Slow. Easy."

"What are you, a doctor?"

"A runner. I've dealt with my share of cramps and charley horses. I researched—"

"I'm sure you did."

"Don't be an ass."

"Sorry. It just... *Fuck!*"

"Talk to me."

"What?"

She continued the gentle massage with a keen eye on the ominous sky. "You're too aware of the pain. Too stressed about the delay. It's making you tense. You need to relax."

"I know what to do."

"Stop being all macho and let me help. Focus on something other than the pain."

"Like what?"

She wanted to ask about the bad stuff, except those experiences were connected to these mountains. In light of their current precarious situation she steered away. "Who's Atahualpa?"

"Don't patronize me."

"I'm not. I seriously don't know—"

"Sun King."

"What?"

"The Lord of the Inca, descended from the sun, the creator god. Everything—the land, the people, the gold and silver—belonged to the Sun King. In 1527 there was a rivalry between brothers, but Atahualpa..."

"Yes?"

"Believed he was the true Inca king. Five bloody

years of battle with his brother Huascar. He believed himself the victor, then Pizarro and a few hundred Spanish conquistadors landed on the coast of Peru. Then everything went to hell."

"Go on."

"River—"

"What happened?" She continued to massage, one eye on the approaching storm as Spenser drank deeply from a water bottle.

After urging her to hydrate as well, he rushed on. "Long story short, Pizarro and his men captured Atahualpa and held him captive in Cajamarca, a small town in Peru. Knowing the Spaniards' lust for precious metals, the Sun King offered to have his people fill a large room with gold and twice over with silver in exchange for his freedom. An offer he honored. But even that didn't appease the greedy bastards. Nor did it quell Pizarro's fear that Atahualpa's most trusted general, Rumiñahui, would attack in retaliation."

"This ends badly, doesn't it?" River shivered in anticipation of something horrible. After all, the ancient kidnapping had spurred a curse. A curse connected with these mountains.

"The conquistadors executed Atahualpa not knowing, at that very instant, a caravan of sixty thousand men protected by twelve thousand armed guards and led by General Rumiñahui were headed for Cajamarca, carrying all the gold from every temple and palace in the empire."

"Atahualpa's ransom," River whispered, entranced by the tale.

"Upon hearing the news of their king's death," Spenser said, "Rumiñahui redirected his troops into the Llanganatis."

River was used to hearing old wives' tales about marriage. Conditioned to handle problems associated with impending weddings, not ancient executions. She processed Spenser's information. "So all that gold and silver, sweat of the sun, tears of the moon, is buried… here."

"Somewhere. Later Rumiñahui was captured and tortured, but he never gave up the location of the buried treasure. The secret died with him."

Spenser had told her about the buried treasure days before. She'd even considered the possibility that there was truth to the legend. But this was the first time she'd actually ached to see that treasure for herself. She could feel the chakana burning against her breastbone. *What if?*

"According to sources," Spenser said, "Henry claimed contact with Rumiñahui."

"The Inca general? But he's been dead for centuries. It's not possible." And just like that, her moment of wonder evaporated. So, what? Her father was hallucinating? Lying? *Crazy?*

"Sources also blame Henry for a guide's death. Said the professor killed the man in order to protect his secret find."

River blanched. Yes, she'd blamed her father for her

mom's death. But it's not like he'd *murdered* her. "I don't believe it."

"Neither do I. But someone drove a spear through that guide's heart."

"A spear?"

The sky crackled. Louder this time. River barely noticed. She was too busy massaging Spenser's thigh and envisioning Indians with primitive weapons.

Spenser nabbed her wrists and nudged her away. "Get going."

"What?"

"Push on, River. I'll catch up."

She suppressed a flutter of panic. "I'm not going anywhere without you." It wasn't solely the fear of being alone in these godforsaken mountains. She couldn't imagine abandoning someone in need. *Ever.* Part of the reason she was here to begin with. No matter her issues with Henry, she couldn't abandon Spenser to some unknown fate.

"If I start to lose sight of you, I'll tell you to stop. Meanwhile, it'll motivate me to move. Mind over matter."

She tugged off her gloves in order to get a better grip on his thigh, a deeper massage.

"Your hands," he said, wincing as she dug in. "Getting dirty."

"Have you taken a good look at me? I'm covered head-to-toe in jungle muck."

"Germs."

She got his drift. Normally she would've been dousing

herself with liquid sanitizer. "I'm more worried about getting zapped." She glanced at the sparking clouds, then back to Spenser. He was struggling to breathe. "I'm more worried about you."

His expression softened. His green eyes smoldered. Back anchored against a wall of vegetation, Spenser pulled River into his arms. He kissed her, passionately, and suddenly they were lost in lust, the ground grumbling beneath them and the sky rumbling above.

This is crazy, River's mind whispered. But she was powerless to break away. Coca tea and Cy's seeds had nothing on Spenser's kisses. She burned for this man. It didn't matter that she suspected his motivations. It didn't matter that they were making out on a precarious mountainside while a thunderstorm loomed or that they were both flirting with acute altitude sickness. The only thing she was in danger of was falling in love.

That thought hit her like a bucket of ice water.

River reared back—heart pounding, lungs seizing, blinded by…rain. They were drenched in a matter of seconds.

"Shit." Spenser shifted into a half crouch. "We have to hurry."

River sleeved raindrops from her lashes, watching as he muscled on the heavy pack. He showed no signs of discomfort but she knew he was hurting. "Your leg."

"It's fine. Thanks to you." He cupped the back of her neck, branded her lips with a searing kiss, then urged her up the slick incline. "Grab hold of whatever you can, anchor yourself. Slow and easy, angel."

"You said we have to hurry!"

"Hurry with caution."

She tried to channel his calm…and failed. "I don't know the way," River said, panic building. Cy was out of sight and she saw no visible path. The rain blurred everything. She pulled her new GPS unit from her jacket pocket, but her thick leather gloves proved a hindrance and she fumbled. The compact gadget fell out of her hands and disappeared somewhere below. "No!"

"Leave it," Spenser said, but she'd already turned and…

The ground gave way beneath her feet. A scream lodged in River's throat as she slid on her back several feet in a river of mud, down the cliff face, limbs flailing. She had a brief vision of a scene in *Romancing the Stone,* when Joan Wilder whooshed down a muddy hill, landing unharmed in a pool of murky water with her hero's face between her legs. River anticipated no such luck. She anticipated impaling herself on one of the nasty, spiky arrow plants. *I'm going to die,* she thought, just before she slammed into a jutting tree.

CHAPTER TWENTY-SIX

SPENSER'S HEART STOPPED beating for the length of time it took him get to River. He cursed himself, cursed fate, and in a moment of bone-deep fury, cursed the ancient Inca legend. "Not this time," he ground out as he navigated the slick cliff. "Not her."

His pulse registered when he saw her wedged in a leafy dwarf tree growing out of the cliff. She hadn't fallen a long distance, but fast and far enough to scare the hell out of him. She looked stunned, but she was alive. *Thank you, Jesus.* "River."

"I'm okay. I'm just…I'm afraid to move. If the branches break…"

"It's okay, baby. Just shift—"

"Can't."

"No problem." She'd frozen in fear. He could see that, sense that, even in the driving rain. "I'm coming, angel. Sit tight."

"No problem."

He smiled. Even though she was scared stiff, she'd retained a sense of humor. His admiration of River Kane tripled. "Take my hand."

"Can't."

"Yes, you can." She was wedged in the tree with

a death grip on the branches. Digging his heels into the soggy, craggy earth, he reached farther down, his fingertips grazing the sleeve of her sodden jacket. "I have faith in you, River. Let go of fear and grab hold of me."

Her gaze locked onto his and jolted his soul with a surge of trust. She let go and grabbed on.

"That's it, baby. Hold tight." He hefted her into his arms and eased into a safe position. "It's okay. You're all right," he soothed as she lapsed into broken sobs. Christ. Ignoring the pounding of his own heart and the inconvenient downpour, he held River close, allowing her time to recover from the shock. Hell, he felt poleaxed himself. If anything had happened to her... He blocked the notion and repressed past issues. He focused on now. On getting River safely to the *páramo*.

Just then the rain ended as abruptly as it had begun. Not surprising, given the unpredictable weather of the Llanganatis.

River's sobbing turned to hiccupping laughter. Concerned she was a heartbeat from hysterics, Spenser cupped her face and studied her gaze. Not glassy or shocky, just teary with relief.

She sleeved rain from her face and instead smeared mud. "I'm sorry," she rasped. "I didn't mean to lose it. That was just... Wow. Talk about a wild ride!"

Spenser laughed, then indulged in a lingering kiss. It was the second time they'd made out on this cliff. The second time he'd lost reason to passion. He fought through the sensual haze, desperate for a clear, rational thought. Drugged on relief and River's addictive kisses, the world had taken on an ethereal quality. He blinked to clear his vision but the misty air still swirled. "Fog." Spenser said. "Shit."

"FUCK." GATOR had a death grip on the dashboard or whatever the hell it was called. The copter was motionless, grounded, but his head still spun like the dying blades.

"Grab the rest of the gear in the rear cabin and get out," Con ordered. "We'll have to hoof it from here."

Gator leered at the man who'd already jumped out and strapped on a massive backpack. How could he look and sound so calm? "We just crashed—"

"Forced landing. Big difference." Con strapped a machine gun over his shoulder. "Rock and roll, soldier."

Gator stared as the madman disappeared into a sheet of mist and rain. Even though they'd been forced to land in shitty weather, in the middle of God-knew-where, The Conquistador seemed confident of his surroundings.

Ignoring his own labored breathing and aching body, Gator hurriedly retrieved the remaining gear and followed. He didn't know which was the greatest motivator—the lure of eight billion dollars or fear of falling victim to a cursed mountain.

"WE HAVE TO HURRY," River whispered, echoing Spenser's earlier dictate. First rain, now fog. What next? Hail? *Don't tempt fate*. Even though she was still rattled from the mud slide and Spenser's soul-searing kiss, River gathered her wits. "How's your leg?"

"I can't believe you're worried about me after what you just went through." He shook his head, squeezed her hand. "Stick close."

If she could've superglued herself to him, she would have. Though shaken and sore, River was determined to get off this damned incline, onto flat ground. Her thoughts blurred as they ascended quickly, trying to beat the encroaching fog. She blocked memories of her adrenaline-charged plummet by focusing on the loss of not one, but two GPS units in less than a week. It's as if the powers that be didn't want her to have direction. Although Spenser had mentioned being able to navigate by nature. Probably by the sun and stars, she thought hazily. Isn't that how sailors used to do it?

Lost in thought, she lost track of time. She was vaguely aware of the cooling temperature, even though she was sweating due to exertion. She still heard the occasional crack of thunder, though it sounded more distant. At least the storm was passing.

Fog, however, swirled all around her. It wasn't thick enough to totally obscure her vision, but the effect was haunting. In the back of her mind it occurred to her that she was climbing out of the Amazon into the Andes. Braving an array of threatening circumstances. River Kane, the woman who normally feared leaving her small midwestern town without a map. The woman who feared infection and disease. The woman who famously encountered disaster.

The mud slide was a fluke, she told herself.

I'm not cursed. I'm not compromised. I can do this.
I'm not cursed. I'm not compromised. I can do this.

River crawled, grappled, clutched and clawed, grabbing onto anything to anchor herself as the sodden vegetation squished and the fog thickened. She ignored the smelly, slimy muck and the occasional lash and poke of branches, the prickles that scratched and stung. She blocked out the pain when her muscles twinged and her lungs screamed for air. *Seed juice,* she thought, but she didn't want to hinder their progress by stopping to "medicate."

I'm not cursed. I'm not compromised. I can do this.
I'm not cursed. I'm not compromised. I can do this.

She repeated that mantra for an hour, maybe two. Then suddenly Spenser disappeared over a ridge. Her heart stopped, but then she felt his hands around her wrists. Felt him haul her up—again. Only this time he set her to her feet. On flat ground. Soggy, but flat.

Hallelujah!

She would've dropped to the ground and kissed the earth, but she'd pretty much been doing that for the last several hours!

Spenser gently cupped her face. "You scared the hell out of me back there."

Worried he might insist on sending her back as soon as they found Cy, she shrugged off the mud slide with a smile. "What doesn't kill you makes you stronger," she rasped, trying to catch her breath. "I'll be Superwoman by the time we find Henry."

"Don't tempt the curse, River."

Her attempt to make light backfired. Touched by the concern in his eyes, she squeezed his hand. "I'm fine. Wet, muddy and sore, but fine." She looked around his shoulder, squinted at the misty landscape. "Where are we?"

"The *páramo*." Spenser shrugged off his pack and stretched. "I admit, I'm surprised and impressed you made it this far, angel."

"Me, too," she gritted out. Her muscles trembled with fatigue. Her body ached to wilt into a puddle, but she was so thrilled to be on level ground, she forced herself to stand and stretch. Through the silvery mist she saw twisted and gnarled trees, thorny shrubs and what looked like fields of prairie grass. The thick jungle canopy had given way to open skies, but because of the fog, visibility was limited.

"I thought I'd be able to see Cerro Hermoso," she said in between gasps for air.

"You would," Spenser said. "On a clear day."

"I have to pee." She blushed as soon as the words came out. It was just that suddenly, after hours of climbing and drinking water to stay hydrated, her bladder was near to bursting. She looked for the nearest bush big enough to squat behind.

"Don't go far," Spenser said. "And talk to me so I know where you are."

She felt ridiculous but at least he was distracted, rooting through his humongous backpack. After grabbing a supply of tissues, River ducked behind a flowery bush just a couple of feet away.

"Talk to me!" he yelled.

What about? The GPS sprang to mind. She felt bad about losing it, especially since he'd refused to allow her to reimburse him. "So that quirk I have about needing to know where I am?" she called out. "It's because I got lost once!"

"I figured!"

"It was after my mom died. I wanted to spend time with Henry. To apologize for some ugly things I'd said. He didn't want me to visit. He was in Mexico, an expedition having to do with Mayan ruins. But I talked him into it and, long story short, I got lost in the jungle. Alone for twelve hours. I freaked out, lost control, ran all over looking for the way back, making it harder for them to find me and..." She trailed off as she flashed on the overwhelming panic. "Let's just say, I confirmed Henry's belief that I'm not cut out for the wild."

"How old were you?"

"Fourteen."

"I don't blame you for freaking out."

"Henry did," she mumbled to herself. She zipped up her muddy cargo pants and squirted her hands with sanitizer, marveling at her timing. She wasn't sure why she'd chosen this awkward moment to reveal one of her worst memories. An experience that had saddled her with one of her biggest phobias. "Losing control was the worst part," she said, more to herself than Spenser, as she stepped out from behind the bush. "The emotional chaos. Can't go there again. Ever."

She stopped talking, stopped moving and simply stared. The fog had thickened and it was moving in all directions. Swirling. Dancing. Hypnotic. Eerie. Various shades of silver and gray. The twisted trees. The howling wind. She half expected the ghosts of General Rumiñahui and his army to emerge from the rolling fog. Haunting. Captivating. She reached for her camera and remembered.

River spun in a circle, searching for the man who'd taken her backpack. "Where's Cy?"

"Brunner's camp or close to it. Once he hit level ground, I'm sure he booked."

"How much farther to that camp?"

"Another hour."

She stared into the fog, her heart still pounding from the strenuous climb and now from the realization that she'd compromised Henry's trust a second time. First the journal. Now this. Physically, she was so wiped out she couldn't imagine walking for another hour. But she *had* to get her camera back. What if Cy snooped?

Temples throbbing, she turned and saw Spenser pitching some sort of tent. He'd already anchored down a floor—rubber? nylon?—and erected an aluminum frame that he was hurriedly covering with heavy-duty fabric. Her first thought was, how did that all fit in his pack? Second thought: "What you are doing? We have to catch up to Cy!"

"Within twenty minutes tops, visibility will be zero. We can't navigate the quaking bogs in dense fog."

"Maybe it won't last that long."

"Or maybe it will last all night. Besides, we're in for another soaking."

"But the storm's blowing over, isn't it?" River looked up and in answer...

Splat!

Splat, splat, splat!

Her heart sank. They couldn't walk safely in heavy fog *and* pouring rain. Plus, it was growing dark. Plus, there were those quaking bogs. What had Spenser likened them to? Marshy mud? Andean quicksand?

Dammit.

She moved swiftly to Spenser's side. She didn't mind the rain. At least it would wash the mud and guck from her clothes. She even swiped off her hat so her hair and face benefited. But she was concerned about the dropping temperature. What if one or both of them caught a chill? "What can I do?"

"Get inside."

"But—"

"I need to secure some cables. Other than that, we're good to go." He tossed his backpack and the remaining gear inside. He waited for her to follow but she refused.

"I want to help," she shouted over the pounding rain.

Glaring, he relayed instructions and ten minutes later the overall tent was secured and they took shelter.

River hugged herself as he attended to details. An extreme-weather tent, he'd called it. Waterproof and durable. Effective in high winds and pelting snow. As exposed as they were, on an open stretch of land, high in the mountains, an electrical storm raging—she worried the tent, no matter how sturdy, wouldn't offer ample protection.

"Take off your clothes," he ordered. "You need to get dry," he said before she could argue.

By the time she'd stripped down to her panties and bra, Spenser had produced an ultra-padded sleeping bag. "Get inside," he ordered as he stripped down to nothing. Buck naked, he slipped in beside her. "Go to sleep."

"But—"

"We're socked in. We're exhausted. You suffered a fall and we've yet to adjust to the altitude. Sleep, angel."

Outside the storm raged and the temperature dropped.

Disoriented and nervous, River closed her eyes and tried to relax.

Right.

"I can't do it. I can't sleep. I'm beyond exhausted. I'm wired. And…" *Scared.* Suddenly, sliding down a cliff and landing in a tree seemed like child's play. What if lightning struck the pole of the tent? What if they got electrocuted? What if the tent caught fire and they burned to a crisp? What if the wind battered the canvas so badly a portion tore away? Exposed to the elements, how would they fair in the drenching rain, wind and cold? What if they…

"Stop thinking the worst."

"I can't help it. Maybe you're used to roughing it under extreme conditions, but this is new to me. Not that I can't handle it, I just can't pretend like it's nothing when it could be a huge something. We need a plan. A backup plan just in case—" Her breath caught when his hand slipped beneath her panties. "What are you doing?"

"Redirecting your thoughts." Spenser pressed his hard, warm body against her, suckled her earlobe and touched her intimately.

Needing a distraction, needing to release coiled tension, she moved her hips, silently begging for more. If they didn't survive this storm, at least she'd die in ecstasy.

"What are you thinking about now?" he rasped as he slid a finger deep inside.

The way he'd taken her from behind in the shower. The way she'd ridden him this morning in bed. The way he'd kissed her on that treacherous cliff.

Her body quivered, her heart raced. "Infinite possibilities."

CHAPTER TWENTY-SEVEN

The Páramo
Altitude 14,000 feet

LONG AFTER SPENSER had pleasured River into exhaustion and sleep, he lay wide awake. Senses sharp, he held River close as the storm continued well into the night. Cocooned in his extreme-weather tent they were safe from the elements, but possible danger lurked in another form. He couldn't shake the feeling they were being stalked. Someone had killed for the other half of Kane's map and here they were alone on the *páramo,* a pair of freaking sitting ducks. Even though he was armed, he had no idea who or what he was up against. What if they got the best of him? What if River...

He told himself to stop thinking the worst. If someone was out there, surely he would have seen or heard something by now.

At one point, the rain stopped and he contemplated venturing outside with his wide-beam flashlight. Between the insulated goose-down sleeping bag and their combined body heat, they were relatively warm. Still, a fire would be good. If the fog had lifted, he'd gather tinder, careful not to venture far from the tent. But he worried River would awaken in the dark, alone. He worried she'd freak out, thinking he'd abandoned her. Every time he thought about her, lost and alone in a Mexican jungle, his gut twisted. Fourteen freaking years old. No survival training. No supplies or weapons. That she'd avoided serious injury was a fucking miracle. How in the hell had Kane lost track of her in the first place?

The more he learned about Professor Henry Kane, the more he lost respect for the man. There were always two sides to a story, but from River's perspective the man had been a piss-poor dad. Spenser marveled that she'd traveled all this way, braved her phobias and risked her life to save a father who considered her cursed, a father who'd, for all intents and purposes, forsaken her. Then again, River, the angelic-faced, delicately boned lamb, had the heart of a lion.

Even though she'd suffered a fright and flirted with death, she'd shrugged off the slide down the cliff. And before that…

She'd stunned him with her cool and calm reaction to his leg cramp. It hurt worse than he'd let on. He'd been paralyzed with pain. Jo would have teased him for being a wuss. He could hear her husky laugh. "Catch up when you can, pretty boy." Jo would have pushed ahead. Not because she was cruel, but because she knew he would catch up. Because she had faith in his survival skills, not to mention his drive to find the treasure. Andy's skills weren't as honed as Spenser's. She would have stopped for Andy.

Spenser's heart pounded as he flashed back on that

doomed expedition. Memories he'd buried kept resurfacing. The guilt was crushing. He wiped sweat from his brow and tried to redirect his thoughts. But Jo wouldn't let up. *I told you he had AMS. But you wouldn't listen. You wouldn't turn back.*

River, who'd been in a spooning position, turned in his arms and rested her cheek and hand against his chest. "Spenser?" she whispered.

"Yeah, baby. What's wrong?"

"I was about to ask you the same thing. Your heart's beating so hard and fast, I thought you were having a nightmare."

"Close," he said.

"Bad stuff?"

"Mmm."

"Tell me," she said in a drowsy voice.

Thoughts and images crowded his mind. A month of memories. Some good. Some bad. Some downright ugly.

"You said you wanted to move on." She slid her hand from his chest to his cheek, then smoothed her fingers over his furrowed brow. "Let it out and let it go."

It was pitch-black inside the tent and her face was nestled against his chest. He wouldn't see her expression when he admitted his sin. He'd feel her disappointment, shock, maybe even contempt. He might even hear it in her tone—if she had anything to say to him. But he wouldn't see the loss of respect in her eyes. That was something.

"I'm not up to the full-blown version tonight, angel."

"I didn't give you the full version of my Mexico fiasco, either, but I feel lighter for telling you."

"Not that your episode wasn't traumatic," Spenser said, "but this is ugly."

"Tell me."

Spenser held River close, cherishing her warmth and compassion. After this she could well turn cold. "Right out of high school, I went into the military. Just four years, but I made two friends for life. Duke, who you met, and Andy Burdett. I'd always had an obsession with lost treasures and Duke had a thing for the Amazon. When we got out of the army, we decided to tour South America for a summer. Andy tagged along. We raised a lot of hell. Had a lot of fun. For the thrill of it we went on a treasure hunt."

"Atahualpa's ransom."

"That was my first expedition into these mountains. We were young and cocky and ill-equipped for the trek. We didn't even make it this far. Got socked in by fog for two weeks. We ran short on supplies, thinking we'd be in and out in six days. When the fog lifted, I still wanted to go on. I had the fever. Not ordinary gold fever. Worse. I burned to lay my eyes and hands on the gold and silver artifacts that had once adorned the temples of the Incan empire. Some say the booty included golden vases full of emeralds. I was obsessed with finding the massive and unique treasure. Figured we could live off the land. I pushed it a day too far and Duke got pretty sick.

"Making our way back was a little rough," he continued, "but we'd survived worse in the army. We vowed we'd take another shot at the Inca treasure someday. Only when that day came, Duke was already involved with Lana and knee-deep in building the Jungle Lodge. He'd never been about the treasure as much as the adventure. Just then he was getting his kicks with Lana.

"Andy and I ended up bumming around Baños for a while. Spent a lot of time at El Dosel hanging out with local treasure hunters and guides, soaking in their knowledge and expertise. If we were going to make a second attempt, Andy insisted we be better informed. Although I think he was more interested in the drinking games than the folklore. That is, until we met Jo."

He felt a subtle tension in River's body. Did she hear something in his voice, feel something in his touch? Suddenly he was twice as leery about sharing this part of his life. It meant admitting he'd been in love, obsessive love, with another woman.

"Tell me about Jo," she said in a soft voice.

"Joviana Mendez. An expert on Andean culture and legends."

"A woman."

"Yes."

"A smart woman."

"Smart and fascinating."

"Young and beautiful?"

He didn't sense jealously as much as curiosity. "Yes." He faltered, not knowing how much to share, unsure of how much he *wanted* to share. He'd never talked to

a woman he cherished about a woman he had once…
worshipped. River was a first in many ways.

"You loved her," she said.

"I was *in* love with her. Not sure that's the same thing.
Although at the time I thought it was."

"Andy fell for her, too."

"Perceptive."

"Just working the puzzle."

In spite of his gloomy mood, he smiled. "Let's fast-
forward."

"Wait." He felt her shift, knew she was looking up at
him. "Which one of you did *she* favor?"

"She didn't say at first. Didn't say for several
weeks."

"She played you off of one another?"

He couldn't see her face, but heard her disgust. "Jo
was a free spirit and a flirt. She was also fiercely inde-
pendent. We were all relatively young and, I'm embarrassed to say, drunk more than sober. Andy, especially,
had a weakness for booze." Duke had once speculated
it had contributed to his downfall, but Spenser blamed
only himself. As did Jo.

"Fast-forward," River said as if sensing she was losing
him.

"Instead of Duke, Jo accompanied Andy and me into
the Llanganatis. She'd been on other expeditions. She
was tough, mentally and physically. Andy and I were
a little wiser, a lot better equipped, but still cocky. The
trek was more of a professional venture for Jo but, make

no mistake, she was as intrigued with the legend as I was."

"And Andy?"

"He was interested in impressing Jo. So was I. Maybe even more so, because, two days into the trek, I realized she had feelings for Andy. Actually, she flat out told me she was in love with him."

"But you didn't give up. You never give up," River said. "Infinite possibilities."

"You've got a hell of a memory, angel."

"More a blessing than a curse. Fast-forward."

"We lucked out the first few days. Great weather. Unusual for this region. We pushed hard. Probably too hard. Or at least too fast. Made it even more difficult to acclimate to the altitude. But Jo introduced us to the seeds and we also chewed coca leaves. We were dealing. Or at least I thought we were. The closer we got to Cerro Hermoso, the greater my obsession. I was certain we'd find at least a portion of Inca gold, if not the lost treasure. In the sixteenth century, a Spanish soldier named Valverde got rich after several visits into these mountains. He claimed he'd located the treasure and before his death crafted a detailed guide for the king of Spain, a work known as Valverde's guide. Throughout time other explorers claimed success as well. A contemporary, though now dead, Eugene Brunner swore the treasure was located on Cerro Hermoso, buried under tons of mud."

"But it was never found."

"He never gave up the location."

"Brunner's camp," River said, working the puzzle.

"Brunner made this trek more than a few times. He set up a few rustic camps. There's also a lake named after him—Brunner's Lake. Or Laguna Brunner. Supposedly the treasure is not far off. Anyway, I kept thinking, if not Valverde, if not Blake and Chapman, Guzmán or Spruce, Brunner and others, why not me?"

"You had the fever."

"A raging fever that compromised judgment. Plus, some arrogant part of me thought that if I found the treasure or any part of it, I'd win Jo's affections."

River squirmed.

"I told you it was ugly."

"I'm just…I'm anticipating something bad."

"Jo warned me that Andy wasn't well," Spenser plowed on. He had to get this out. His chest hurt. His gut ached. "Hell, we were all suffering headaches and nausea, loss of appetite. But Andy seemed disoriented at times. I thought it was booze. I was certain he had a flask hidden away. Alcohol at high altitudes is dangerous. I was pissed at him for compromising the expedition. We fought. Over booze. Over Jo. She expressed fears that Andy was suffering AMS—acute mountain sickness. Severe symptoms include difficulty walking a straight line, confusion."

"You thought it was the alcohol."

"I thought it was a contributing factor, yes. But that's no excuse. I should've listened to Jo, should've turned back, descended to lower altitudes at least a day or two before. But Andy was furious and adamant, swearing he was fine, egging me to keep going. And I was…"

"Obsessed."

Spenser wanted nothing more than to put distance between him and River when he told her the worst of it, but he didn't want to deprive her of his body heat. His emotional comfort wasn't worth risking her health. He resisted the urge to pace off his nervous energy. Resisted the urge to shut down completely. He hadn't talked about this in a long time and each word scraped his throat like a razor blade. Each shared memory cut deep. He'd been talking a blue streak, thinking the faster he got it out, the less painful it would be. But this part…

River slipped her hand into his and squeezed. "Tell me."

He braced for her contempt. "Later that day a fog rolled in. I suggested making camp, but Andy wanted to go on. Too dangerous, I argued. Jo agreed."

Being here, in the Llanganatis, brought stifled memories back to life. Spenser relived the worst day of his life in vivid detail. He could *feel* the tumultuous emotions. The frustration and contempt. The heightened anxiety. He could *see* Jo's panic and Andy…

He wiped sweat from his forehead and forced out the rest. "Andy took off in a rage. I saw it then. I knew he wasn't in his right mind. Knew we had to turn back. Jo twisted her ankle running after him. I made sure she was okay, then followed cautiously, my senses on overload as the fog thickened.

"When I spotted Andy he was talking to himself. I

tried to reason with him but he was agitated and confused and…I watched as he turned the wrong way. I called out. I lunged and reached…but he walked right off the fucking cliff."

He'd watched his friend fall hundreds of feet to his death. Through the swirling mist into nothingness. It had been surreal. Horrifying and surreal.

He realized then that River had a vice grip on his hand. She didn't speak. Didn't move. What was she thinking? Feeling? Did she think him a monster? A jerk? *An immoral treasure hunter?*

He punched through a wall of shame, determined to finish. "I got Jo back to Triunfo, but Andy… Although we initiated an extensive search, his body was never recovered. Jo refused to speak to me. She left and…I never saw her again. I tried to call her once but…"

"You never had closure," River said in a raspy voice. "Not with Andy or Jo." She fell silent for several seconds, then said, "When we leave here, you should find her, Spenser."

It was the last thing he'd expected her to say. "I know exactly where she is." He'd kept tabs throughout the years. A morbid obsession.

"Then go to Jo and make peace."

"I'm not sure that's possible. I don't think she'll ever forgive me."

"It would help if you forgave yourself first."

Heart pounding, Spenser stared down at River in awe. "Aren't you shocked by what I just told you? Horrified?

Disgusted? Didn't I just verify your suspicion that I'd do anything, sacrifice anyone, for a legendary treasure?"

"I wasn't there. I can't judge. As to your character…I admit I had my doubts, based purely on your profession, but…I think you're a good man, Spenser. Your sister certainly sings your praises, and Kylie's one of the nicest people I've ever met."

He was torn between relief and disbelief…and still smarting from the vivid memories.

"If you need to place blame," River said, "try these mountains, the altitude, the curse."

Spenser kissed River's forehead and pulled her close. "I didn't expect you, given the circumstances, to be so understanding."

"I guess it's because I can relate."

After a few seconds of tense silence, she elaborated. "My mom died on one of Henry's expeditions," River said in a tight voice. "I blamed him. I publicly blasted him at her funeral. It was…ugly. Things were never the same between us, not that they'd been great to begin with. But after a while, I realized Mom was the one who chose to go to Africa instead of staying home with me. She was the one who'd insisted on driving the jeep so he could go over his notes. She was the one who lost control of the vehicle. Henry was thrown free. She wasn't. Not his fault. Not directly. I regret the things I said, and I need to say I'm sorry. Even if we never mend our relationship. I need closure so I can move on with my life. Closure with my father. With David. I'm here to make peace. You should do the same."

Spenser was at a loss for words. A rarity.

River cuddled closer. "Thank you for sharing the bad stuff. I know it wasn't easy."

"Easier than I expected, but I suspect that has something to do with you." He caressed her cheek, found her mouth. He kissed her. "River, I—"

"Please don't say anything incredibly romantic."

"What about semi-romantic?"

"No."

"Straight from the heart?"

"Absolutely not."

"Why?"

"Because I don't trust it. I don't trust…me." A tense hesitation, then, "I'm worried I slept with you to get back at David."

Blindsided, he leveled on one elbow. Even though he couldn't see her face, he still stared down. "A revenge fuck?"

"You're laughing at me."

"I'm not laughing."

"You're amused. I hear it in your voice."

He should've been insulted, but it was a welcome distraction…and ludicrous. "You're not the vengeful type. It's not in your nature."

"How do you know? You've only known me for one week. Has it even been a week? What day is it? So much has happened so fast. I can't keep track—"

He squelched her nervous chatter with a kiss. She gave over, just as he knew she would, wrapping her arms around his neck as he suckled her tongue. *Revenge, my ass.* Her desire was genuine and that wasn't his ego talking. His gut and heart concurred. He connected with River. Physically. Intellectually. And on some level, emotionally.

His thoughts melted around the edges as the kiss went on and on. God, he loved the taste of her, the scent and feel of her. He cradled the back of her head, his fingers tangled in her messy curls, while his free hand explored her shoulders and back. He trailed his fingers lightly over her smooth skin, brushing, stroking, eliciting goose bumps and a sigh.

His dick throbbed. His heart pounded.

She tensed and eased away. "It's worse than I thought. I'm not vengeful," she said in a ragged whisper. "I'm a slut."

He would've laughed, but she sounded so goddamned miserable.

"When I'm with you...when you kiss me and touch me...I...I want the most wicked things. All I can think about is sex and I want it to go on forever. I...I never felt that way with... He never drove me to the brink with a...a kiss. He..."

"He wasn't the one."

"You *can't* be the one."

"We'll fight about that later." Spenser suckled her earlobe, smiled when she shuddered and moaned. He rolled her onto her back, skimmed his fingers over her taut belly. "Tell me what you want."

"Damn you, Spenser."

"Tell me."

Instead, she grasped his hand and guided it to the lacy edge of her cotton panties.

He peeled them away, his fingers brushing over her inner thighs, her calves, her feet.

She shivered. "Stop teasing."

"That's half the fun, angel." He retraced his path, skimming his fingertips up her toned calves, the backs of her knees, her silky thighs. He lingered there, urging her legs apart, tracing feather-light circles over her skin, softly brushing her feminine curls.

She whimpered.

"Say it. Tell me what you want, River. Tell me what to do."

"I can't," she panted, moving restlessly beneath his touch. "I don't…"

"Talk dirty or I'll talk hearts and roses."

"Make me come. Make me delirious with ecstasy," she pleaded. "Can you do delirious?"

His mouth quirked. "Desperate for me not to speak my heart? Or desperate for an orgasm?"

"Yes!"

Charmed and aroused, Spenser dispensed with talk— dirty or otherwise. He kissed River hungrily and, for the second time that evening, stroked her to a shuddering climax. He ached to touch her breasts, to feast on her nipples, but he refused to touch her bra. The map, he assumed was still hidden there. He didn't want her to think he was after that map…or the chakana looped around her neck.

He was after her heart.

He relished the aftermath of her orgasm. Stilted breathing. Subtle trembling. The lusty groan as he slid his finger into her tight wetness. "I need to be inside you."

"Wait," she whispered.

In one fluid move, River rolled onto her side and fondled his erection. She stroked. Fast then slow. Spenser willed himself to breathe, ordered his self not to come. Not a kid. Not… Then…his balls tightened as she tickled and cupped them. His lungs seized. "Tease."

"Half the fun."

Undone, Spenser flipped the devilish angel onto her back. Before she could catch her breath, he plunged deep. Hard and fast. Slow and hard. He made love with bone-deep intensity, kissing her passionately, holding back as long as he could, which wasn't long. Tonight, he had the control of a boy. Tonight confirmed what he'd suspected all along.

This was love.

Spent and more content than he'd been in ten years, he rested his forehead to hers. "You slept with me because you're attracted to me, River. I slept with you because I—"

She pressed her fingertips over his mouth. "I still don't trust this."

Smiling, he kissed her fingers, her nose, her cheeks, her lips. "You will."

CHAPTER TWENTY-EIGHT

RIVER WOKE UP FEELING like crap. Her head throbbed and her body ached. Exhausted and queasy, she refused to open her eyes. She didn't want to get up. She wanted to stay in bed, sleep all day.

Only she wasn't in a bed, she thought hazily.

She cracked open her lids.

"You're not in Kansas anymore either, Dorothy," she whispered.

She was in the wild. In a tent. In a sleeping bag.

Alone.

River bolted upright, tamped down a surge of panic. She looked down and noted she was still wearing her bra. Felt inside the cup and, yes, thank God, the map was still hidden there. For a blip of a second she'd worried Spenser had stolen it and run off. Her cheeks flushed with shame. Then again, he was the one who kept harping on his obsession with the lost treasure.

She shook off her anxiety, breathed deep. She smelled burning wood and…oatmeal?

A campfire.

He was out there. Cooking breakfast, watching over her.

I won't abandon you.

River sat there for a moment, gathering her thoughts and wits, reflecting on the night before. She worked backward, her skin heating as she recalled their love-making. Playful, passionate, tender. A combination that warmed her heart and set off warning bells. Just like Spenser's insinuation that he was her soul mate. She skipped right over that memory. Her life was complicated enough.

Instead, she focused on Spenser's past. He'd touched her deeply with the story of the ill-fated expedition. If she thought about it too much, too hard, it shook her conviction to push on. Even though she knew he'd fight it, what if Spenser had a relapse? What if he succumbed to the fever? She also worried about the altitude. What if she got severe AMS? What if he did? Then there was the matter of forcing him to walk through the area where his friend had died. Would he relive the moment? Would it cause him to wallow in guilt for another ten years? Or would he be able to make peace?

The possibilities were endless.

Her mind jumped tracks. Again, she flashed on their lovemaking. Her blood sizzled as she reflected on the sinful sensations. Spenser's hands, his mouth, his... She squeezed her thighs together and sighed. The man was well-endowed, well-skilled and tireless.

He was also impetuous.

More than once over the last few days, he'd intimated he had deep feelings for her. Last night he'd wanted to say something straight from the heart and she was almost positive that involved three simple words. Except there was nothing simple about love.

She'd never understood the obsessive love between her mom and dad or the undemonstrative love between her grandparents. Just now she wasn't sure if she'd know honest-to-gosh true and healthy *love* if it bit her in the butt.

This morning, she was clear on one thing only. She hadn't slept with Spenser to get back at David. David couldn't have been further from her mind last night. He couldn't have been further from her heart.

Clearly, she did not love David T. Snodgrass.

Now *that* was a troubling realization. How could she have been so set on a lifetime with a man she could so easily disconnect with?

Because you never loved him. You loved the idea of him. Stable. Conventional. Three children, a two-story single-family home on an acre of land, yearly vacations to Disney, a 401K plan…

"Oh, God."

She hadn't used Spenser. She'd used *David*.

"Morning, angel."

Once again, all thoughts of her ex-fiancé, the man she dated for five years, the man she'd been primed to marry, evaporated the moment she laid eyes on Spenser McGraw. He stepped into the tent and stole away her breath. Dressed in his typical baggy layers, unshaven, hair tousled, he looked like a walking ad for, well, the Explorer Channel. A rugged, handsome, charismatic hunk.

She, on the other hand, no doubt looked like she felt.

Crappy. Self-conscious, River smoothed her matted curls from her face wishing desperately for a breath mint, a shot of Pepto-Bismol, and a bar of soap—in that order. "Hi."

He moved toward her carrying a cup of something. Coffee? She wasn't sure her stomach could take the acidity, although the caffeine might help her headache.

"How do you feel?"

"Hungover."

"It's the altitude. I felt the same way." He crouched next to her. "Drink this."

"What is it?"

"Alka-Seltzer."

"Seriously?"

"Never travel without it."

She drank eagerly, burped. "Sorry."

He grinned. "Now these." He passed her a small water bottle and three tablets. "Two Motrin—you're allergic to anything else, right?—and your antimalarial meds. I kept a supply with me. Just in case."

She blushed, remembering how she'd duped him into going to the drugstore for her while she'd fled Baños with Mel. To add to her chagrin, he'd not only hunted down her requested pain reliever, he'd also hoarded some of her primaquine. *Just in case.* She lowered her gaze and downed the meds. "Thanks."

"Sure."

She drank more water, waited for him to broach the night before. He didn't. She was okay with that. She didn't need to rehash the story about Andy and Jo or to expand on her mom's death. She wasn't ready for his straight-from-the-heart declaration. But she *did* miss the physical intimacy they'd shared. Instead of saying something mushy or kissing her good-morning, Spenser hurriedly packed gear and invited her to use his toiletries. She appreciated that, but there was a nervous energy about him that made her uneasy.

"I aired out your cargo pants," he went on. "Grass-stained but dry. You can wear one of my tees and my hooded sweatshirt."

"Don't suppose you have any clean underwear in your gear?"

"Only if you don't mind wearing men's briefs."

"I'll take them."

"Once you're dressed," he said, tossing her a pair of white Hanes, "join me by the fire. A quick breakfast, then we'll be on our way."

"Why the rush?"

"We lucked out. It's cold, but clear. If the weather continues to cooperate we can meet up with Cy in under an hour and make the volcano by late afternoon."

River's mind had been so jammed with Spenser's bad stuff and the love stuff that she'd somehow pushed Cy and that potential disaster to the back of her mind. Suddenly it was all she could think about. "Is Cy trustworthy?" she asked as she wiggled into Spenser's briefs.

"What do you mean?"

"Do you think he'll be waiting for us at Brunner's camp?"

"Why wouldn't he be?"

"Did you tell him about the map?"

He didn't answer right away, which suggested he had.

"Damn." She dressed quickly, ignoring her aching body. Holy heaven, every muscle in her body screamed. She was paying for yesterday's strenuous walk and climb, but she'd eat mud before complaining. She had to get her camera back!

"I was indiscreet," Spenser said. "I'm sorry. I had your best interest at heart. Your safety."

"I don't doubt that." She honestly didn't. "But we're talking about a potential fortune and Cy's not with us now. He's *ahead* of us." She shoved her feet into a pair of socks, then the pink boots.

"Granted," Spenser said as he rolled the sleeping bag, "Cy's made several expeditions in search of the treasure, but he doesn't have the map. You do."

This time it was her turn to hold silent.

Spenser slowly stood and faced her. "Tell me you didn't put the map in your backpack."

"I didn't. But my camera's in there."

"So?"

"I took a picture."

"Of the map?"

"Yes!" she snapped. "Yesterday morning while you were loading up the jeep. I couldn't make out some of the tiny words in the margins and I didn't have a magnifying glass so I took a picture. That way I could zoom in on any section."

"Smart."

"Also, I wanted backup. What if something happened to the actual page? What if I lost it? Or someone stole it? Or…"

What if it got wet?

Yes, she'd put the map in a baggy but she'd gotten soaked in the downpour. Not clear through to her undies, but still.

She reached under the tee she'd just pulled on, nabbed the treasured baggy from the cup of her bra. She couldn't open it fast enough.

Spenser just watched.

"It's smudged." Her heart dropped to her toes. "I guess some moisture seeped in. Or maybe my body heat? I worked up a sweat climbing that jungle wall. And then last night when we, well, you know. Between that and the folded page rubbing together…" She trailed off, desperate for another hit of Alka-Seltzer.

"How bad is it?"

She blinked up him. He hadn't moved. She remembered how she'd accused him of looking at the chakana like the Holy Grail. He wasn't looking at the map or the amulet, but directly at her. He wanted her to trust him.

"Here," she said, moving to his side and displaying her father's detailed drawing. "The writing in the margins. It was tiny to begin with and now it's smudged. And this part here."

"Could prove a problem," Spenser said, staring hard at every detail. "Or maybe not."

"You're just trying to make me feel better."

"You have a backup, remember?"

"Cy has the backup."

Spenser passed her the map and started breaking down the tent. "He doesn't know you took pictures of the map, angel. I didn't know. Why would he scroll through your camera? I'd be surprised if he even knows how to use a digital. He's pretty old-school."

He was still trying to make her feel better.

She set down the map long enough to pull on his green hoodie, then shoved her arms through the sleeves of her turquoise coat. "What if he does scroll through?" She froze. "Oh, my God. The nude photos of you."

"Nothing Cy hasn't seen before. Figuratively speaking."

"Okay. Fine. But the *map*. What if he decides to go it alone? Screw us. Screw Henry. Hello, eight billion?"

Spenser wrapped her orange scarf around her neck and nudged her outside.

She shivered as a brisk wind whipped her hair, squinted against the bright morning sun. No fog. No rain. The twisted and gnarled trees were still twisted and gnarled. There were still countless flowery bushes and cactus-like plants. There were oceans of prairie grass, too, but gone were the eerie shadows and silver-gray tones of the day before. Colors were vibrant. The sky was clear. And toward the east… Whoa. "Is that Cerro Hermoso?"

"Impressive, huh?"

It took her breath away. Majestic and daunting, the snowcapped volcano towered high above all else in the

Llanganatis. A vast mountain of lush green and stark craggy regions, untouched by human influences and surrounded by a patchy cloud bank. Primitive. Intimidating. The Inca general had chosen his hiding place well. "How would someone survive up there alone for several months?" she wondered aloud. Every other person involved in her father's expedition was dead. Logically, Henry was dead, too. She'd considered the possibility, but she'd held out for a miracle. Staring at that formidable volcano, it was hard to keep the faith.

"Sit by the fire while I finish packing," Spenser said softly, as if sensing her mounting distress. "I made oatmeal and coca tea. I know you're not keen on the tea, but it'll be another physically demanding day and we'll be ascending."

She heard the rough edge to his voice. Slight, but there. "I'll drink it." After hearing his story last night, she'd do anything to avoid a severe case of AMS. So she'd get loopy and maybe embarrass herself. It was better than walking off a cliff.

"The oatmeal will give you energy, along with that protein bar."

"Oatmeal, protein bar, tea. Got it." She pulled her attention from the volcano and back to the problem at hand. "Back to Cy. What if—"

"He'd have to decipher Henry's code," Spenser said as he continued to break camp. "Figure out the clues. That would slow him down."

"Did you decipher the code?" she asked with a mouthful of sweetened oatmeal.

"Haven't studied it enough. I'll cross that bridge when we get there. It's easier to spot clues and visual markers when you're in the thick of it."

She was still holding the map in her free hand. "What should I do with this?"

"I could hold on to it. Or not," he added when she frowned. "Just stash it where you did before."

"But what if it smudges more?"

"I could take a picture with my phone. Backup for the backup."

She liked the idea of having another copy of the map—insurance—but...he could send that picture to another phone or even a computer.

"It was just a thought," he said.

She was being paranoid. Either she trusted this man or she didn't. She took a leap of faith. "Do it," she said. "Take a couple of shots. Make sure you get the whole thing."

He didn't say anything, just took a few pictures, then folded the map and passed it back to her.

"Don't suppose you've got a fresh baggy in that backpack."

He handed her one.

"It's like a clown car," she joked to lighten the mood. "Stuff just keeps coming out of there."

He grinned while stashing the remainder of the tent. "You forget, Gordo and I travel like this all the time."

"I didn't forget." She poured a second cup of tea, surveyed the daunting landscape, thought about the legend, then looked back to Spenser.

No wonder his show was such a hit. The man was fascinating. His way of life…fascinating.

No wonder Kylie was so crazy about her brother. There was plenty to be crazy about. River remembered how the woman's face had lit up when she'd said she couldn't wait to see her earthy brother in a sophisticated tuxedo. *"He'll hate it,"* she'd said with a giggle.

And Kylie would hate it if Spenser didn't make it home in time for her wedding. She'd be positively crushed if anything bad happened to him.

So would River.

Brain buzzing, she glanced at the Cerro Hermoso, considered infinite possibilities.

She had to get back her camera.

She chugged a third cup of tea while Spenser doused the fire.

Seconds later he was shrugging on that massive pack. "Ready, angel?"

Stuffing a coca leaf between her cheek and gum, River nodded. "Let's book."

CHAPTER TWENTY-NINE

THE CONQUISTADOR WENT through blondie's backpack a third time. Every pouch. Every pocket. He even ripped out the lining. Clothes, camera, soap, medicine, sunblock, hand sanitizer, insect repellent...

Gator remembered how blondie had begged for bug spray instead of her wallet or expensive camera lenses during the roadside robbery. Fucking loon.

"It's not here," Con said.

Of course not, Gator thought bitterly. That would have been too easy. They'd searched the treasure hunter's backpack, too...and his person. No map. It had to be on blondie or McGraw, and they were both missing.

Hands on hips, Con surveyed the primitive campsite. "They should have been here with Lassiter."

"Maybe they got an early start," Gator wheezed. Christ, the air was thin up here. "Maybe they're up ahead."

"Why would they separate? Why would she leave her provisions and camera? I don't see additional tracks or evidence that they slept here." He shook his head, shoved his aviator shades higher up his nose and peered out at the sun-drenched landscape. "No. They're behind."

"Maybe they turned back."

"McGraw wouldn't turn back. Not after getting this far. He wants that treasure as much as I do."

Gator raised a brow. "Know him well, do you?"

Con didn't answer. He hadn't answered any of his questions last night, either, not that Gator had been all that talkative. He'd been too preoccupied with adjusting to the altitude, nursing his various injuries and catching snatches of sleep. Con had been focused on Kane's journal.

"Maybe blondie couldn't keep up," Gator said, offering an alternate scenario while Con shoved her belongings back into her pack. "Maybe they got trapped by that fog, like us."

Gator had never seen anything like it. After he and Con had deserted the copter, they'd humped it through mist, rain and wind, but when the fog had gotten so dense Gator couldn't see his hand in front of his face, Con had stopped cold. It was the first time Gator had sensed apprehension in the man. They'd taken refuge in a cramped cave and that's where they'd spent the night.

"Get rid of the body," Con ordered. "I'll dispose of Lassiter's pack. We'll take River's pack with us."

Gator frowned. "So we're going to hide and wait for them to show up?"

"No, we're going to hurry ahead and wait for them at Brunner's Lake."

"How do you know—"

"Because Kane drew the lake in the center of the map. Part of it is on my half, the other part—"

"But you have the first half. The half that tells you how to get there. Will McGraw know—"

"He knows."

"But why there and not here?"

"Poetic justice." Con gathered Lassiter's supplies. "Hide the body where no one will find it."

Two hundred pounds of dead weight. Gator usually prided himself on his strength and endurance, but these were unusual circumstances. "Boss—"

The man slowly turned and glared.

If looks could kill.

Gator was beginning to wish for death anyway. He'd exhausted his supply of herbal salve on his bruised neck and throbbing ankle. His nose hurt. His lungs and muscles burned. It was hard to think straight. High altitude and brutal terrain, plus it was fucking freezing. The Conquistador didn't look cold. He wasn't breathing hard, either. *Fucker.* Gator was beginning to wonder if the man was human.

"So we hike to this lake and wait," Gator said, straining not to wheeze. "Then what?"

"We get the map."

"Without killing River."

"That's right."

All because he wanted her for himself. With that treasure in his possession, The Conquistador could do a lot better than skinny-ass, paranoid blondie—an observation he kept to himself. "What about McGraw?" Gator asked, tipping a flask to his lips. He'd been counting on whiskey to dull his aching body and warm his chilled bones. If only it could help him breathe.

The Conquistador shot him another one of those death stares. "He must live to mourn the loss of Miss Kane."

Gator would have rolled his eyes at the overdramatic drivel, but he wouldn't put it past the man to poke them out with that damned silver spearhead he kept in his pocket. It was all he could do not to break The Conquistador's neck, the way he'd broken Lassiter's. But Gator needed him in order to get to the treasure. The freak navigated this region like a native, knew shortcuts and tricks that enabled them to move swiftly and silently. He'd cracked the journal's code. Bragged he had the key to the Inca kingdom. All he needed was the map…and River Kane.

"Since you've repeatedly bungled this job," The Conquistador said, "I'm going to give you clear direction and assistance. Although you're no good to me in your present state." Disgusted, he tossed Gator a bottle of pills. "Take one of these. It will ease your discomfort. Then I'll help you dispose of Lassiter and share my brilliant plan."

Gator hated the man's arrogance. He hated the man. The Conquistador paid others to do his dirty work while maintaining anonymity. While dodging risk. Gator swallowed a pill and gathered his wits. Con's arrogance, he thought in a passing moment of clarity, would be the man's undoing. Until then Gator would do his bidding. Afterward, Gator would have it all.

CHAPTER THIRTY

"This is disgusting," River said.

"I know."

"I mean it. This is gross. All this muck and mud. Do you know how many germs—"

"I can imagine."

"Have you had your shots?"

"I'm not a freaking dog, River."

"Bet that depends on who you ask." She snorted, sighed. "Sorry. That was rude."

"And you're never rude."

"Only when I'm not myself."

"Like now."

"You're the one who insisted on coca."

"Guilty." *But not sorry,* Spenser thought. The altitude was a bitch and they were pushing hard. If a coca high kept River from hurting, he'd happily deal. She'd been talking his ear off for the last twenty minutes. He didn't mind—she was funny and interesting and, when buzzed, refreshingly unguarded—but it had been a long time since he'd been in these mountains and he was working hard to keep his bearings. He was also concentrating on the marshy terrain. Trekking across the *páramo* was a challenge.

"So how many women *have* you been with?"

"River—"

"Sorry. So?'

"Just keep walking," he said.

She saluted him and...walked right out of her boot and into the bog. "Gross!"

"For the love of—" Spenser steadied the woman before she fell face first. He freed her pink boot from the thick, sucking mud and bit back a smile as she yanked her stocking foot from calf-deep slime.

"It's cold and—"

"Disgusting. I know. Hold on." He worked a pair of wool socks from the side pocket of his pack and helped her swap her slimy, wet sock for a thick, dry one. He slaked mud from her pant leg and shoved her foot back into her boot.

"Thanks," she said.

"Sure." He glanced up. "No tirade on germs?"

"Too distracted."

"By?"

"You."

She was peering at him over the rims of her sunglasses. He chalked up that dreamy-eyed look to coca. Even so, his heart skipped. *Skipped,* for Christ's sake.

She smiled. "You're awfully handsome."

"You're awfully pretty."

"Sure I'm not too delicate for you?"

"Sure I'm not too old for you?"

She scrunched her brow. "Where'd that come from?"

"Forget it." He brushed a kiss over her mouth. "Come on, angel. Cy's waiting."

"Cy! Right. My camera. Henry. Stop dawdling, McGraw." She pushed out of his arms and tromped forward.

He raised a brow when he saw her stuff another coca leaf in her mouth, but said nothing. He'd been chewing on one himself. "Let me lead," he said, tugging her behind him. "Walk where I walk."

After a whole second of silence, she asked, "How old are you, anyway?"

Damn. "Turned thirty-seven last month."

"Happy belated birthday."

"Thanks."

"I thought you were older."

"Ouch."

"It's just that you're so confident and worldly. So masculine and mature and…skilled. You know. In bed."

He chuckled. "Keep talking."

"And you've got all those lines. The crinkles at the edges of your eyes. The brackets framing your mouth."

"Okay. You can stop now."

"You don't smoke, so I'm guessing it's a combination of sun and wind exposure and a lot of smiling. Laugh lines. They're sexy."

He grunted.

"Why are you so touchy about your age?"

"Because I'm the host of a cable television series and

the entertainment industry is obsessed with physical perfection and youth."

"Since when is thirty-seven old?"

Spenser angled his head. "That's what I'd like to know." *Fuck you, Necktie Nate.*

"Is that why they airbrush your promo shots?"

"Yes." He noted a particular rock formation in the distance, eyed the sun, then made a hard left.

"I wouldn't retouch your photos," she grumbled, sounding distracted. "Your face has character. *You* have character. I—" She let out a squeal.

What now? Spenser turned. "Shit."

"I'm thinking this is bad. What did you call it? Andean quicksand?"

She was waist-deep in marshy mud. *What the hell?* "Don't panic."

"Don't come any closer," she said in a strangled voice. "What if you sink, too?"

"I won't." He shrugged off his gear.

"Do you have a rope in that clown-car backpack?"

One hundred sixty-four feet of double-dry coated mountaineering rope. He tossed her one end. "Grab hold and I'll pull you out."

She gave him a cocky salute then grabbed hold.

He pulled…and the rope slid right through her hands.

"Can't get a good grip," she said, holding out her slimy palms. "Too muddy, too slick."

"It's okay, hon. We'll attack it another way." Instead of trying to drag her across the sluggish muck, better to pull her straight up and out. He eyed a nearby tree, the rope, River. Her silence bothered him. But if she panicked, she'd struggle. If she struggled, she'd sink. He searched his pack for a carabiners. "I'm going to rig something."

"Okay."

"It'll take a couple of minutes. Talk to me."

"I...I can't think of anything to say."

Indicating her fear had trumped the coca buzz. "How did you meet my sister? You haven't been friends for long, right?"

"A few months."

"Go on." He looped one end of the rope and tied a bowline knot.

"I...I needed shoes. For the wedding. My wedding."

Christ. "Yeah? And?" He tossed the rope over a sturdy branch of a nearby tree.

"Everyone in a three-county radius was talking about the recently refurbished shoe store in Eden. McGraw's Shoe Shoppe. *Walk in comfort, walk in style.*"

His sister's new logo. Actually, the man she'd hired to renovate the family store had come up with that logo. Spenser didn't like to think about the trouble Travis Martin had brought into Kylie's life. Thank God Jack had been there.

"I heard you could get designer shoes at a bargain price. So I drove over. Maple Grove's only about forty minutes from Eden."

"I know. Reach up and grab the lasso, River. Pull it over your head, under you armpits."

"Kylie had a limited but amazing selection of high heels. I wanted four-inch stilettos," she said as she gingerly positioned the rope. "Because I'm short and David's tall and—"

"I get the picture."

"Anyway, we just sort of hit it off. Kylie and me," she clarified as she adjusted the lasso. "We were both planning weddings and—"

"Got it." Spenser channeled his explosive jealously and, with the rigged pulley, easily hauled River from the muck. He refused to think of it as quicksand. Refused to imagine her going under. "Swing and drop," he said, and seconds later she was safely in his arms.

"Are you going to cry?" he asked as he held her close.

"No. I knew you'd get me out. But I am going to kiss you."

"Okay," he said….and kissed her first.

THOUGH THE TEMPERATURE was brisk, the sun shone bright. It was a beautiful clear day. *Dammit.* In between reassessing her priorities and future, River had prayed for rain. She'd cleaned up as best she could after that unexpected dip in the marshy mud pit, toweling off the slime without the aid of soap and water. Spenser had helped her change into fresh underwear and a pair of his Levi's. Yes, they were clean and dry, but she still felt filthy. Rain would wash away the remaining mud that was now dried and caked on her body and in her hair.

She refused to think about things like jungle rot, fungus infections and rashes—obsessing wouldn't do. Instead, she pretended she'd been the recipient of a luxurious mud wrap, compliments of the Llanganatis outdoor spa. She also pretended that her spirits weren't flagging and her thighs weren't cramping. It seemed like they'd been walking forever.

"Almost there," Spenser said as if sensing her impatience.

Five minutes later, she spied what looked like three thatched huts. Small, primitive and still several yards away. She pushed her sunglasses to the top of her head for a clearer look and pointed. "Is that it?"

"Brunner's camp."

Yes!

She didn't see Cy, but he could be inside one of the weathered shacks. *Please be inside.* She would've sprinted the rest of the way, but she'd learned her lesson about treading haphazardly in the quaking bogs. Up until now the coca had eased her breathing and anxiety. But now...

Please be there.

She had a plan. A new plan. Not perfect, but sensible. Something she could live with...*if* she got her camera back. "Cy!"

No answer. Her pulse raced as they neared the huts. She had a bad feeling.

Spenser tugged her to a stop. "Stay here."

He moved ahead and pulled a handgun. A freaking semiautomatic! Obviously, he had a bad feeling, too. He looked more like a mean street cop than a celebrity treasure hunter as he carefully circled, then peered inside each dilapidated shack. She thought about the road bandits, about the burglar who'd killed Bovedine. She held her breath, waiting for a spear to sail out of one of those straw huts. But then Spenser signaled her to come ahead and her adrenaline shot to the clouds.

"Cy's not here," he said, holstering the gun beneath his jacket.

"I knew it."

"No signs that he even slept here."

"I *knew* it! He found the picture of the map, sucked more seed juice and just kept going!"

"That doesn't sit right with me."

"Me, neither! I can't freaking believe this!" She realized suddenly that she was pacing and punching the air.

"Get hold of yourself," she could hear Henry saying. *"This is why I don't want you with me."* He'd said it over and over after finding her in the jungle. She'd hated him for that. She couldn't help it that she couldn't stop crying. She'd been scared out of her wits. But instead of comforting her, he'd scolded.

Spenser said nothing. He was walking around the camp, gaze intent on the ground.

"What are you doing?"

"Looking for signs of a struggle. But…" He shook his head.

"That's because there *was* no struggle!"

"*Or* last night's rain washed away the evidence."

"*Or* he's halfway to Cerro Hermoso!"

Spenser shrugged off the pack. "Why do you want to believe the worst about Cy?"

"Because it makes sense. He's a treasure hunter. He's been looking for this particular treasure for years. He doesn't care who he hurts as long as he gets what he wants. And he doesn't want me!"

"Whoa," Spenser said. "Who are we talking about? Cy or your dad?"

"Grandpa Franklin didn't want me, either, but at least he didn't kick me out. And David…" She kicked a stump. Kicked it again. All the hurt she'd shoved down on her wedding day and the days after spewed like molten lava. It was hot and destructive and she was helpless to stop it. "That selfish, insensitive…jackass! How could he *do* that to me? At the altar. In *front* of everyone!"

"Easy." Spenser tenderly grasped her forearms. "You're going to break your foot, angel."

She whirled and punched his shoulder. "I'm not an *angel*. I'm difficult. I'm…quirky!"

"I like quirky."

Tears stung and flowed. "What's *wrong* with me?"

"Nothing."

She was sobbing now. She couldn't stop.

Spenser pulled her into his arms, made gentle shushing sounds that only made her cry harder.

"I had a plan," she sobbed.

"Disney time-share. A house in the best school district. I know."

"No, a new plan. Cy ruined it." She could feel her legs giving way. "Now we'll have to go after him."

Spenser lowered himself to the ground, rocked her in his arms.

"I wanted to go back," she hiccuped over a sob. "The risk is too great. Henry made his choice and…there are more important things…other ways to find closure."

"We can still go back."

"Not without my camera. I already lost Henry's journal, now the camera, with the picture of the map," she wailed. "After all these years, he finally trusted me with his work, with a secret, and I blew it."

"You didn't blow it. We'll get the camera."

She grabbed a fistful of his jacket and glared up at him through a sheen of tears. "If anything bad happens to you—"

"It won't."

She'd drown in the depth of his tenderness if she weren't already drowning in tears. She dragged a sleeve across her wet cheeks and sniffled. "I don't love David."

"Glad to hear it."

"I wouldn't know love if it bit me in the butt."

"Is that an invitation?"

"What?"

He winked and a split second later she laughed. A scratchy, hiccuppy laugh, but at least it wasn't a sob.

"Better?" he asked, mopping her face with a bandanna.

"Ella warned this would happen." She took the kerchief from him and blew her nose. "She said I'd explode. That it was only a matter of time. Said you can only keep things bottled up for so long."

"Something tells me you've been keeping a tight lid on your emotions ever since you lost control in Mexico."

She quirked a watery smile. "Perceptive."

"Boils down to listening and observing. I'm pretty good at both. So are you."

She raised a brow. "You didn't add, *we're a good match.*"

"Waiting until you're ready to believe that."

Her heart thumped. *Infinite possibilities.* "You should write passages for Hallmark. You'd be rich."

"I'm already set for life."

"Oh, right. You're a star."

His lip quirked. "I invest my money wisely."

"Money you made from *Into the Wild.*"

"A top-rated series for five seasons." He raised a brow. "Seriously? You've never seen even a few minutes of one episode?"

"A dent to your ego?"

"More like a boost. Means you love me for me."

"I don't—"

"You do."

"We can't—"

"We will."

Her head spun, her heart hesitated. The treasure hunter and the wedding photographer. She couldn't imagine. River chewed her bottom lip, looked toward the volcano. "I can't think beyond this treasure fiasco, Spenser. If there's the slightest chance Henry's still alive… He entrusted me with his map, a secret. If it's connected to whatever he sent Professor Bovedine, I…I can't let whoever killed Bovedine benefit. I can't let them near Henry."

Spenser caressed her flushed cheek. "Heart of a lion."

Smiling a little, River sniffed back the last of her tears. "That's the nicest thing anyone's ever said to me."

After a sweet kiss, Spenser helped her to her feet. "If you're right about Cy, he's headed for Brunner's Lake. If I'm right and someone got the best of him, if they scrolled through your camera or if they have the first half of the map, they're headed in the same direction." He hefted his backpack and took her hand. "Let's book."

CHAPTER THIRTY-ONE

GATOR FELT LIKE A CAGED animal. He itched to pounce, but there was no one to pounce on. He'd followed The Conquistador's dictate. They'd hauled ass. They'd set a trap and then they'd waited.

And waited.

Hiding behind a tangled wall of vegetation, Gator sipped whiskey and hugged his rifle close. Once again he'd been assigned to do the dirty work. Con, who'd retreated to his own hidey-hole several hundred feet away, refused to show himself until McGraw was subdued and Gator had the map in hand. Then he'd make his *grand entrance*. Whatever the crazy-ass bastard had in mind, Gator hoped he'd make it quick. The sooner they got the map, the sooner they located the treasure, the quicker he could carry out his *own* plan. Skin itching with anticipation, Gator squinted through thorny vines willing their prey to show.

Where the hell *were* those two?

What if he was right? What if blondie and McGraw had turned back? But his employer was convinced they'd show. Con got a crazy gleam in his eyes every time one of them mentioned the famous treasure hunter. If Gator didn't know better, he'd think Con was more interested in hurting McGraw than finding the gold. Come to think of it, he *didn't* know better. He didn't know anything about The Conquistador, other than he was rich, ruthless and obsessed with the Lost Treasure of Llanganatis. That's how the nut-job had referred to the buried gold. Only it wasn't just gold. He'd also mentioned silver and emeralds along with fame, respect and revenge.

All Gator cared about was the monetary windfall.

Eight. Billion. Dollars.

So he ignored his doubts and fears. He concentrated on the fortune and popped another pill. Con had said the illegal meds would set him right. Hell, yeah. One had done the trick. Two would heighten the effect. He was feeling no pain and flying high on visions of living like a king.

Focused and determined, he hunkered down and waited.

Eight. Billion. Dollars.

A SENSE OF clusterfuck dogged Spenser as he led River toward Brunner's Lake. He kept expecting, hoping, to catch up to Cy. But they'd been walking for hours and there'd been no sign of the seasoned treasure hunter—dead or alive. He couldn't have disappeared into thin air, although in a way that had been Andy's fate. Fallen off the cliff, through the mist, never to be seen again. Spenser shook off a twinge of guilt.

Stay focused.

He squeezed River's hand and tugged her clear of a hostile-looking thornbush. Still on the *páramo*, they navigated the boggy desert with effort and caution. There were pockets of wild beauty—scattered lakes and streams, rolling hills, low clouds surrounding distant peaks—and River was quick to point them out. He remembered how entranced she'd been on the zip line, photographing the wildlife and fauna. Given her parents' backgrounds, if they'd kept her under their wing, nurtured her confidence and talent, she'd probably be shooting for *National Geographic* instead of nervous brides.

Then again, if he'd followed in his parents' footsteps, he'd be selling shoes.

"Have a power snack handy?" River asked. "I'm sort of losing steam."

Spenser dipped into his jacket pocket and passed her a protein bar. He noted her flushed face, her labored breath. "I've been pushing too hard. We should stop. Rest." This was River, for Christ's sake, not Gordo. Gordo, he thought with an inner smile, would've demanded a *frickin' break*.

River bit off a chunk of granola and shook her head. "Have to find Cy, besides," she pointed ahead, "look."

As they watched, blue skies muted to steel-gray. Fog rolled in and around, cascading down the volcano like a frothy tidal wave.

Shit.

He got his bearings, calculated. "We're ten, fifteen minutes from Brunner's Lake." And the shoulder of Cerro Hermoso. It was as far as he'd gotten with Andy and Jo. It was also close to where Blake and Chapman had claimed to discover a cave of gold back in 1887. And the location of the first visual marker on the map tucked inside River's bra. They were as close to Atahualpa's ransom as he'd been in nine years. He was torn between pushing on and marching River back toward Triunfo. To safety.

That fucking fog.

"Maybe it's a good thing," River said as they plowed forward. "The inclement weather, I mean. The fog's a lot thicker up there. Cy knows these mountains. Knows it's unsafe to venture in the fog. Maybe it slowed him down. Maybe he's at the lake. You said there's shelter there, right? More huts? Who built those huts, anyway? Brunner? Isn't he dead? How long have they been there? Can you teach me to navigate by the stars?"

"How are you feeling?" he asked, alarmed by her disjointed chatter.

"Better," she said without meeting his gaze.

"Do you have a headache? Are you dizzy?"

"I'm fine," she said, but she had a vice grip on his arm.

"Don't lie to me, River."

"I'm…I'm a little light-headed."

"A little?" He caught her as she stumbled. "For how long?"

"For a while," she said in a soft voice. "I didn't want you to worry." She stumbled again, only there was nothing to stumble over.

Dammit!

His heart hammered as he scooped her into his arms.

"What are you doing?" she asked.

"Sweeping you off your feet."

"That's sweet. No. Wait. I'm too heavy."

"Not even close."

"But with the clown-car backpack. That thing must weigh a ton."

"Shush."

"You're thinking about that fog. About that mountain. You're worried I have AMS. I don't. I'm just…loopy. Maybe I OD'd on coca."

He was closing in on the camp. He could see the huts. No sign of Cy.

Arms around his neck, River rested her head on his shoulder and sighed. "I bet you'll look hot in a tux."

He smiled in spite of his concerns. "What are you talking about?"

"Your sister's wedding. Do you have a date?"

"I do now."

The fog rolled and swirled, patches of varying thickness. He didn't want to carry her inside one of the huts without making sure they were safe. Where in the hell was Cy? He could feel the presence of Andy, here the voice of Jo, *"Get her out!"* He sensed the ancient Inca curse rolling in and around him, alive like the fog.

Spenser set River to her feet. Held her steady with one hand while shrugging off his pack. "Here. Sit on this, hon. Don't move."

"Okay."

"I'm serious."

"Serious. Got it." She saluted then dropped her forehead to her knees.

He hustled toward the first hut, gun in one hand, satellite phone in the other. "Gordo."

"Miss me?"

"Initiate and stand by."

"No small talk? That's bad. *A* or *B*?"

"*B*."

"I'll get there as soon as I can. You know Bingly. Won't fly in foul weather."

"He will if you pay him enough."

"Hate to ask, but... Everyone alive and accounted for?"

"One missing. Cy. And River's showing signs of progressive AMS."

"Shit. What about you?"

Spenser glanced at the mountain before peering inside the first hut. He thought about the treasure, Andy. "Fighting demons."

"Get the hell out of there, Spense."

"Working on it." He disconnected, slipped out of the first hut, turned for the second...and saw River running.

"My stuff!"

Near the third hut the fog had swirled upward, revealing a small, colorful pile of baggage. Belongings she'd had with her at the airport. Things stolen by the road thieves. Namely, her sling pack. "River, stop!"

Spenser dashed across the field and lunged just as she disappeared into a fog bank…and screamed.

He heard a hard thud and fell to his knees. Again the fog swirled. He saw it then. A hole, maybe six feet deep. River was lying at the bottom tangled in thin netting and covered with straw and grass. A camouflaged pit.

Trap.

He eyed the fog, eyed River. He listened.

She moaned and moved.

"River," he said in a calm, low voice. "Give me your hand."

She tried to push herself up, yelped and faltered. "Think I sprained my wrist."

"Don't panic."

"What's that stink?"

He smelled it too. B.O., whiskey and medicinal salve.

"Bandit," she said at the same time Spenser rolled and aimed at the foul smell.

"Toss your weapon," the man said, "or I'll kill her."

Spenser saw his worn combat boots first, then the automatic rifle.

Pointed at River.

He tossed his handgun.

"You have something I want," the man said in a gruff, scratchy voice.

"You have something *I* want," River said. "My father's journal."

"You're not in a position to bargain," he said.

"You speak English well for someone who pretended

to be Spanish," River said. "I'm glad, because I have a question. Did you kill Professor Bovedine?" she asked in a fiery voice.

"I've killed a lot of people. Uncooperative people top the list. So don't test me, blondie."

The man's upper half was still veiled by fog, but Spenser could tell he was tall and muscled. His brain scrambled for a plan of attack. "Where's Cy?"

"Your crazy-ass partner? The one you sent ahead? Alone?"

Spenser's conscience winced. Had he misjudged and reacted irresponsibly yet again?

"He was almost as arrogant as Bovedine and twice as stubborn." The man spit in the dirt. "Collateral damage."

River gasped. "No!"

Stay down, angel. Stay still. Spenser eyed the fucker as the fog swirled higher, to his waist, his chest. "What do you want?"

"Don't play dumb, McGraw. Dumb's kin to stubborn."

"Do we know each other?"

"I've seen your show. Give me the map and maybe you'll live to film another episode." He turned the rifle on Spenser.

"Don't!" River screamed while pushing unsteadily to her feet. "I have it."

"I have it," Spenser countered as calmly as possible. Damn River's lion heart. "In my backpack."

"Nice try." The bandit fired into the ground, inches

from Spenser, then aimed at his head. "Give me the map, blondie. Now!" *Cough.* "Or loverboy dies."

Spenser sensed another presence a half second before something whistled through the air, out of the fog, and straight through the bandit's chest. The man didn't make a sound, just slumped into the pit along with River.

She screamed and, in spite of her injured wrist, tried to scramble up the dirt wall. Spenser reached down and hauled her out just as two fierce-looking natives brandishing intricately painted faces emerged through thick, swirling fog. It was like a scene out of a movie.

Or a dream.

They wore sleeveless tunics with cloaks secured over their broad shoulders, the two corners knotted at their thick necks. Braided sandals, gold cuff bracelets, bows and arrows...

Ancient warriors.

"Rumiñahui and his men," River whispered.

More likely members of a lost tribe, the Sambellas maybe, although even that was far-fetched. Spenser couldn't be sure. No one had ever seen them.

Except maybe Professor Henry Kane.

Too late, Spenser saw one of them raise a blowgun. *Necktie Nate would love this.* He shielded River even as the dart hit its mark and the world went black.

CHAPTER THIRTY-TWO

Cerro Hermoso
Altitude 14,500 feet

RIVER DREAMED ABOUT far-off places. She dreamed about places she'd been, places she'd read about and places that made no sense. All remote. All wild. But none so beautiful as this place, she thought hazily. She stared up at the towering trees, the tops hidden in a swirling mist. She saw ferns and moss and exotic orchids. She smelled cinnamon and raspberry and the smoke from a campfire.

She heard birds and monkeys—soothing—and human voices—troubling. She couldn't make out what they were saying. It was as if cotton was in her ears, as if she were looking through a kaleidoscope—pretty, but abstract.

Am I in Shangri-la?

No. That couldn't be right.

Shangri-la was in the Himalayas. She was in…the Andes.

River forced her heavy lids open. Heart pounding, she blinked slowly to dispel the dream, but she still saw the mystical forest, still smelled the sumptuous scents.

She still heard the birds, the monkeys and the voices. Only, now those voices were angry.

"I specifically wrote, tell no one but Bovedine."

Henry. They'd found him! She tried to sit up, but her muscles wouldn't cooperate. Tried to speak, but no words came. Was she dreaming? Drugged? Dead?

"I told you, Henry. Professor Bovedine was murdered."

Spenser. At least she wasn't alone in this heavenly hell. He was somewhere to her left, beyond the heat of the campfire.

"Unfortunate and troubling. He was a dear friend. I regret—"

"Regret? That's all?"

"—that I perhaps contributed to his end. I hate that he died without knowing. I wanted him to know. I wanted River to know."

"Yet you expected them to keep news of this historical significance secret?"

"Yes."

"Quite the burden," Spenser said.

"A gift," Henry said.

"Your friend's dead. Your daughter's injured and was almost killed by a thieving murderer. You call that a gift?"

"I warned her. Beware of the hunters."

"People like me? And you?"

"No! People like…that thieving murderer."

The bandit. A self-confessed killer. Even given his

sins, River cringed at the memory of that spear sticking out of his chest. Of the blood.

She closed her eyes, shuddered.

"And she'd know this difference how?" Spenser asked, a hard edge to his voice. "Instead of educating her, you abandoned her."

"I saved her, you sanctimonious ass. She wasn't cut out for this life."

"Wrong," Spenser said. "You weren't cut out to be a father."

River's pulse raced as she waited for Henry's reply. *Defend yourself,* the little girl in her cried. *Refute him.*

"You're right," Henry said. "Nurturing a child, especially one as fragile as River, did not come easy."

"Did you even try?"

"How do you protect a child who's unable to function and thrive in primitive situations?" Henry asked. "By sheltering her. If I'd kept River with me…she would have fallen prey to some disaster. She would have died. Because of me…she's cursed."

Tears welled behind River's lids.

Spenser swore. "You're a man of science. Don't tell me you actually believe some witch doctor—"

"I know what I saw, what I heard and what transpired after," Henry said in a gruff voice.

"You could have amended your lifestyle," Spenser plowed on. "Taken a path closer to Bovedine's. Taught at a university—"

"My wife wasn't meant for that kind of life any more

than I was," Henry said. "We did the best we could. Did what we believed was best for River. Tell me, Spenser, would you be able to turn your back on your passion, on the work you were born to do? Could you stomach a lifetime of regret, of discontent? Don't judge me, boy, until you've walked in my shoes."

Tears leaked from the corners of River's closed lids, streamed down the sides of her face and tickled her ears. Instinctively she reached up to swipe them. She could *move*. And feel. "Ow!"

Suddenly Spenser was at her side. "Easy, angel." He helped her into a sitting position while shielding her right arm. "Pretty sure your wrist's broken."

"Set it as best we could," Henry said, hunkering down in front of her. "But you need X-rays, a cast. Hopefully, not surgery."

Instead of concerned, he sounded angry. For a moment she couldn't speak. The relief of knowing her dad was alive and well warred with the hurt his words and expression inspired. She hadn't seen Henry in years. His weathered face sported deeper wrinkles and some sort of tribal tattoo. His salt-and-pepper hair had turned full-blown silver. Aside from that, he looked much the same. Fit and healthy, dressed in baggy brown pants, a long-sleeved shirt and the vest with a gazillion pockets, and when he looked at her, she still saw disappointment in his intense hazel eyes.

He blew out an exasperated breath. "Why in blazes are you here, River?"

Her heart hammered as she glared at the man who'd

doomed her with quirks and insecurities. The man who'd chosen career over family. The man who'd broken her heart again and again and, as of a few second ago, *again*.

Could you stomach a lifetime of regret, of discontent?

That's how he would have felt if he'd curbed his wanderlust and obsessions to spend more time stateside with his own daughter? To keep his family intact? Even if only for a few stinking years? To hear his thoughts in blunt terms was almost too painful to bear. River tabled the gut-wrenching hurt and focused on his rude question.

"I came here to personally inform you about the death of your closest, probably *only* friend," River gritted out. "I came here because I was worried about you. I came here to apologize for the horrible things I said to you at Mom's funeral."

Henry's deeply creased brow furrowed. "Your first motivator was thoughtful but reckless. Your second—unnecessary. The third…also unnecessary. I've long forgotten words spoken in anger."

She blanched at his insensitivity. "Well, *I* haven't."

Spenser squeezed her shoulder. "I'm going to make you hot tea—regular tea. Give you two some privacy."

"No," she said. "Stay. Please." Aside from feeling physically ill and sluggish, she very much needed Spenser's emotional support. Yes, she could handle this confrontation without him, but she didn't want to. She was sick of handling "the bad stuff" solo. Managing her fears and insecurities, internalizing, keeping friends at arm's length, living in an emotional cocoon. She realized suddenly that even when she'd been with David, she'd been very much *alone*.

Henry settled on a rotting log, jammed his hand through his thick, unkempt hair. "Let me rephrase. When you accused me of killing your mom…your spiteful words cut deep, River. Some of what you said was true. Bridget was in Africa because of me. She was driving the jeep because of me. I didn't kill her literally, but…if I hadn't asked her to join me for that expedition. If *I'd* been driving…your mother might've survived the wreck. Or maybe we wouldn't have wrecked at all and she'd still be alive, we'd still be together. I *chose* to forget your hurtful accusation because it only intensified my guilt." He looked away. "I miss your mom very much."

"So do I." Tears stung her eyes. She missed Henry, too. Or at least the idea of two loving parents. She felt Spenser gently massaging her lower back. Subtle comfort. She gathered her scattered emotions and choked out what she'd traveled all this way to say. "I'm sorry for the awful things I said…at the funeral. Logically, I know Mom's death wasn't your fault."

"That makes one of us." Henry rose to his feet.

No "apology accepted." No hug.

No closure.

River felt more ill by the second. She trembled with anger, shivered with cold. The temperature was drop-

ping with the sun. She must have been unconscious for
two or three hours.

"We'll camp here for the night," Henry said, affirma-
tion that evening approached. "You need food, drink
and ample rest. Tomorrow you'll be escorted to safer
ground. The longer you're here the greater the threat."

River glared. She hadn't come all this way to be
brushed off, to be *insulted*. Ignoring her queasy stomach, her throbbing wrist and head, she pushed unsteadily
to her feet and faced her father's coldhearted indiffer-
ence head-on.

"For your information," she growled, "I made it all
the way from Maple Grove, Indiana, to—" she looked
around "—wherever we are…without serious illness or
injury. Yes, I was challenged at times, but that doesn't
make me fragile, just human. According to Spenser, few
have the fortitude to withstand a trek into the Llanganatis. Well, *I* beat the odds. I'm here. I'm alive. Maybe
not thriving, but that's because I was drugged." That
had to be why she was so sluggish, why her tongue felt
thick and her brain hazy. She remembered tribesmen,
blowguns. She remembered feeling a sharp sting in her
shoulder. She glanced at Spenser. "Right?"

He nodded. "I just recovered more quickly than
you."

"As for this," she said, supporting her injured arm,
"I didn't sustain a broken wrist because I'm a lightning
rod for disaster. It's the result of trying to break my
fall when I plunged into a pit. It could've happened to
anyone."

Henry quirked a brow. "You've changed."

"I'm still me," she countered. "It's just that I've learned to recognize my potential, as opposed to believing what was pounded into my head for years. I'm not cursed. I'm not compromised. I'm River Kane and, at heart, I'm an adventurer. As soon as I get out of here, I'm going to…explore infinite possibilities!"

Spenser squeezed her good hand and kissed her temple.

Henry looked back and forth between them. "It's like that, is it?" He shook his head. "The irony."

"What's that supposed to mean?" River snapped.

"You hate me, my profession and my passion, yet you hooked up with someone exactly like me."

She flushed for a dozen reasons. "We didn't hook up. We're just friends."

"The hell we are," Spenser said as he dug a water bottle from his pack, "and I'm sure as hell not a carbon copy of you, Henry." He handed River the bottle.

She didn't refuse. She drank deeply, knowing she needed to hydrate. She felt weak and sick. Damn drug. Damn altitude. Goddamn Henry Kane.

Henry zoned in on Spenser. "Not like me, huh? Tell me you're not dying to see Atahualpa's ransom."

Spenser didn't answer, but River felt his body tense. "Of course, he is," she said. "We both are. Who wouldn't want to see a treasure that's eluded the world's greatest explorers for centuries? But mostly," she said, "I'm curious to see what you're willing to sacrifice your life for."

"You already have. In part, anyway."

River blinked.

"The two indigenous people we saw, the men who killed the bandit?" Spenser speculated.

"They, and others like them, patrol the region," Henry said, "and when people get too close or pose a threat…" He spread his hands wide.

"They meet some debilitating accident or grisly end," River said with a shiver. "How did Spenser and I luck out?"

"They recognized you," Henry said. "One day when trying to establish communication and trust, I showed them your picture. They protect family as fiercely as the treasure. And they consider me, and by extension you, family. Apparently they've been watching over you for a couple of days."

"That would explain the sensation of being followed," Spenser said. "Amazing. I never saw them."

"They move like ghosts," Henry said.

"Where are they now?" River asked.

"Patrolling. Always on the move. Always watching."

"I still don't understand. *They're* the precious treasure you mentioned in your letter?"

"They're part of a lost tribe," Henry said. "Direct descendents of General Rumiñahui and a few of his most courageous warriors."

"Holy shit," Spenser said. "If that's true—"

"It's true."

"How can you know for sure?"

"I've been living with them for months," Henry said. "Learned their language. Listened to their stories, saw…" He trailed off, worked his jaw. "I'm sure."

River gestured to Henry, then the rotting log. "Sit. I don't want tea or rest. I want details." Not just for herself, but for Spenser. He'd risked so much to bring her this far, and now Henry's claims had ignited his curiosity and stoked the fever. The suppressed excitement and anxiety rolling off Spenser knotted River's already nervous stomach. Desperate to somehow quench the treasure hunter's thirst, she narrowed her eyes on her father. *"Details."*

"Details are in my journal."

Her cheeks flushed. The journal he'd trusted her with. The journal she'd lost to the murdering thief who'd been speared. She noted her sling pack was near the fire. Maybe the journal was with her belongings. She resisted the urge to look. "I want to hear it from you," she told Henry. That much was true.

He mulled that over for a second, then sat on the log.

River, with Spenser's help, sat, too. She felt weaker by the second, but refused to pass out. She tuned out the exotic sights, sounds and scents and zoned in on Henry. She wanted to understand his obsession and motivation. She desperately needed closure, and this could well be her only means.

"They've lived on Cerro Hermoso for centuries," he said, lowering his voice and leaning forward. Even though it was dusk now she could still see excitement dancing in his eyes. "Successfully sequestered from civilization, the tribe lives to protect the legendary lost Inca treasure. They practice the ancient traditions and speak a form of Quechua. They live..." His face glowed with wonder as he spread his arms wide. "Imagine a working village similar to the ruins of Machu Picchu, but on a much smaller scale."

River had seen pictures. Master stonemasons, the Incas had built impressive structures—temples, sanctuaries, residences, water fountains and irrigation systems...

"For a primitive culture, they're quite advanced," Henry said, sounding almost giddy. "Communal, highly structured."

Spenser angled his head. "Fascinating."

River raised a skeptical brow. "How is it no one's ever stumbled upon this village?"

"There are parts of the Llanganatis—so wild and remote—that have never been mapped. Aerial views are faithfully obscured by a massive, thick blanket of clouds. The village is well hidden."

"Like the treasure."

Henry smiled.

"You honestly expect us to believe that you've been living in an ancient village with a lost tribe, guardians of a legendary treasure?"

"If you had read my journal—"

"I *tried*. It was too cryptic. I didn't recognize half the words—"

"Bovedine would have translated."

River refused to blow her top, refused to waste the energy. She was already operating on fumes. "Then why didn't you send it to him in the first place?"

"Because I wanted you to have it. It was a gift."

"The family photos were a gift," River gritted out. "The journal, *that* was your way of trying to convince me, or maybe yourself, that your chosen lifestyle, one without me, was justified. A discovery of a lifetime. *Eureka!*" River's head was going to explode. Overall, none of this made sense and Spenser wasn't helping to work the puzzle. He was just soaking it all in, apparently taking Henry on his word. "Since we're discussing your journal," she snapped, "just so you know—"

"It was stolen," Henry said.

"I filled him in before you woke up," Spenser said.

"Maybe it's in my bag," River said, gesturing to her recovered sling pack.

Spenser shook his head. "I looked. And according to Henry, the guardians searched the thief who attacked us and found nothing of consequence, except his wallet."

"His name was Gator Wallace," Henry said.

The name meant nothing to River. "Did you know him?" she asked both men, and both responded no.

"At least you thought to tear out the map," Henry said. "Hopefully, whoever is in possession of my journal will chalk up the contents to gibberish. If they do break my code, then we must hope they consider my data a hoax, or at the very least, the ravings of a lunatic."

"Everyone we've encountered so far definitely thinks you're mad," River said.

"Or dead," Spenser said.

He rubbed his hands together in a maniacal fashion. "Another victim of the ancient curse. Excellent."

"How so?" River asked.

"If they think your dad's crazy or dead," Spenser said, "no one will bother to look for him."

Oh, right. She knew that. She massaged her temples, alarmed by her muddled thoughts. She squinted at Henry. "So your secret's safe. Maybe."

"Hopefully." Henry wiggled his fingers at River. "I want my map back."

"I only have the second half."

"The most important half."

"If you didn't want me to have it, why did you send it to begin with?" She struggled with her jacket zipper. Her right hand was useless. Her left was shaky. Finally she ordered Henry to look away so Spenser could retrieve the map from her bra. Her skin tingled when his fingers brushed it. She would have cursed herself as shallow, except she had a weird tingling sensation head to toe. Nothing sexual. Just pins-and-needles. As if her whole body was falling asleep.

She nailed Henry with bleary eyes. "If it's such a big stinking secret, why did you document the location of the gold?"

"I documented the location of the lost village and I did so because that's what scientists and explorers do."

She felt sick when Henry took the map and tossed it into the campfire. She wondered how Spenser felt.

Wondered why he didn't protest. Then remembered they had backup. Somewhere.

Can't think straight.

Henry regarded River with a bizarre mixture of pride and anger. "You weren't supposed to come here, River."

Of all the insensitive… "Bastard," she mumbled. She realized suddenly that, deep down, she'd hoped for some sort of emotional, affectionate reunion with her dad. To form some sort of father-daughter bond. She'd been an optimistic fool. She'd risked so much, and for what?

Her thoughts and emotions grew more chaotic. Losing control wouldn't do. Not here. Not now. "I came because I thought you were in danger," she rasped. "I wanted to help. And I wanted I wanted to say I'm sorry. Sorry for damning you to hell when Mom died. Sorry for not being the son you wanted. Sorry for…" Her mind went blank. She palmed her forehead. "I know there was more. I know…" She focused on Spenser, saw the anguish in his eyes. "I'm sorry about Cy," she managed before twisting in his arms and retching into the dirt.

CHAPTER THIRTY-THREE

SPENSER SOAKED A BANDANNA with water and wiped River's clammy face. "You're okay, angel. Hang on."

"Tougher than I look," she mumbled.

"Fucking superwoman," Spenser said close to her ear.

Henry, the eccentric bastard, at least had the decency to look concerned. "Is it a reaction to the guardians' tranquilizer," he asked, "or severe altitude sickness?"

"Don't know." Spenser eased River back on the blanket. "Maybe a combination. She definitely exhibited signs of AMS earlier today."

He'd been watching her closely for the past few minutes, more focused on her well-being than Henry's discovery. It's not that he wasn't intrigued. He burned to see that Inca village—if it truly existed—and to meet that lost tribe. As for the treasure, the air vibrated with an unusual energy. An energy that twisted Spenser into a feverish knot. His gut said Atahualpa's ransom was buried nearby. That the lost tribe and village existed. His mind warned there was no proof, no evidence to support any of this. Just Henry's word, and the professor didn't strike him as wholly competent. His daughter, on the other hand, struck him as fully compromised.

"Can't afford to wait until tomorrow. Need to get River to a lower altitude now." Spenser surveyed the area. He couldn't distinguish familiar landmarks. Given the dense forest, the darkening sky and disorienting mist, he couldn't even determine east from west. The guardians had carried them here, wherever *here* was. Though he hadn't been unconscious as long as River, he'd definitely lost track of time and direction. "I don't know where I am, Henry."

"As was intended by the guardians. They meant to disorient you. The village isn't far from here, but the location—"

"Is secret. Got it."

"They brought you this far as a courtesy to me. I can't direct you."

"You realize that's warped, considering two minutes ago we were in possession of a map *you* charted."

"A map intended for River and Bovedine's eyes only."

"Bullshit."

"Fine. A map intended for future generations. Later down the line. Just as there was Valverde's guide and Brunner's map and—"

"At some point you wanted your place in history," Spenser said. "I get that, Henry. But we're talking about River, your daughter. Her health—"

"We've come so far," she said. "Must see treasure."

"Forget it," said Henry. "Even *I* haven't seen the treasure."

River forced herself up on one elbow. "But the amulet you sent me...sweat of the sun."

"A small sampling of the buried treasure," Henry said, eyes bright. "Given to me by the tribe council. One of a few gifts. Along with tears of the moon, which I sent to Bovedine. As I've chosen to live out my life here, I have no need for such things. I thought—"

"For Christ's sake, Henry. I have to get River down from here. At least point me to Brunner's Lake."

The older man pushed to his feet. "I'll summon the guardians. They'll take you, but you'll have to be drugged."

"Whatever it takes."

Henry fled.

River squirmed. "I have to pee."

Spenser helped her to her feet. "I'll come with you."

"Just get me somewhere private, then leave. I may be loopy but I have my pride."

"To hell with pride."

"I just threw up in front of you," she said in a shaky voice. "At least spare me another indignity. Besides, I feel a little better. Guess it helped to get whatever out of my system."

"Fine." Spenser guided her to a private area. "I'll give you space, but talk to me."

"Fine."

He propped her against a tree. He distanced himself, but not too far. He had a bad feeling. Not just because she was ill, but because Henry was unreliable and the heavy mist that had been hanging high above now swirled in a downward motion. Between the fog and the encroaching dark... "Talk to me, River."

"Are you sure the journal wasn't in my sling bag?"

"Positive."

"What about my camera?"

"Negative."

"I don't understand," she said. "Maybe, what was his name? Gator? What kind of name is that? Maybe he wasn't working alone. Maybe he had a partner. Kind of like I have Ella. I inherited my grandfather's headache. I mean, business. Did you know that?"

"Tell me." Christ. Her thoughts were all over the place. Not good. He listened to River ramble incoherently about Forever Photography while he worked the puzzle.

She was dead-on about one thing. Gator must have been in cahoots with someone. Someone other than the second road bandit killed by Mel. Someone on the outside. Someone with connections. How did Gator know where to intercept River on the day she'd left Baños? How did he know she was staying at the Jungle Lodge? Who could have alerted the thug in both instances?

Mel-fucking-Sutherland.

Spenser's mind worked double time. When Mel had asked about River's well-being, when he'd asked if they were headed back to Baños, Spenser had mentioned he was taking her to the Jungle Lodge.

The night before that, the Aussie had spent time with River before Spenser had arrived at El Dosel. He'd plied her with liquor. How much had she told him about her hunt for Professor Kane? Had she mentioned the journal? The map? She must have. But then, why not take it from her himself? Why stage a shoot-out and pretend he'd been injured? To keep his identity secret?

Spenser was still pondering the mystery when he realized River had stopped talking.

He spun around, thinking she'd passed out, but instead she moved toward him.

She wasn't alone.

They moved as one through the swirling fog—River and her captor. He half carried, half dragged her, holding a gun to her head.

Spenser locked down a frenzy of panic and fury. He mourned the loss of his Beretta, taken by the guardians, he assumed, or left behind. He met River's wide eyes as they moved closer to the campfire, noted similar emotions—panic, fury—and overall confusion. He willed her calm while his mind spun for alternative ways to thwart the bastard holding her captive.

Then his brain froze.

Not Mel, but…

No. It couldn't be.

"Look like you've seen a ghost, Spense."

It couldn't fucking be.

"Had some reconstructive surgery done. The fall fucked up my face, but surely you recognize your old army buddy."

Andy Burdett.

He looked different, older, altered, but Spenser

recognized his voice, his eyes, the way he moved. His friend was alive. The only thing that kept Spenser from rushing forward and catching the man up in a bear hug was the fact he was holding a gun to River's temple. Confusion and fury pulverized his being. "What the hell, Andy? Let the woman go."

"Not on your life." He tapped the gun to her head. "Or should I say, her life."

Spenser drew on his military training. Hostage situation. Establish communication. *What does the gunman want?* He blurted the obvious icebreaker. "I thought you were dead."

"You mean you wanted me dead. With me out of the way, Jo was yours for the taking."

Spenser didn't answer. Couldn't answer. He felt as though he were in the middle of any one of the hundred nightmares he'd had over the past few years. Disturbing dreams involving Andy. He suddenly wondered if he himself was suffering ill effects from the altitude. Surely this was a hallucination.

"Obviously," Andy said, "I didn't fall as far as you thought. Landed on a jutting ridge, part of an old Incan path—so I was told."

"The fog," Spenser said. "You fell through it and disappeared. I couldn't see…I thought…" He dragged a hand through his hair and blew out a breath. "We searched when the weather permitted but—"

"I'd already been saved by an Andean farmer and his son. I don't remember anything between falling and waking up under the loving ministrations of a beautiful young Indian woman. The farmer's daughter," Andy said with a sardonic gleam in his eyes. "I don't remember much of the first few months after. In addition to a broken body, my memory was fractured. But this family practiced old Indian ways and, because of their care and my stubborn determination, I healed."

"Why didn't you let your friends and family know you were alive?" River choked out.

Her shaky, frustrated voice shredded Spenser's soul. That's when he knew for certain this wasn't a dream. This was real, this was now, and River was in mortal danger.

"Because, sweet thing," Andy said, while tightening his grip, "death was preferable to life. My old life, anyway. I was in dire financial debt. A couple of loan sharks had threatened my life, and my ex-wife had promised to make my world hell for the rest of my days. As for friends, they're fickle and fleeting. Even old friends. Duke was obsessed with his lodge and his woman, and Spenser here was obsessed with lost treasures and my woman."

"Jo loved you," Spenser ground out. "She was traumatized by your death. How could you let her suffer all these years?"

"Suffer guilt knowing she'd called out *your* name when we'd made love the night before my fall? Knowing she'd driven me to drink more than I should have?" Andy smirked. "I have no regrets. Meanwhile, I married that native girl. She educated me on the Llanganatis, the history, the landscape. She showed me places where the ancient Incas would smelt gold. These mountains are full of trinkets." He smirked at Spenser. "If you know where to look."

"Let me guess," Spenser said, wishing Kane and his spear-chucking, dart-blowing guardians would show. "You got rich off of those *trinkets*. Sounds familiar. Valverde married an Indian woman and, after multiple visits into these mountains, became a wealthy man. Sure you're not borrowing from his history?"

Andy just smiled. "On the contrary, old friend. I'm going to *make* history. Unlike all the adventurers and explorers before me, including you, I will unearth the Sun King's ransom. People will remember me long after they remember some hokey treasure-hunting celebrity, and I will be as wealthy as, well, a king."

"You're crazy," River whispered.

"Crazy as a fox," countered Andy. "I have the first half of the map—compliments of Professor Bovedine and that dead idiot Gator. I have your dad's journal—"

"Thanks to Mel?" Spenser asked.

"I'd applaud your brilliant deduction," Andy said with a taunting smile, "but my hands are full." He tightened his grip on River. "Sutherland's been my ears and eyes in Baños for quite some time. All transactions were made over the phone and he was reliable until sweet thing here got under his skin. He went ballistic when Gator's hired help reneged on the plan and tried to abscond with Ms. Kane. I had to double his pay and promise no harm would come to her in order to get him to obtain further information on her whereabouts." His cosmetically altered face purpled with anger. "Sutherland's no longer in my employ."

"Did you kill him, too?" River snapped.

"Didn't you know?" Andy chuckled. "No. How would you? He should have visited a more reliable doctor. Back to the journal," he said coldly, and Spenser had no doubt his old friend was indeed mad. "Took a little time, but I cracked the code. A lost tribe of noble roots. Interesting reading."

"*My* journal," River said with more fire than Spenser liked. *Don't agitate him, angel.* "Give it back," she demanded.

"It's in my pocket, sweet thing, and, like your addled dad I will gift it to you. After."

"After what?" Spenser asked with dread.

Andy smiled and spoke close to River's ear. "I also have your camera, which contains a beautifully detailed shot of—"

"I can't find the guardians." Professor Kane pushed through thick foliage. "I don't understand. I…"

"They're dead," Andy said. "I watched them kill Gator. Watched them carry away River and Spense. I bided my time then…they were no match for me. And no, I don't feel bad. They owed me. The world owes me."

Henry took in the scene. His face burned red. "Who are you?"

"A ghost from the past," Andy said. "You may call me The Conquistador."

Spenser frowned. *What the hell?*

Henry narrowed his eyes. "As in the Spanish soldiers who massacred innocent Incas in their quest for gold?"

"Seemed fitting. I harbor the same desires and determination as Pizarro, and you, Professor Kane, are my ticket to glory."

Spenser held River's worried gaze as the two eccentrics exchanged words. Their dialogue sounded like something out of a B-movie adventure. Or something scripted by a ratings-motivated producer like Necktie Nate. He'd give anything if a film crew lurked in the dense foliage, if he and River were the victims of a warped version of a reality show pilot. Anything was possible. Hell, Andy had risen from the dead. Unfortunately, Spenser's gut screamed this wasn't staged, but real. Bizarre payback for his obsession with Atahualpa's ransom. He never should have led River into these mountains. He should have found a way to talk her into returning home. Although his affections were true and his need to protect her sincere, deep down he still suffered the fever. He still wanted to see the legendary treasure—sweat of the sun, tears of the moon. River had been right not to trust him.

"You're holding a gun to my daughter's head," Henry said. "Do you mean to bully me into sharing my secrets?"

"I know your secrets, old man. Read your journal. I also have both halves of the map."

"Impossible."

"Possible," Spenser countered, spying River's 35mm strapped over Andy's shoulder.

"I could kill you all here and now," Andy said. "Proceed to the village on my own. But I fear I would suffer the same fate as Gator and the countless others who ventured too close."

"I marvel you even made it this far," said Kane.

"Thanks to my wife, rest her soul, I know these mountains well, and, like your guardians, I, too, move like a ghost."

"Even if I led the way," Henry said, "they'd kill us within a mile of the village."

Andy shook his head. "According to your journal, you're beloved by an elder's daughter. Amazingly, the high council is not opposed to marriage. You have won their trust, established yourself as a god of sorts."

"Not a god," Henry argued.

"Still," Andy said, "you are…cherished." He aimed his gun at Henry, then quickly trained it back on River. "They will do what they must to protect you," Andy said, "and your offspring."

"They will protect the treasure at all cost," said Henry.

"I can persuade them otherwise."

Henry fisted his hands at his sides, "I won't help you."

"Then your daughter dies."

The air swirled with mist and tension. Henry had indicated earlier that his devotion to his passion was greater than his devotion to River. Spenser could see by the pained look in River's eyes that she didn't expect Henry to budge on this matter. At this point, neither did Spenser. He had to make a move. He thought about taunting Andy with lies about Jo, drawing his anger and fire. But what if he took out his anger on River instead? Warped revenge.

"Pity," Andy said. "I had hoped to keep River alive. I had plans. She smells so…sweet." He intensified the pressure of the gun, shrugged. "Ah, well. You know what they say about best-laid plans. And I can buy any woman, sweet or raunchy, even without the ransom."

"Wait!" Henry shouted. "I'll help you. I'll lead you to the village and do whatever I can. Just don't hurt my daughter."

River gasped, then burst into tears.

Relief surged through Spenser. The old man really did love his daughter. *Fucking A, Henry.* He'd not only soothed River's soul, he'd bought them some time. Still…Spenser didn't trust Andy with River's life. Even if Kane got them all the way to the village, even if they persuaded the tribe to reveal the location of the treasure, no way in hell would Andy allow any of them to live. He'd existed the past nine years in anonymity. He spoke of his wife in the past tense. Had he killed her, too? He'd had a hand in Bovedine's death. In Mel's and Gator's and at least two Andean guides'. How many other deaths had he contributed to in his feverish quest?

"Douse the fire, Professor. Spense, grab your gear. My supplies are beyond that tree. You'll have to tote those, too." He kissed River's cheek. "I'll handle this package."

Murderous thoughts ran through Spenser's head, but instead of acting rashly, he spoke reasonably. "She'll never make it. Relying on my memory and the *X* on the map, we'll have to ascend another hundred or so feet to reach the village. Am I right, Henry?"

"Yes," he gritted out.

"River's suffering from AMS," Spenser went on. "Remember what that feels like, Andy?"

The man frowned. "She'll make it. I have experimental medication in my pack. It'll alleviate—"

"If she doesn't pass out first," Spenser said, willing River to read his mind. "She looks like shit."

"I feel like shit," she whispered in a thin voice. "Feel like…" She went limp. Dead weight that caught Andy off guard.

Spenser lunged.

CHAPTER THIRTY-FOUR

Somewhere in the jungle...

RIVER DRIFTED FOR A LONG time. Eternity. A soothing, silent blackness that later gave way to twisted images of betrayal and revenge. When she could stand it no longer, when she had the strength, she clawed her way through the hazy fog. The closer she got to clarity, the more she panicked.

Danger!

She bolted upright with a gasp and almost retched from the pounding in her head.

"Easy, angel."

Spenser!

He was lying on the ground next to her, looking dazed. His face was bruised and cut, his shirt torn. A moment of sheer panic registered in her brain.

Andy.

Heart pounding, she inspected Spenser for a bullet wound. "Are you all right?" she rasped, throat thick with worry.

"Feels like my worst hangover times twenty. What about you?"

"Sluggish. Sore." Knowing he'd escaped severe

injury, her anxiety kicked down a notch. Her pulse, not so much. She glanced around. No Henry, no guardians, no Andy. "What happened to us?"

"I remember Andy and I beating the shit out of one another, wrestling for his gun. Other than that..." Spenser curled his fingers around hers. "Give me a sec, hon. My body's not the only thing that's numb just now."

She rolled back her left shoulder, winced. "I think we got tagged with another blow dart."

Spenser grunted. "More guardians must've showed. I didn't see them, but that would explain my draggy reflexes and lapse of memory."

River's own memory was hazy. The last thing she remembered was a gunshot—just as Spenser plowed into her and Andy.

She still couldn't believe the friend Spenser had thought dead was alive. Insane, but alive, and obsessed with the same legend as her father. What were the chances?

Then she remembered more.

Talk of her father. Of an elder's daughter. Of marriage. Is that why Henry was so willing to turn his back on modern civilization. For *love?*

The notion confused and intrigued River. Was Henry back with the tribe? Back with his woman? Had he seen River safely to this point, or had he entrusted her solely to the guardians? It shouldn't matter, but it did. She shoved the troubled and complex feelings aside.

She focused on Spenser and Andy beating the hell out of one another, a struggle for his gun. Also troubling.

She remembered blood.

Andy's blood.

She remembered another gun.

Spenser's gun.

Only it was in Henry's hands.

Her eyes brimmed with tears as her memory sharpened. At one point Andy had bested Spenser, pointed his gun at River and... "My dad shot Andy to save me!"

"With my Beretta. Thank God Henry's got decent aim. The way Andy and I were tussling, he could've winged me instead." Spenser pushed himself into a sitting position, graced her with a tender smile. "Do you remember what happened seconds before the shooting?"

I'll help you. Just don't hurt my daughter.

Her heart swelled, her eyes burned. "Henry had been prepared to risk his precious secret to keep me safe," River whispered. She let the tears flow. "He loves me, Spenser."

"I think he always has in his own eccentric way." Spenser pulled her against his chest, stroked her hair.

She clung to him, trying to assemble her scattered memories and emotions. She would have thought the face-off a terrible dream except for the makeshift splint on her wrist and the very real pain shooting up her arm. She took in the surroundings. The trees looked different.

The smells and sounds were different. And the sun was shining. "We lost a night."

"So I see." Spenser rubbed the back of his neck. "They really souped up those darts second time around." He glanced at his watch. "Damn. We were out for over sixteen hours."

"Where are we?"

"Don't know."

Using her good hand, she unlooped her scarf and unzipped her jacket while Spenser reached for her sling bag. It was lying alongside his bulging backpack. He pulled out her GPS, the one she'd lost in the road robbery.

"I have a headache," she said. "But I can breathe easier and…I'm not as light-headed. Or cold." In fact, she was burning up.

"No wonder. We're at twelve thousand feet."

"What were we at before?"

"Fourteen and a half at least." He thumbed more coordinates. "Unbelievable. Somehow they transported us from there to here in less than a day, and here is as good as home." He glanced at River, smoothed his hands over her face. "You're feverish."

"I'm fine." A knee-jerk response. She didn't want him to think her weak. At the same time this was a possible problem she was unable to ignore. "My wrist is throbbing and my arm hurts. Bad."

"We need to get you to a doctor," Spenser said calmly. "Can you walk?"

She was still feeling the effects of the tranquilizer.

But she'd zip-lined on coca tea and scaled a flipping muddy jungle wall under the influence of a mysterious seed juice. Surely she could conquer flatland on the remnants of…whatever. "A straight line might be asking too much, but, yes," she said, allowing him to help her to her feet. "I'm mobile."

He traded the GPS for his satellite phone. "Yeah, Gordo. I know. I *know*. Where are you? Great. Stop bitching. I'll fill you in later. On my way. ETA fifteen minutes."

River's mind whirled. Again. "Gordo? Your cameraman is nearby?"

"I asked him to arrange transportation in case I needed to get you out of here quickly."

"When?"

"The day we left Triunfo."

She'd lost track of time, but one thing was clear. "You didn't expect me to make the trek. You thought I'd wimp out or chicken out."

"I worried we'd run into trouble," he said, hurriedly guiding her through hacked vegetation. "When Cy went missing and you started exhibiting signs of AMS, I wanted the option of flying you out."

"Airplanes steer clear of the Llanganatis, don't they? Too much cloud coverage?"

"Typically, that's true. Occasionally there are exceptions. Especially with daredevil chopper pilots."

"I take it you know one of those."

"Bingly."

"First name? Last?"

"Both."

"Bingly Bingly?"

"Keep walking."

River walked. She contemplated a chopper pilot with two last names. She contemplated the discussion she and Spenser both seemed to be avoiding. Maybe he was trying to get his thoughts straight, his emotions in line. She knew *she* was reeling. "It doesn't seem real."

"I know."

"But it all happened, right?" she asked as they neared a clearing. "A dead man walking, warriors from a lost tribe stalking, my father—"

"It happened."

She swallowed hard at his tense tone and less than forthcoming answer. What was he thinking? Anxious, she whirled and planted her good palm against Spenser's chest. "Henry shot Andy, right?"

"Right."

"Dead?"

"If not by Henry's hand, then probably by the guardians'."

"But you don't know for certain."

"No."

"So again you're left with no closure regarding Andy."

"That's right."

"And I'm left with…what? His cryptic letter and one photograph. I lost Henry's map, the journal, the family photos tucked between the pages."

"You have the memory of him standing up for you, protecting you," Spenser said reasonably.

"But I didn't get to say goodbye. And he didn't... I wanted... I was hoping... I feel like...like I was cheated somehow. Like I came all this way and... How long was I with my dad? An hour? Two? And I'll never see him again." She choked back a sob. "I don't feel it, Spenser."

"What?"

"*Closure*. I still have questions. Unresolved... needs."

He threaded his fingers through her hair, cupped the back of her head. "You apologized for blaming him for your mom's death. He chose you over his 'treasure.'"

"In that moment."

"That moment has to be enough, River. Let it go."

Frustrated, she punched his shoulder with her good fist. "I want to let it go. I *want* to move on. And I will. I just wish... I wanted more."

Spenser stared down into her eyes, his expression unreadable. He leaned down and kissed her—soft and sweet, hot and desperate.

It felt like...goodbye.

He eased away, squeezed her hand. "Get in the chopper."

River jerked out of her emotional daze, surprised by the loud whir of the helicopter blades. The whir of the engine. The churning air blasted her as she turned and, prodded by Spenser, moved closer to the whirlybird.

Disoriented, she squinted up at the redheaded, scruffy bearded stranger offering her a hand up. "Gordo?"

"River? Wow. You're pretty."

She was covered with mud, sweat and jungle debris. She was wearing Spenser's jeans—several sizes too big, baggy, the hems rolled high. She didn't even want to think about the state of her hair. "I'm a mess."

"A pretty mess."

"River's got a broken wrist and a fever," Spenser shouted over the noise. "She's also suffering lingering effects of AMS and a tranquilizer of unknown origin. Fly her to the best hospital in Quito."

"You're coming with, right?" Gordo asked as if reading River's mind.

"Have to go back."

"Why?" Gordo and River railed as one.

"It's personal."

"Don't give in to the fever, Spense. Not this fever," Gordo snapped. "Get in the chopper and let's get the hell out of here. Necktie Nate called. He's got an idea for a shoot."

"So do I."

River pinned Spenser with anxious eyes. "Don't go."

"Bingly!" he shouted. "Got a survival kit handy?"

The chopper pilot jerked a thumb toward the rear seat.

Spenser nabbed an army-green backpack from beneath, then locked on Gordo. "Got your minicam with you?"

"Goddammit, Spense."

"Give it to me."

Instantly River thought the worst. She envisioned Spenser risking the guardians' wrath in exchange for a chance to shout *eureka!* She envisioned him with a spear through his chest. She nabbed Spenser's jacket. "Some tales are best forgotten."

He kissed her hard, then looked over her shoulder at Gordo. "Take good care of her."

"Take me with you!" she demanded.

"Can't."

"You mean you won't!"

"Sorry, angel."

"If you do this," River shouted as he backed away, "if you don't come with us right now, Spenser McGraw, I...I won't wait for you in Quito. I won't wait at all!"

He started to back away and her stomach dropped to her toes.

"Wait!" she screamed.

All along she'd known they weren't meant to be. She'd sensed the end of the adventure would mean the end of their relationship. She was logical and practical, after all. But she refused to let him walk off like David, leaving her stunned and speechless. If this was the end, she'd have some sort of say. "Take this," she said, pulling off her Inca chakana necklace.

"Your dad gave that to you."

"And I'm giving it to you. The tree of life," she shouted over the helicopter's whir and roar. "A positive talisman, yes?"

"River—"

"Take it, dammit. Wear it." Even though he was breaking her heart, she wanted him safe.

He looped the Inca gold cross around his neck. "I love you," he mouthed, then shouted to Bingly, "Take her up!"

CHAPTER THIRTY-FIVE

Cerro Hermoso
Altitude 14,500 feet

IT TOOK SPENSER SIX DAYS to get back to Lake Brunner—twice as long as it had taken to get there with River. The weather had been particularly fierce. A constant mix of rain and sleet hindered his progress. He'd spent two full days at Brunner's first camp, socked in by an eerie, relentless fog. Knowing the danger of straying too far when he couldn't see his hand in front of his face, Spenser had spent nearly forty-eight hours inside his extreme-weather tent—alone with his thoughts.

Lots of thoughts.

On the emotional and physical trek back to Cerro Hermoso, Spenser relived his previous three expeditions. The first with Duke and Andy. The second with Andy and Jo. The third with River. He didn't suppress a single memory. He embraced every one—the good and the bad. He embraced the fever. Let it burn.

As he navigated the rugged terrain, while he holed up in his tent, Spenser likened the South American Llanganatis to a North American sweat lodge. A spiritual refuge. A place to heal mentally and physically. A place to attain answers and guidance.

Screw the curse. He wanted closure.

When he left here, he was determined to leave with a light heart and healed conscience.

For himself. For River.

This trek was for both of them.

He knew she was pissed off. He knew she thought the worst. When he'd called Gordo to make sure she'd gotten top-notch medical attention, he'd asked to speak with River. She'd refused. That's when he'd decided the best course was space and silence. She didn't trust this. *Them.* And if he was brutally honest with himself, time apart would also clarify and confirm *his* intentions. Henry had pitched a viable concern. How much was Spenser willing to give up for a lifetime with River—a woman with a Disney time-share and visions of a conventional family?

He immersed himself in the solitude, contemplated the future and came to terms with the past. By the time he reached Lake Brunner, Spenser had conquered his demons. But, like River, he still had questions.

He pressed on, utilizing the map stored on his phone. He pushed, he climbed, knowing all the while the guardians were watching. They'd *been* watching. For days.

If he'd experienced a crippling accident, forcing him to turn back—he wouldn't have been surprised. If a spear had pierced his chest, he would've been disappointed, but not surprised.

The surprise came in the form of nothing. *Nothing* happened.

Not when he reached Brunner's first camp, or Brunner's Lake or the base of Cerro Hermoso. Not when he navigated the mysterious cloud forest.

Noble intentions drove him forward, but so did the lure of the lost Inca treasure. A battle raged within. The fever burned and Spenser persevered. "Where are you, Henry?"

Spenser was just beyond where he thought he'd spoken with the professor and faced down Andy. *That's* when he sensed them. Spied them. Ancient warriors. A lost tribe. Historical nirvana.

He stroked the Inca chakana looped around his neck. A gift from River. A sign of affection. A woman worth dying for.

He envisioned her angelic face and braced. Felt the sting of the dart and crumpled willingly into oblivion.

CHAPTER THIRTY-SIX

Maple Grove, Indiana, USA
Altitude 810 feet

"I'VE NEVER BEEN SO nervous in my life," Ella said as she and Ben loaded the last of the photography equipment into her Ford hatchback. "I hope I don't blow this."

"You won't." River smiled at her assistant, a woman who'd run the office single-handedly while she'd been in South America. A woman with a natural flair for photography. A woman who'd promised to respect River's wishes never to discuss her whirlwind nine-day trip. *Ever.*

"I have total faith in your abilities, Ella. So do Kylie and Jack. Otherwise they would have taken their business someplace else."

River had returned to Maple Grove two weeks ago, sporting a cast that covered her right hand and extended up to her elbow. She wouldn't be shooting any professional pictures for at least another four weeks. Kylie and Jack's wedding was today. They were set on Forever Photography and, after seeing samples of Ella's work, hadn't balked at her being the chief photographer.

It was a big day for Ella. A big day for Kylie and Jack. But an even bigger day for River.

Today, for the first time since she'd watch him head back into the Llanganatis, River was going to see the man who'd challenged and charmed her. The man who'd rekindled her adventurous spirit and sparked her sensual being. The man who'd crushed her by succumbing to temptation. Part of her wanted to avoid Spenser. She worried her cherished memories would shatter the moment she saw him. She wanted to cling to the good stuff, not the bad. But she'd promised Kylie she'd attend the wedding as a guest, a friend. Plus, though it might hurt like hell, better to have some sort of closure.

I love you.

He'd spoken straight from the heart and broken *hers*. She wanted to cherish those words, but instead they taunted her. If Spenser truly loved her, he would've resisted a chance at his *eureka* moment. She'd begged him not to go back into the Llanganatis and he'd done just that. He'd gone back—armed with the map on his phone and Gordo's minicam. She could only assume he hoped to catch that lost tribe and maybe even the treasure on film. The historical find of a lifetime. She could think of no other explanation for his actions.

"Are you sure you don't want to ride with us?" Ben asked, as if sensing River's anxiety.

"The church is forty minutes away," Ella said. "A cab's going to be expensive."

"No worries," River said. Unable to drive and unwilling to trouble friends, she'd been cabbing it a lot lately, thus Barney, the sole driver of the town's only taxi service, had promised her a discount. "Now, get going. You need to arrive early in order to photograph the bride and groom preceremony."

River didn't want to be at the church any longer than necessary. Bad enough she'd have to endure four hours of Spenser's presence at the reception.

"I know the drill, boss." Ella swished pink gloss over her lips. "You can count on me," she said with a wink, then hesitated. "Wish me luck, River."

"You don't need it, but, *luck*." River hugged the younger woman, then waved left-handed at Ben. "Drive safe!"

Pulse racing, River moved back inside Forever Photography. She had twenty minutes to kill before the cab arrived. Twenty minutes plus forty to prepare for her face-to-face with Spenser.

She knew he was alive and well because he'd called Gordo to ask about her and he'd been in touch with his sister—who said she'd never heard him sound more jazzed. River read all sorts of things into that. She even watched two episodes of *Into the Wild,* fully expecting a breaking news special edition, featuring "A Lost Tribe and Atahualpa's Ransom."

Instead, she'd seen two reruns, one of Spenser and Gordo in Scotland and another in Tibet. She'd watched Spenser's every move, inhaled his every word and expression. She'd been entranced by his passion and the wild landscapes. She'd imagined how she would have photographed certain aspects of each quest. She'd imagined trekking alongside Spenser by day and making love at night. She'd relived the Amazon/Andes adventure a hundred times, and although she regretted all the associated deaths, she honestly couldn't wish that adventure away.

She just wished she'd responded to Spenser's declaration of love with one of her own. Maybe then he would have gotten on the chopper. Now they had two weeks and two worlds—his and hers—between them.

River scanned the perfectly organized reception area, the framed wedding photographs on the wall. She silently thanked her mom for her artistic streak, her father for her adventurous streak and her grandpa for her photographic training. And although she was grateful for this studio, she could feel the walls closing in day by day. "I'm capable of more," she whispered to herself. "I want more."

She started at a firm knock on the door, glanced at her watch. Barney wasn't due for another ten minutes. Ella must've forgotten something. "Why didn't you use your key?" she asked as she let her in.

Only it wasn't Ella. Or Barney.

"Oh," she said.

"Hi," he said.

Her memories didn't shatter. They blossomed in her mind, one after the other. Vivid, terrifying, inspiring and wondrous. For a moment River couldn't speak. It wasn't solely due to the tidal wave of adrenaline-charged recollections. It was the heat of the moment.

Spenser in a tuxedo.

He looked…amazing. Dashing and charming, like a cover model for Armani or a movie star glammed up for the Oscars. She thought about the rugged body beneath the refined clothes. She noted the twinkle in his vivid green eyes, the ornery tilt of his mouth.

Her breathlessness had nothing to do with the altitude. Her racing pulse wasn't due to coca leaves or seed juice.

She was high on love.

Blindsided, she dug deep for the sense of betrayal she'd suffered, for the anger she'd nurtured over the last several days, but all she felt was relief. Relief and joy and a fluttery feeling in her stomach.

"You look beautiful, angel."

"I have a cast." What a stupid thing to say.

"A pretty pink cast."

"The nurses in Quito thought my pink muckers were a hoot and, well, they thought a pink cast might cheer me up. I was a little cranky and mopey and…" The closer he moved, the more she rambled.

"How's your wrist?"

"Healing." One word. Succinct. Good.

"I liked the pink boots, but I like these sexy heels even more."

Four-inch purple stilettos to match her clingy purple-satin dress. Full makeup and a flirty updo. Her skin heated as his gaze moved over every primped inch of her. "What are you doing here?" she squeaked. "I mean, I know you're in Indiana for Kylie and Jack's wedding, but what are you doing *here? Now?* As best man, you should be with Jack. Calming his nerves."

"Jack doesn't get nervous."

"Maybe not. Even so—"

"Where I'm from, it's customary for a gentleman to pick up his date."

Even though he was a globe-trotter, he'd been born and raised in Eden—Paradise in the Heartland. A small town with…old-fashioned sensibilities.

It suddenly occurred to River that even though she was ten years younger than Spenser, they probably knew some of the same people—people aside from his sister and Jack. They'd probably shopped at the same mall and eaten at the same pizza joints. Suddenly their worlds shifted just a little closer.

"I stopped at your house," he said, "but your neighbor directed me here." He looked over her shoulder. "So, this is Forever Photography."

She realized then that she'd kept him standing on the threshold, in the sun and heat. "Yes, I… Won't you come in?" Her skin sizzled as he brushed past her and set a canvas bag on Ella's desk. She wanted to throw herself at him, to tear off his jacket, his shirt and tie. *Ever done it in a darkroom?* she wanted to ask. "I'm sorry. Did you say *date?*"

He raised a brow. "You forgot."

"I…"

"On the *páramo,* you asked if I had a date for my sister's wedding. I said, *I do now.*"

"I…"

"I shouldn't have assumed you'd remember. You were light-headed and—"

"You swept me off my feet." River blushed. "I remember. Most of it."

"Are you going with someone else?"

"No."

He smiled. "Good. Then it's settled."

"We can't just…" An unwelcome vision of him traipsing back into the mountains soured the moment. "We need to talk."

"I agree."

Instead of pacing, she sat on the edge of a flowery cushioned chair. She tried to organize a dozen scrambled thoughts and concerns. She tried not to obsess on his handsome face and the fantastic sex they'd shared. Her mind jumped back to Quito. The hospital. Her alone with Gordo, and Spenser alone in the wild. "I'm sorry I didn't take your call. That was childish and rude."

"You were angry with me," he said, perching on the corner of the desk. "I didn't realize how angry until I didn't hear back from you. I thought maybe you'd call me to give me hell or…to make sure I was all right." He rubbed a hand over his recently cropped hair. "Christ. That sounded pitiful."

The mushy, vulnerable side of the tough and confident adventurer. Her heart swelled. "I wondered and worried, a lot, if that makes you feel better. Gordo and your sister assured me you were fine."

He smiled a little at that, focused on his polished oxfords—so unlike his dusty hiking boots. "I was surprised when Gordo told me you got on a plane bound for the States instead of Peru."

"You thought I'd try to patch things up with David?"

"I thought you wanted closure."

"I found closure on the *páramo,* at least as far as David was concerned. The moment I realized I didn't love him. When I realized…" *I love you.* River fidgeted in her seat.

Spenser regarded her with a small smile, his green eyes shining with relief and a dash of amusement.

He knows, she thought. He's always known.

"David got back last week," she rushed on. "We had a talk. He apologized for the way he ran out and I apologized for trying to control every move we made as a couple. I wouldn't say we're friends, but…we're okay." She hadn't been able to confess she'd never loved him, not deeply and madly. It seemed too cruel.

Uncomfortable with the subject, she switched the focus to Spenser. "What about you? Did you make peace with Jo?"

He met her gaze, the smile gone. "No. I couldn't see the good in telling her Andy had been alive all these years and that he'd purposely kept that secret to punish her. I also saw no good in telling her what a demented man he'd turned into and that he died a violent death. Again."

"That's kind of you, Spenser, except she'll still blame you for his first death."

"I'm okay with Jo not forgiving me. I've forgiven myself. I've moved on."

Their worlds inched a little closer.

"So is Andy really dead? Are you sure?"

He nodded. "I saw him. Don't ask details."

River swallowed. "Okay."

"That's just one of the reasons I had to go back, River. I had to know for sure that Andy was no longer a threat to you or anyone else. Another reason…Cy. I couldn't leave him up there like that. He deserved a decent burial, a few kind words."

River blinked back tears. "Did you find him?"

Spenser nodded.

"I'm so sorry."

"Cy died doing what he loved best—treasure hunting. And doing what came naturally—protecting a woman. I guarantee his soul is restful."

She fell silent, processing everything, trying to get a handle on her emotions.

Spenser angled his head. "Why don't you ask me what you're dying to know?"

"Did you see Henry?"

He quirked a tender smile. "Let's cut to the chase, angel. You assumed I took Gordo's minicam back up Cerro Hermoso to get footage of the lost tribe and maybe even the lost treasure itself." He held up a hand, cutting off her words. "You had good reason to suspect that and I admit the temptation was strong, but as you said, some tales are best untold."

"Did you see the village?" River whispered, gripping the edge of her seat in anticipation.

Spenser rubbed his brow, blew out a breath. "It was everything Henry described and more, River."

"Did you meet the woman he…the one…"

He nodded. "I don't speak the language but…she was very kind and she adores your dad."

"That's good. That's…I'm glad." Surprisingly, she meant it. "I think Mom would approve."

"He's happy, River."

She smiled at that, her heart blossoming more by the second. "So…did you catch them on film? Did you see the treasure?" Part of her hoped so. Part of her burned to see with her own eyes what had eluded explorers for centuries.

"No and no." Spenser scraped a hand over his clean-shaven jaw. "Here's the sad truth and the motivation for Henry keeping the existence of the tribe secret. They'd be in mortal danger if they were inundated with civilized people. The entire population could easily be wiped out by the common cold. Do you know how Andy planned to threaten the tribe into revealing the treasure?"

She shook her head.

"He had a vial in his pack. A vaccination."

"For what?"

"Swine flu."

River frowned. "He was going to expose them to swine flu? That's despicable!"

"Andy isn't the only one who'd go to villainous lengths for eight billion dollars. That's why I convinced

Henry to keep his journal. It's why I deleted the picture of his map from your camera and my phone."

River gawked. "You buried a once-in-a-lifetime story."

He shrugged as if it was no big deal, although she knew it had cost him mightily.

"Old-fashioned sensibilities?" she croaked past the lump in her throat.

"Something like that." He shoved off the desk and closed the space between them. "Henry's not coming back, hon."

"I know."

"Ever."

She licked her lips, nodded. "I know. It's okay. I've thought about it, a lot. I'm okay with how things ended between us. I told him I was sorry and…he saved my life. In his own way, he loves me. I've moved on, too. You were right. I have the memory of him choosing me over his precious treasure."

"I wanted you to have more." He reached into his inner jacket pocket and handed her a DVD.

Her heart hammered. "What is it?"

"I filmed your dad…. I asked him to share some of his favorite memories of you."

She blinked. This was so unexpected. So…unreal. "Did he have any?"

He stroked her cheek. "Several."

She could scarcely breathe. "Were they good?"

"Yes. He also included a personal message for you."

"Is *it* good?"

"Oh, yes."

"Is it going to make me cry?"

"Definitely."

She blew out an anxious breath and stood, marveling that her shaky legs withstood her weight. "Then maybe I should wait to watch it until later. In private."

"Whatever you want."

She wanted to savor the anticipation, even though she was dying of curiosity. Something good from Henry. Something nice about her! Heart full, she wrapped her arms around Spenser and hugged. "Thank you."

He kissed the top of her head, smoothed a palm down her back. "I love you, River. I know you don't trust this, us. But we'll figure it out. We'll make it work. I can amend my lifestyle. I've already started."

She eased back and stared up at him in awe. "What have you done?"

"Taken a hiatus from *Into the Wild*. I own stock in the Explorer Channel, so it's not like I'm throwing away my future. I'm exploring—"

"Infinite possibilities?"

He smiled.

"Me, too."

"How so?"

"I researched and found out that the Explorer Channel owns a travel magazine. I want to apply as a staff photographer, only my portfolio is all wrong. If only I hadn't lost my camera in the mountains. I must've taken four or five hundred pictures while in Ecuador. I'm not saying they're all good—"

"Mostly they're very good. Your camera's in that bag on the desk. All photos intact, except for the map."

Her brow rose. "What about the nude shots of you?"

He grinned, a sexy grin that heated her naughty regions. "Anxious to revisit those photos?"

She quirked a shy, teasing smile. "Maybe."

He laughed. "God, I missed you."

"I missed you, too, Spenser. Terribly. And now…it's like we've never been apart. Like we've known each other forever. It's weird and wonderful and I…I think I fell for you the moment I saw you at the airport in Quito. We haven't known each other very long, but I know without a doubt I…I… *Dammit*."

"It's okay, hon. You don't have to say it. I see it in your eyes."

"I *want* to say it. I *feel* it. It's just that…I think I'm intimidated by it."

"Then *it* must be damned impressive." He brushed a kiss over her lips. "We need to head out or we'll be late for the wedding, but after…I'm going to kiss you for an hour or four."

Her heart danced. "I think I can handle that." River moved out of his arms and into her office. She put her dad's DVD in a safe place, lingered for a sentimental second, then rushed back to her *date*.

Spenser caught her up and held her close. "One kiss to get me through the day."

River gave over as he stole away her thoughts and breath with a passionate, achingly beautiful kiss. "On second thought," she rasped as he broke away, "I'm not sure I'll survive an hour or four of that."

"Me neither."

"I love you, Spenser."

"Looks like I finally discovered a precious treasure." He gazed into her eyes like like a man besotted. "Eureka."

EPILOGUE

Eighteen months later...
Quito, Ecuador, South America
Altitude 9,214 feet

"I'M GLAD WE FLEW in early," Kylie said. "I felt like crap yesterday. Today I'm just slightly off. Morning sickness stinks."

"You weren't sick at home, tiger." Jack poured his wife another glass of water from the chilled bottle their server had left behind. He sounded calm, but River could see the concern in his eyes. "I'm thinking it's jet lag," he said. "Long flight. Time change."

"It's the altitude," River said. "Some bear it better than others." Spenser had said the same thing to her when they'd first met. Here in Quito. Over a year and a half ago. She got all weepy just thinking about it. Then again, these days she cried at the drop of a hat. Wacky hormones and all that. Like her soon-to-be sister-in-law, River was pregnant. Only she was twice as far along.

"I'd suggest coca tea," Lana said to Kylie. "But since you're carrying..."

River winked at Kylie, who was four months along

and barely showing. "Unless you want to zip-line over a jungle, forgo the coca tea."

Kylie laughed. "I'll never tire of that story."

"My wife gets into enough trouble on her own," Jack said, giving Kylie's hand an affectionate squeeze. "She'll pass on the coca."

Duke smiled. "Good call."

River looked at the people sitting around the dining table and beamed. She loved this restaurant—a favorite of hers and Spenser's—and she loved these people. Kylie and Jack had flown in from Indiana. Lana and Duke had driven over from the Jungle Lodge. They were all here to witness River's marriage to Spenser. She'd put him off for over a year. She'd taken marriage too lightly before and refused to do so with Spenser. He was her world.

They'd spent several months traveling to exotic locals, places he'd been before, looking for treasures that continued to elude him. Two major projects had been in the works. A non-fiction book and an Explorer Channel spotlight miniseries. River had been the photographer, Gordo the videographer and Spenser the writer. The three of them had worked side-by-side by day, exploring, creating. The nights had belonged to River and Spenser.

Those months had been the most exciting times of her life and, even after they'd settled for a spell, setting up house just outside of Quito, she knew she'd travel again. Photographing wild regions and exotic people was in her blood—like Spenser. She loved him fiercely, even though he gave her crap for dodging his multiple marriage proposals.

Although she'd conquered most of her fears and quirky, obsessive habits, somewhere along the way River had become a tad superstitious and was afraid to rock the boat where their relationship was concerned. They were deliriously happy as they were—just *being* together, traveling and living together. They were a couple in every sense of the word. Why did they need to make it "official"? Worried a ceremony would somehow curse their relationship, she kept hedging—even after she'd become pregnant. Maybe it was her insecurities. Maybe it was because of her background. She didn't want Spenser, of all people, to feel trapped.

Eight months pregnant, she'd finally caved. All of a sudden it was supremely important to her that she was *Mrs.* McGraw when their baby was born. Eager to make it so, Spenser had rushed things along, pulled a lot of strings. The ceremony was tomorrow—exactly four days after she'd said yes.

Tonight they were having dinner with the few people they'd invited to share in the moment. The only ones missing were Spenser and Gordo, who'd be along any minute, and Spenser's mom and grandma.

"Did you check with your mom today?" River asked Kylie. "How's your grandma feeling?"

Kylie snorted. "Cantankerous. She's driving Mom crazy."

"Not that that's unusual," Jack said, thanking the waiter when he served their appetizers.

"Kylie's grandma broke her ankle a few days ago," River told Lana and Duke.

"Square-dancing in stilettos," Kylie said. "What was she thinking?"

"She wanted to impress her boyfriend," Jack told the gang with an amused grin.

"She's crazy," Kyle said. "If you've ever wondered where Spenser got his wild streak…"

"Speaking of Spenser," Lana said, glancing at the plentiful appetizers. "It feels weird to eat before the guest of honor arrives."

"He texted me a couple of minutes ago," River said. "Said we should start without him. Still tied up in traffic." She dug into a dish of tapas so that their guests would follow suit. "He was all the way on the other side of town, greasing palms or something. Some sort of legal snafu. Since we're not citizens—" She glanced over at Jack. "You probably didn't want to hear that, *Chief* Reynolds."

Jack's lip quirked. "Spenser ever tell you about the time he arranged Kylie's and my *first* wedding ceremony?"

River chuckled. "Oh, right."

Duke sipped his beer while Lana helped herself to char-grilled artichokes. "I'd like to hear that story," she said.

Duke agreed.

River chowed down on her spicy food, feeling all warm and fuzzy as Jack and Kylie relayed their impromptu wedding at Mount Fuji. She reveled in the laughter, the tender moments, in the affectionate looks passed between each couple. She thought about how Spenser had used his sister and Jack's and Lana and Duke's happy marriages as examples while trying to assure her it would be the same for them.

She placed a hand over her huge belly and smiled. *Mommy and Daddy are going to live happily ever after as man and wife. We'll be together,* she mentally assured her unborn child. *All of us. Forever.*

Her peace of mind shattered two seconds later when she felt a sharp pain. The another, sharper pain. Then *whoosh!* "Oh, no!"

"FUCK!" SPENSER disconnected, tossed his cell on the dash and slammed his hand on the steering wheel.

"I only got one half of that very brief conversation," Gordo said, tightening his seat belt as Spenser swerved into the opposite lane. "River's in labor?"

"Yes."

"But it's too early."

"I know." Spenser spun the jeep in the direction of Metropolitano, the private hospital they'd planned to visit for the delivery of the baby *next* fucking month. Heart pounding, he swerved in and out of traffic in his panicked haste. His sister's shaky voice still rang in his ears.

"It'll be okay, Spenser. Duke's driving. He said he knows a shortcut to the Metropolitano. Lana already phoned River's doctor and Jack, well, he's trained in

these sorts of things. If it comes to that, which I'm sure it won't."

He'd heard River cry out his name. An anguished cry that tore at his heart.

"She's okay," Kylie had assured him. *"Just a little scared and… I have to go. Meet us at the hospital, Spenser. Hurry."*

"Calm down, Spense," Gordo said. "You can't help River if you're dead. You're driving like a freaking lunatic."

"If anything happens to her…or the baby…" He couldn't go there. Christ. Over the past year and a half, River had risked treacherous landscapes, extreme weather and heights. She'd survived journeys to Egypt, China and Australia with minimal scrapes and dicey moments. When they'd discussed settling in one place for a while, she'd insisted on Ecuador. She wanted to be close to her dad. It was where she and Spenser had fallen in love. She'd listed a dozen reasons and he'd given in. "I knew we should've settled in the States."

"Get a grip, for fuck's sake," Gordo ordered as Spenser jumped a sidewalk and cut through an alley. "Metropolitano's a fine hospital and Dr. Perez is top-notch."

"I know. But what if she doesn't make it that far?"

"Jack's with her. He's a cop, remember? If he has to—"

"I know, dammit." His best friend had delivered more than one baby in the course of his law enforcement career. He trusted Jack, but if there were complications…

In spite of Gordo's warnings, Spenser punched the accelerator.

Ten minutes later, he stalked into Metropolitano with a frazzled Gordo on his heels. Duke had his arm around Lana. Jack was lecturing Kylie to calm down. Heart in throat, Spenser looked to his childhood friend. Jack was a freaking rock. "Where is she?"

Jack pointed down a hall just as a nurse came around the corner. "Mr. McGraw?" she said in heavily accented English. "Come with me."

Gordo slumped in a chair beside Duke. Spenser followed the nurse. He heard River's pained cry as they entered the delivery room. Mouth dry, he followed the nurse's orders—sterilized his hands, put on a surgical mask.

"She's in good care," the nurse told him. "But you've got to calm her."

Spenser nodded. He acknowledged Dr. Perez, who gave him a reassuring look, before returning to business. Spenser moved to the head of the table, his heart aching at the sight of River's anguished expression. Eyes squeezed shut, she cried out his name.

He smoothed her curls from her sweaty face. "I'm here, angel."

She nailed him with her lovely green eyes. "You made it."

"Wouldn't miss this for the world."

"Too early," she rasped.

He listened to the nurses and doctor converse in Spanish, while corralling his own emotions. "Dr. Perez said you're fine. The baby's fine. But you have to calm down, River. Remember your breathing techniques."

"It hurts."

"I know, honey." If he could take on the pain, he would. "Maybe you should reconsider an epidural."

"No! No drugs!" she shouted. "I can bear it. I can bear anything now that you're here."

He smiled and stroked her forehead, and even though she'd been studying Spanish, he translated Dr. Perez's instructions.

Tears streamed down her cheeks.

"River, you have to push. Listen to Dr. Perez—"

"But it's too soon. He or she won't be big enough and you and I aren't married. I shouldn't have put you off. I wanted...I wanted..." She lapsed into a delirious tirade, something about their baby being illegitimate. Well, hell.

Spenser flashed back to a few years ago, broached a solution with Perez. The man nodded and Spenser flew out of the room, down the hall. "You," he said pointing to Gordo, "come with me." His friends and family blinked in confusion. Gordo turned white. Spenser hauled him up by his jacket and practically dragged him toward the delivery room. "You're going to marry River and me."

"What?"

"Wash up. Put this mask on."

"But, Spense—"

Spenser dragged his friend into the room, held him steady when he swayed.

River caught sight of the cameraman, blanched. "You're going to *film* this?"

"What?" Gordo said, glancing at the doctor, the sheet. "Hell, no."

"Then why are you here?"

He swayed. "Good question."

"Gordo's going to marry us, angel," Spenser said. "He went through this spiritual phase a few years back, indulged in a mail-order ministry."

She screamed when another contraction hit, then stared at Gordo. "Is that true?"

"Yes," he rasped, looking greener by the minute. "But—"

"You're certified?"

"A long time ago…"

Dr. Perez spoke calmly but firmly. It was time.

"Do it," River told Gordo, then she did as Dr. Perez ordered.

"I think I'm going to pass out," Gordo said.

"Stop being such a girl!" River snapped, which made Spenser laugh.

"The sooner you do this," he said to Gordo, "the sooner you can leave."

Gordo launched into a stilted, streamlined marriage ceremony.

One of the nurses turned up the Latin music, a powerful, moving ballad that had been playing in the room. From now on, Spenser thought, *Imaginame Sin Ti* would be "their" song.

River squeezed the hell out of Spenser's hand. He

stroked her cheek. They listened and responded to both Dr. Perez and Gordo.

To have and to hold.

To honor and cherish.

"Almost there," Dr. Perez said.

"You've got no ring!" Gordo said.

Spenser calmly took the gold Inca chakana from around his neck and looped it back around River's. "Full circle," he said close to her ear. "Tree of life." He brushed a kiss over her lips.

"I now pronounce you man and wife," Gordo said, then crumpled to the floor in a dead faint.

"It's a girl," Dr. Perez announced. "Congratulations, Mr. and Mrs. McGraw."

River burst into happy tears when the baby voiced her first, bawdy cry.

Spenser swallowed an emotional lump as he watched the nurses clean and fuss over his tiny daughter.

"She's small, but strong," Dr. Perez said. "She'll be fine. You'll be fine," he said to River.

She thanked him on a hiccupping sob, then looked up at Spenser as the doctor left to conduct preliminary tests. "Poor Gordo," she said as a nurse worked to revive him.

"He'll be okay. Although he'll never let us live this one down."

"I don't care. We're married. And our daughter has a proper mom and dad."

"I don't know about *proper*," Spenser said with a

wink, then focused on her mouth. "I could kiss you for a lifetime."

"Hold that thought," she said with a shy smile. "About our daughter—"

"I'm going to spoil her rotten, you know."

Her smile widened. "I know we tossed around a few names," River said, gasping his shirt. "But I'd like to name her after my dad."

He frowned. "Henry? Henrietta? Ah, sweetheart."

"No. *Kane*." She beamed up at him. "Kane McGraw. It sounds adventurous, don't you think?"

Spenser smiled. "I like it and I love you, *Mrs. McGraw*."

"We're married," River said on an exhausted, joyous sigh.

"We're a family," Spenser said as the nurse placed his swaddled daughter in his wife's arms.

They stared down at their baby, then met each other's wondrous gaze.

They spoke as one. "Eureka."

* * * * *